# THE HOLIDAY

## JOHN NICHOLL

Boldwood

First published in Great Britain in 2024 by Boldwood Books Ltd.

Copyright © John Nicholl, 2024

Cover Design by Head Design Ltd

Cover Photography: Shutterstock

A CIP catalogue record for this book is available from the British Library.

Paperback ISBN 978-1-80426-408-9

Large Print ISBN 978-1-80426-409-6

Hardback ISBN 978-1-80426-410-2

Ebook ISBN 978-1-80426-406-5

Kindle ISBN 978-1-80426-407-2

Audio CD ISBN 978-1-80426-415-7

MP3 CD ISBN 978-1-80426-414-0

Digital audio download ISBN 978-1-80426-413-3

Boldwood Books Ltd
23 Bowerdean Street
London SW6 3TN
www.boldwoodbooks.com

*For Ava Rose Nicholl. I told you your name would be in the book!*

# 1

Suzie Reynolds had never seen anyone look more out of place on an economy flight. Suzie watched as the woman she thought in her mid- to late twenties – a similar age to her – strolled down the aisle. She was the last person to board the plane, taking her time as if keeping everyone else waiting was of no concern at all. Suzie looked on with an immediate sense of resentment that she knew only too well stemmed as much from envy, as the inconvenience the woman caused. She herself was a little over five feet tall, some would say overweight and a little awkward. Yes, most of all, awkward. But the stranger, in contrast, was moving with a feline grace – despite the restricted space and her smart red hand luggage – almost gliding on her high heels, as if on a catwalk, a tight blue dress yelling for attention, clinging to her curves, as if painted to her body: such an attractive woman, such a beauty. And Suzie thought the woman knew it, too. Everything about her conveyed an evident confidence Suzie had rarely experienced in her own life.

Suzie stared, fixated, feeling dowdy by comparison, dull and ordinary in her blue jeans, white cotton blouse and green wool jumper, but unable to look away. And she knew her husband was staring too, as the beauty stopped, reaching up, placing her small red case in the luggage rack, then took her seat immediately next to the couple on the other side of the aisle.

Shaking her head slowly, Suzie sucked in the air and emitted a long, deep, audible breath, one self-deprecating thought after another invading her troubled mind as the beauty slowly crossed one long alabaster-white leg over the other, her dress rising high above her knee, sensual, and, in Suzie's opinion, no doubt deliberately so.

Suzie studied the woman's red-painted fingernails, her perfectly manicured hands, and the expensive-looking, delicate, key design gold bracelet around one wrist as she fastened her seat belt around her ridiculously slim waist. And sunglasses, really? No doubt, designer. On a cold, wet Welsh autumn afternoon, waiting on the runway at Cardiff Airport in the middle of October? Where did she think she was? Bermuda? Malibu? Dubai? And that makeup, it was immaculate. And the long, blonde hair tied back with a shiny ribbon matching her dress looked natural, not dyed like her own, with no dark roots. A virtual vision of female perfection, as if all the woman had to worry about was herself.

Suzie knew she was obsessing, focussing on the stranger with an unreasonable and wholly over-the-top intensity. But it was a thought process she couldn't stop. Why compare the stranger to herself? What did it achieve? Nothing, nothing at all. No good would come of it. So, why torture herself? *For goodness' sake, Suzie, get a grip. Let it go.*

The black dog of depression threatened as Suzie sat there overthinking, very close to tears. She felt inclined to run for the nearest mirror. To turn on a bright light and stare, taking in the reality, coming to terms with whatever bitter truth her reflection held. But she told herself such things were best avoided. Recent months hadn't been easy. Their events had aged her. There were lines where there weren't lines before, and shadows under her eyes that no makeup could hide. Stress could do that to a girl. It could blunt your edges. Perhaps things could have been different if she had a more understanding husband, someone more supportive, someone with even an ounce of empathy, a man she could trust. But, no, she had George, with all his many flaws. A man who seemed to think sensitivity was a weakness, a character flaw unbecoming in males. Something to be avoided at almost any cost.

Suzie wiped away a tear, still deep in thought, unable to silence her mind. George, she pondered, had once seemed to be very different, before time revealed his true nature. She'd been initially attracted, not only by his undoubted good looks, but by his personality, too: the attention he gave her, his gusty enthusiasm for life. She hadn't seen him for the man he truly was. She'd loved him back then and she still loved him now, God help her. Love! But why, after all he'd done, letting her down so very badly time and again? Her younger sister, Isobel, had asked her that question only days before, clearly perplexed. She didn't have an adequate answer then, and she didn't now, nothing that made any sense, nothing logical she could put her finger on. But the feelings were still there, nonetheless, undeniably so. And maybe one day George would change for the better, mature, if she clung on in there, if they were lucky enough to have the child she so craved. And at the end of the day, she wasn't perfect either. She wasn't the fun young woman she once was. The one she'd so like to be again if only she could. What did George even see in her? She wasn't a looker, not like the woman who'd so recently boarded the plane. Not even close.

Suzie looked directly ahead now, then closed her eyes for a second or two. She pictured what she considered her very average face and told herself that looks weren't everything. There were far more important things in life. And anyway, the beauty's attention-grabbing persona was all about the show, all red shoes and no knickers, so contrived. Maybe the beautiful stranger was insecure too, under her disguise. Perhaps life had affected the stranger as it had her; the sunglasses and makeup a mask behind which to hide. Things weren't always as they seemed, not at face value. Forget her, that was best, although easier said than done. Sometimes, Suzie observed, her thoughts appeared to have a life of their own.

Suzie opened her tired eyes, then popped a boiled fruit sweet into her mouth for the second time in under ten minutes and started sucking. But her attention soon returned to the woman, despite her resolution just a minute or so before. Suzie surmised the beauty must have taken an absolute age to create such a flawless image, sitting in front of an illuminated mirror for goodness only knew how long, focussed only on herself, and never looking away until she achieved the desired transformation. She probably didn't look half as good without all that painted slop on her face. Surely such an obvious effort was all so unnecessary before a holiday flight to Tenerife. They weren't going to some red-carpet event; there were no TV cameras, no paparazzi baying for the next cover photo for some glossy magazine. Who on earth did she think she was? What was so special about her?

Suzie shifted her weight from one plump buttock to the other, unable to get comfortable as her rumination continued, a thought process seemingly beyond her control. Yes, the woman was all about image. There was no substance to any of it.

Suzie glanced at the woman again, still obsessing. Look at her, taking her phone from her flash handbag, taking off her sunglasses, and texting when her phone should be on flight mode. What on earth was that about? Surely she was showing off, trying to make an impression again. That must be it. That was the only explanation that made any sense at all.

Suzie looked away now, no more glances, quickly unwrapping another sweet, offering one to her husband, who declined with a subtle shake of his head. She tried to focus on the holiday to come. Escaping the grey, windy autumn, a welcome week in the Canary Islands sun at a spa hotel that looked fabulous in the online photos, even those posted by other travellers on Tripadvisor. But her thoughts quickly returned to the woman, who was still looking at the phone held in both hands a few inches from her oh-so-pretty face, as if totally unaware of the impact she'd had on those sitting close. On anyone who'd made the comparison between themselves and her.

Maybe, Suzie thought, if her husband paid her more loving affection, she'd hardly have noticed the woman at all. She wouldn't have spent the last few minutes thinking about her. It was their wedding anniversary, for goodness' sake, just two years, and he'd been staring, he'd definitely been staring from his aisle seat. When the woman reached up, placing that smart cabin bag in the luggage rack, he'd been focussed on her bum, eyes on stalks, almost drooling, no doubt picturing her naked or imagining what sexy underwear she was wearing under that tight dress.

Suzie had never been more certain of anything in her life. And it ate away at her, leaving a sour taste in her mouth despite the sweet sugary treat. She briefly recalled the first happy days of their marriage not so very long ago. But, she ruminated, it may as well have been an age. He wasn't always all bad. There was good in him. She'd been flattered by his attentions. And he used to make her laugh. But so much had changed. Did George really have to make his sexual interest in other women so blatantly obvious? Did he ever consider her feelings even for a second? Men, she sighed, were so very predictable, as transparent as polished glass, slaves to their hormones, thinking with their dicks. And George was no different to the rest of them. He'd proved that well enough. He was worse than most if anything. Marriage wasn't an easy institution. So much to put up with, so much to forgive.

Suzie swivelled in her seat and turned her head, glaring at her husband, sadness enveloping her, beating her down. She briefly considered saying nothing, not commenting at all. But the hurt was too deep. The words poured out of her, harsher than she'd intended, more confrontational. And once she started, she couldn't stop, despite knowing deep down that nothing good would come of it. It never did.

'Shame you didn't get a photo,' she said, eyes narrowed, a pinched expression on her face. 'You could have had it blown up, had it framed on your office wall, or made it your screensaver. You'd like that.'

George Reynolds raised a hand, rubbed the back of his neck, and crossed his arms as if trying to form a barrier.

'What are you talking about now?' he said, sounding a little apprehensive. As if he knew what was coming next.

Suzie lowered her tone, whispering her words directly into his ear, her warm breath on his face, not wanting to be overheard.

'Oh, you know exactly what I'm talking about,' Suzie replied. 'Don't play the innocent with me. You couldn't take your eyes off her bum. I know what you're like. You must think I was born yesterday. At least be honest about it. Surely, you can manage that.'

George began twisting his wedding ring, looking down rather than meeting Suzie's eyes. He'd reacted much as she thought he would. And now, of course, he'd go on the attack. Making it seem as if she was in the wrong. Another tactic he used all too often. So typical of the man.

George let out a brief snorting laugh that had nothing to do with humour.

'I wonder what goes on in that silly head of yours sometimes,' he snapped back a lot louder than she'd have liked. 'I wasn't looking at anything.'

'Like hell you weren't looking,' she said, fighting back tears.

'Maybe you'd like to talk to her instead of me. You could get to know her then. And have a really good look. I'm just your wife, that's all. Don't you go worrying about little old me and my feelings. I wouldn't want to cramp your style.'

The contours of George's familiar face had changed as muscles tensed.

'Oh, come on, not this again,' he said, almost pleading, his hands now pressed together as if in prayer.

Suzie thought George looked more anxious than irritated, but there was a flash of anger, too. Just for a fraction of a second before he composed himself. She asked herself what on earth he had to feel aggrieved about? She was the wronged one, not him. He always seemed to think he was so hard done by for no good reason at all.

Suzie glared at George again with unblinking eyes now, the tiny hairs on her forearms standing to attention. She silently pondered that George was all about denial, as if his thoughtless actions, upsetting her as he had, hardly mattered to him at all.

'Don't ever go thinking I've forgotten about your office Christmas party,' she said. 'Kissing that tart like that. Dancing with her, putting your hands all over her. And just two months after I lost the baby. You should be ashamed of yourself. My sister warned me not to trust you. I should have listened to her. She was right all along.'

George dropped his chin to his chest, his face reddening as it often did in similar circumstances.

'Please don't go ruining the holiday before it's even started, Suzie. You know what parties are like. I was seriously pissed, letting my hair down, drowning my sorrows after a difficult time. And one of the boys I work with laced my lager with vodka. The idiot's idea of a joke. I didn't know until it was too late. I've told you all this. I've tried to explain. I've said I'm sorry time and again. I wish it hadn't happened. I didn't know what the hell I was doing. I don't even fancy the girl. I was mortified the next morning when I remembered what had happened. I'm sorry! I don't know what else I can say.'

Suzie narrowed her reddened eyes, far from convinced, thinking she'd heard it all before.

'So, you didn't actually fancy the girl?' she said. 'Not even with her short skirt and low top?'

He shook his head with an exasperated look.

'No, how many times do I have to say it? No!'

Suzie paused, letting him suffer for a few seconds before finally speaking again, saying what she had planned to say all along. Their conversations on the matter always followed the same pattern. 'So, you claim you didn't fancy her. Really? Is that so? I saw the photos. The filthy tart put them all over Instagram. You had your tongue down her throat, lipstick all over your face.'

'Are you ever going to let me forget it?'

'How can I?' she sobbed. 'You hurt me, George. More so than ever before.'

'I was legless. I've explained. I wish I'd never gone to the party at all.'

'You were all over her. How do you think that made me feel? What if it was me kissing some other bloke like that? And everyone has seen the photos. Even my family. The girl tagged you. It's shameful; I've never been so humiliated in my life.'

He glanced at his chunky, stainless-steel divers watch, a black face with white numerals and a red bezel. Bought years before, after a winning bet on the horses.

'Please let it go, Suzie,' he said. 'I've said I'm sorry so many times. Talking about it over and over isn't going to change anything. Look, we'll take off soon; they're about to give the safety briefing. We're running a few minutes late.'

Oh, so he was trying to change the subject, she thought. What a surprise. Same old story. No change there.

'Do you think you can distract me that easily?' she asked. 'Do you really think I'm that stupid?'

'I kissed the girl. And I danced with her. I haven't denied it. It was the drink, just the drink. That's it, nothing more. Just a stupid drunken mistake I regret. You talk about your Catholic faith often enough. About how we should live. Doesn't that include forgiveness?'

Suzie paused for a beat.

'You hurt me, George.'

The skin bunched around his eyes in a contrite expression. 'It will never happen again,' he said, as if he meant it. 'If I could turn back time, I would. It's you I love, nobody else.'

Suzie asked herself why his talk of love never convinced her. She sometimes wondered what the word meant to him. If it was just something he said because it sounded right. If he understood love at all.

Suzie began unwrapping another sweet as a grey-haired stewardess dressed in smart blue livery began her presentation. Seemingly going through the motions with practised efficiency. A process she'd likely followed many times before.

Suzie placed her mouth close to her husband's right ear again, whispering, 'If I ever find out you had sex with that tart, I may never forgive you. You do understand that, don't you? There's only so much I'm willing to put up with.'

He screwed up his face.

'Oh, come on, not this again. I did not screw her, and I wouldn't, however drunk I was. That's the truth; I swear to it, nothing but the truth. I don't know how many times I need to tell you the same thing.'

Suzie wanted to believe him. But there were still doubts as the

photos came back to mind, big, bright and bold. The colour images
playing behind her eyes fed her insecurities, not letting up. She so
wanted the holiday to be an amazing new start for them. The
beginning of better times. But were such things even possible after
all that had gone before?

She gripped his wrist, digging in her fingers. 'You insist you
didn't have sex with her. Swear to it on your life.'

'Oh, come off it, Suzie, that's enough. We've had this exact same
conversation so many times.'

Her expression hardened as she resisted the impulse to yell.

'Swear to it!'

'Okay, okay, I swear to it. I didn't have sex with the girl. Never
have and never would. I swear it on my life.'

## 2

Take off came as a relief to George. Suzie was nervous about flying, always had been. And the roar of the plane's powerful engines silenced her in an instant as they lifted from the runway, rising higher towards the grey clouds above. It was precisely what he'd hoped for. A small win. Her whinging over. Sometimes it seemed she'd never shut up.

The approximately four-hour mid-morning flight from South Wales to Tenerife South Airport in the Canary Islands off the west coast of Africa passed slowly, with George making repeated attempts to overcome his wife's resentments in the interests of an easy life and Suzie seemingly holding onto her grudges, which didn't surprise him at all. It was, he thought, no different to other recent days. Although now he was stuck in a seat next to the silly cow with no means of escape, other than a brief toilet visit that ended all too soon.

As the flight continued, George made intermittent attempts to talk to Suzie about ordinary uncontentious things he thought may interest her. But her responses were limited to a nod, or a little shake of her head, as she spent the majority of her time nervously sucking one fruit sweet after another, drinking strong black coffee when available, and perusing a well-thumbed Tenerife travel guide she'd bought second-hand on eBay to save a few miserable pounds despite her recently acquired wealth. A Premium Bond win. The top prize! A million quid invested, thought George, and she was still as tight as a duck's arse. Maybe if Suzie learnt to live a bit, she wouldn't be so miserable; perhaps then she wouldn't be such a morale-sapping drag.

George said a silent prayer of thanks when Suzie finally put the book aside about twenty minutes before landing, the prospect of arrival seemingly softening her mood. So, the moody mare was finally ready to make peace, thought George, as she held her half-empty sweet packet out, offering to share for the second time since boarding. And this time, he accepted. Not because he particularly wanted a sweet. He wasn't a fan of confectionery. He had more savoury tastes. But simply because it seemed the right thing to do in the circumstances. Refusal, he thought, might set her off again. God knows, it didn't take much these days. He felt like he was walking on eggshells all the time.

George thought about Suzie and their relationship now as he so often had, as if rumination would somehow change something. As if by thought alone, he could manifest a new reality. He thought the same things most days. He asked himself the same questions. Often more than once, whether at work at the gym, at home or anywhere else. Where, oh where, had the fun young woman he'd once known gone? The one who knew how to enjoy herself and have a good time, not to worry about anything and everything to the nth degree. Before depression and anxiety blunted her edges, popping one prescription pill after another, dulling what had once been a creative mind. Before she became the judgemental bitch she now was, making his life as miserable as hell. It was as if she'd become another person entirely, constantly playing the blame game –

about his gambling, or his having a few miserable drinks and a dance now and again when he needed to raise his spirits. What was the big deal? It wasn't as if he didn't need the alcohol. He had to live with the bitch. It was surprising he wasn't pissed the entire time.

George continued his thought process for a few seconds longer before finally reaching the same conclusion he always reached. The only one that made any sense at all. Okay, so things weren't great. His long-gone attraction to Suzie had turned to indifference, then to resentment, and now, occasionally, to hate. There was no denying that sad reality. Sometimes, he loathed her with a burning intensity nothing could extinguish. And who could blame him? No one in their right mind. No one at all.

George sighed as he contemplated. So, she'd miscarried a couple of times, so what? Such a big deal over so very little. It wasn't even as if the babies were planned. He'd never even wanted to be a father and still didn't. Why did parenthood mean so much to her? And the second miscarriage had all happened months ago. Get over it, for fuck's sake. So very miserable. Such a total downer. If she wanted a damned baby so very much, why didn't she do a proper job of holding on to it? Millions of women managed it. The silly bitch couldn't even get that right.

George asked himself if only an evil bastard would have such thoughts. Is that what he'd become? Maybe yes, or perhaps no. He really wasn't sure. He frowned hard, then smiled, his reflections suddenly changing direction, briefly raising his mood. At least now Suzie had cash in the bank, he said to himself. Lots of the lovely stuff. And that was cause for hope. A reason for continuing the relationship for as long as necessary. It was so unreasonable of her to keep the wealth to herself. And so like her, typical, so unfair and so unjust. But his hope wasn't unfounded. He had a right to that cash. It was as much his as hers. Why couldn't she understand that? That's the way marriage was supposed to work. He'd undoubtedly suffered enough. Living with her, putting up with her moaning. So, now almost anything was justified. He had to hold onto that belief. There had to be a way.

George forced a thin smile he suspected was less than convincing. Then finally removed the sweet's clear plastic wrapper. He popped the hard candy into his open mouth, moving it to the side with his tongue, preparing to speak when the moment seemed right.

He turned his head now, momentarily meeting Suzie's eyes, thinking he was finally winning, on top for once, glad when she didn't frown or look away as was often her custom. And he was so cautious not to look at the beautiful young woman sitting so elegantly alongside him, on the other side of the aisle, so near and yet so far. He so wanted to look, to stare, linger, study her form, her shapely breasts, long legs and everything else. But he had to resist. However difficult, he had to resist; another limitation Suzie forced on him. She'd probably like to castrate him if she could, like her parents did their poor dog. But not before she'd had a baby, of course, not before then.

George laughed at the thought. A baby! Good luck with that. He glanced at the beauty. Don't look, don't look. Easier said than done, he said to himself, as he pictured her naked, imagining touching her, enjoying her body, sensual delights. Wow, lovely, just lovely. What red-blooded male wouldn't think such things? He was miserable, not dead. And Suzie hadn't been interested in sex since the latest miscarriage. And then came the party. She'd kicked up such a fuss. A huge overreaction. So unjustified, so unfair. But, of course, she'd never understand that, not for a single second, however convincing his explanations. She didn't have the capacity for reasoned thought. Not like him. So, he had to keep all that to himself.

George smiled again, a distraction more than anything else,

then quickly placed an inflight magazine on his lap to hide his swollen cock as he glanced at the beauty again, erotic imaginings on his mind. Oh, she'd taste so good, honey on his tongue. He'd like to lick every inch of her body.

Focus, George, focus, you have to focus, push the fantasy from your mind, think of something else; now wasn't the time. Suzie would notice something was up. Something best avoided because he'd be spending an entire week with the cow, seven whole days in the same room, around the same pool, going to the same restaurants, on the same trips – no doubt of her choice – with no opportunities to head to work at the gym, his usual means of escape. Shit, a whole week. Shit! Avoiding further friction had to be the best form of defence. Make the best of a bad situation. That's all he could do. And hopefully all his plans would work out for the best. He had to be patient.

George felt a sinking feeling deep in the pit of his stomach as his rumination continued. There'd been so many arguments since the Christmas party, with him on the receiving end, offering mitigation, pleading his innocence despite the evidence in front of Suzie's eyes. Damn those photographs and the needy bitch who posted them. The stupid cow. Talk about moronic. Eighteen or not, she should have known better. She knew he was married. He told her. He'd even showed her his wedding ring, for fuck's sake, held up his hand. He hadn't taken it off as he sometimes did on a night out. Cameras everywhere these days, easy evidence the downside of modern technology. Why the hell did the girl let a friend use her phone? And insisting on a selfie! The bitch must have known she was creating a shit storm. It was all her stupid fault. And she wasn't even that good a shag. It was all over so very quickly, in the back of his car. With a few hard thrusts, he'd pulled out, lifted himself off, come over her stomach, and that was it. And for some inexplicable reason, the stupid bitch wanted to date him. As if they were a couple. As if she didn't know the score. Females could be such drama queens, obsessing over nothing at all.

George crossed his arms, the magazine falling to the floor, no longer necessary despite him glancing at the beauty again for a fleeting moment, then urgently looking away. It would, he contemplated, have been so much better if his cocaine-fuelled night-time dalliances had remained a secret. But, no, they didn't. No luck there. The photos were there for all to see on Instagram and even a short video on TikTok. So, avoiding Suzie's wrath as far as possible had to be the best option left open to him. Maybe the holiday wouldn't be the disaster he'd feared when she told him she'd booked and paid. The selfish cow hadn't even asked where he wanted to go. It was all about her, always about her, as if she was somehow the boss of him. No change there. Just because she was the one with cash in the bank, as if his views, opinions, wants, and feelings didn't matter at all.

Why the hell did he marry her in the first place? Stupid! So, she was pregnant, so what? His mother's pressure confused him, twisting his mind with her talk of hell, piling on the guilt. In truth, he was trapped. And Suzie lost that baby, too. But not soon enough. After the wedding, when it was too late to back out as he should have all along. He should have run a mile. She didn't even have money back then. And now that she did, he didn't see much of it. What was he thinking? He was a good-looking guy and could have had any woman he wanted, lots of them, any number, one after another, without complications. But it didn't work out that way. Not even close. Now he had to play the cards he was dealt. Who knew? Some people believe everything happened for a reason. It could still all pay off in the end. Good could come out of bad. He had to try.

George chuckled quietly to himself, looking at Suzie's face, thinking she seemed almost incapable of smiling.

'Good book?' he asked, hoping she wouldn't somehow find a way to return the conversation to his recent infidelity. It sometimes seemed she almost always did. Such a pain in the arse, so very unpleasant.

Suzie nodded twice, and he suspected the worst of her mood was over. About time, he thought. He really couldn't have stood much more.

'Um, yeah, not bad at all,' Suzie replied, looking first out of the cabin window and then at him. 'I'm only about halfway through, but I've learned quite a lot about the island. It really is an awe-inspiring place. The mountain behind our hotel, Mount Teide, is the highest in the whole of Spain. And there's snow on the top, even in summer. It looks amazing. It's a dormant volcano; we can go on a tour. Maybe tomorrow or the day after, depending on how we feel.'

George could hear the sudden enthusiasm in his wife's sing-song Welsh voice, and now he knew he was winning. The earlier tension was melting away; she was thawing, at least for a time. Now all he had to do was keep it that way for as long as possible. Best keep her onside, build on the progress he'd made.

He told himself they'd no doubt go on the mountain trip when she wanted to, always her agenda, never his. But so be it; he'd make the best of the week away. He'd satisfy himself with the scraps tossed from her table, escaping when he could, time to himself. He'd hang on in there, hoping she'd finally share her riches as she should have in the first place. So what if he'd lost a few quid on the horses? A lot of people had IVAs. He was making the monthly payments. It wasn't a crime. And Suzie could clear his entire debt with ease if she wanted to, tight cow.

'Sounds good to me,' George replied, patting Suzie on the knee, saying what he thought she wanted to hear.

'And the resort looks amazing,' she added with evident enthusiasm. 'It's a bit of a walk down the hill from our hotel to the seafront. But there's a regular complimentary shuttle bus if we need it. Not that we will. And there's a small black sand beach and a harbour not too far away. The beach is a little dangerous for swimming but popular with surfers. It's surprising how big the waves are.'

Would she ever shut up? George tapped his foot repeatedly against the plane's grey carpet, trying to remain patient, fighting the impulse to tell her exactly what he thought of her and her mundane observations. He wished he'd never asked. It was a challenge, always a challenge, but he somehow held it together, despite a tension headache that had started at the base of his skull and spread. Her fault, all her fault, he thought. Like most things were.

'I went there when I was a kid, remember?' he said as calmly as he could. 'With my mum and dad. Puerto De La Cruz. The main resort on the north coast. I've told you all this. It translates from the Spanish as Port of the Cross.'

Suzie shook her head with a quickly vanishing smile.

'Yes, I know what you said, but you were only seven,' she said. 'It will have changed a lot since then. And you stayed in a small apartment, not a 5-star hotel like we're going to. Your mum told me that before she died. Your parents didn't have the money for anything better. It's going to be very different this time. And a bit of pampering will do us both some good. It's been a long while since we went away. And things haven't been easy. I hope the holiday can give us a new start.'

George swallowed his resentment, biting his tongue, focussing on the pain as a means of silencing himself. Why slag off his childhood holiday? And why the reminder of her expense? So, she'd paid for the trip; big deal, she could afford it. And one week? When they could have gone for two. They weren't even staying in a suite. Just a double room.

He broke up what was left of his fruit sweet, crunching with his back teeth, swallowing hard and stalling for a beat rather than saying something he might later regret. Another argument, or worse still, that passive-aggressive silence she often resorted to, was the last thing he wanted or needed. God, why was she so very sensitive? Was it the miscarriages, her hormones, the anxiety? Or was she the same miserable woman she'd always been, despite her win? All that cash in the bank. It seemed nothing was ever good enough for some people. Certainly not her. It would have been better if he'd never met her at all.

George ended his thought process, choosing his words with care.

'It was good of you to pay for such a nice place for us to stay. I'm grateful; honestly, I am. I'm sure we'll have a nice time. It's a new start for both of us, you and me. Although it would be so much easier if I had access to the money. Then I could arrange things, too. I could share the burden. It wouldn't all fall on you.'

Suzie frowned now, and he could tell there was something else she wanted to say. Something he strongly suspected he wouldn't appreciate in the slightest. He rarely did. Talking to her these days had become something of a minefield. He waited silently for her to speak, as he knew she inevitably would. If only he could gag her, keep her quiet forever.

'I took out 800 euros in cash from the post office last Saturday when I was in town with my mum,' she said. 'I'll give you some as and when you need it. I think that's the best way. And, of course, I've got my cards. A few more months, and you'll be able to have one of your own. For your own money, I mean. Once you've paid off what you owe.'

He felt his body tense. It was always the case with the talk of money. Her tone always sounded accusatory, every time, never different.

'Okay, thanks,' he said, resisting the impulse to bite. Sometimes a simple restrained response was best. And it was all he could think to say.

There were a few seconds of silence before Suzie spoke again, this time her voice faltering as if she doubted the wisdom of her words. 'I'm sorry we can't have a joint account, George,' she began. 'But you know what my dad said. It's not safe with all the debts you ran up. The temptation might be too much for you. Best to keep things separate for the foreseeable future.'

He clenched and unclenched his fists, picturing himself punching her father hard, bang, right on the point of the nose, hitting him to the floor. 'I went for counselling, Suzie,' he said. 'You know that. Compulsive betting's an addiction – an illness I conquered. I'm well now. I stopped gambling over a year ago. A lot of what I owed is paid off. There's only four or five thousand to go.'

She made a face, and he knew what was coming next. It was always the same crap. 'Yes, but only because I'm paying all of the household bills month after month. I could pay off the remainder of your debt for you like you asked, but Dad says it's important you do it yourself. It's for your own good. We're doing it this way because of how much I love you. You do understand that, don't you? Imagine how proud you'll feel when you make the final payment. It'll be such an achievement. And then, maybe we can talk about a joint current account a year or two after that. I'd just keep my investments separate.'

George shook his head. He'd heard it all before. How many damned times had she said the same thing? And it was always 'Dad this' and 'Dad that' with her, as if his pronouncements were unquestionable. As if her father was some genius, never to be challenged. He was an accountant for some Catholic charity, for fuck's sake, not the Pope.

George sighed, reluctant to enter into an argument he knew he couldn't win. God only knew he'd tried so many times before and failed. And the silly bitch always seemed to think she was in the right, however ridiculous her point of view. Persuading her to see sense seemed a virtual impossibility he'd almost abandoned. Almost, but not entirely. He silently committed to giving it one final push when he thought the time was right. But now was not that time. 'What do you think is best when we land?' he asked, changing the subject. 'A taxi or a rental car? From what I read online, it's about an hour's drive to the resort.'

Suzie raised two fingers to her chin below her lip. 'A taxi, I already decided. I'll pay,' she said. 'We can always rent a car later in the week if we think we need one. You have got your licence with you, haven't you?'

He was quick to reply. 'It's always in my wallet.'

She frowned.

'I wasn't sure if you'd got it back after your last speeding fine.'

He blew out the air. Oh, shit, another implied criticism. Would she ever let up? 'I've got it,' he replied insistently, wondering if he had.

Suzie smiled thinly. 'That's good, but I still think a taxi. Let someone else take the strain for a change. We do more than enough driving at home.'

Just agree, George, he thought, anything for an easier life. She'd have it her way anyway, whatever he said. She almost always did. And it was beginning to grate. Was she worse since Christmas? Even more demanding than before? Yes, she very probably was.

'Whatever you want, Suzie,' he said. 'Whatever you want.'

She looked back as if unsure of his meaning. He wasn't sure, but he thought his tone might have betrayed his irritation. A part of him hoped it had.

# 3

Suzie was glad to stand after landing, although she calmly waited until the illuminated seatbelt sign finally switched off. She stretched, arms raised above her head, frowning when her lower back stiffened and complained, as it so often did in the colder months. She knew George would prefer to remain seated until all the other passengers had disembarked. And she could see some logic in that. It was a far-from-ridiculous option. But she told herself that just wasn't her style. She'd had enough of sitting, enough of the sedentary life, the holiday beckoned, and she was keen to get going.

The island had looked so alluring from the cabin window as the plane descended towards the black tarmac runway. High mountains, wonderful sandy beaches lining much of the coastline, a dark blue ocean topped with galloping white horses, and what she knew was a year-round sunny climate, an eternal spring that kept the waters warm. Tenerife was, she silently acknowledged, significantly more built up than she'd envisaged, certainly much more so than Lanzarote, the strangely volcanic neighbouring island she'd visited as a teenager. But it was no less attractive for that.

Suzie briefly glanced down at the beautiful young woman who had so dominated her thoughts at the start of the flight, quickly looking away when the woman returned her gaze, with what seemed a friendly smile. That surprised Suzie, that smile, and the slight nod of the beauty's head. That brief, unspoken interaction had made the woman seem all the more human, almost approachable. Not some exotic unreachable creature living on a very different level from her. Perhaps, Suzie said to herself, she'd made unfounded assumptions she wasn't entitled to make. First impressions could be notoriously deceptive. How long had she actually taken before reaching an initial judgement? Four, maybe five seconds at most. Maybe Little Miss Perfect wasn't so bad after all.

Suzie shrugged, still far from convinced by her internal argument, then turned her attention to George, tapping him on the shoulder as he sat there, as if he had all the time in the world. She studied him closely, his body language, his eyes, the direction of his gaze. And he didn't look again at the beauty, which pleased her. It seemed his mind was focussed on other things. She suddenly thought of her medication. It often came to mind.

'Pass me my handbag please, George,' Suzie said insistently. 'Quickly, I need a tablet.'

He pushed up his sleeve and checked his sports watch, making it obvious.

'What, another one? You only took one at the airport before we had breakfast at the café. Remember? You haven't forgotten, have you? You don't want to overdo it. I'm not even sure those things are doing you any good at all. And if you run out, where will you get more? You need to make sure they last you the week.'

Suzie stiffened, snapping back her response, as a grey-haired elderly couple standing immediately in front of her turned to look. She felt her face redden, but her embarrassment wasn't enough to change her tack. And the more she considered her husband's response, the angrier Suzie felt. She wasn't even sure he had her best interests at heart. Sometimes being awkward seemed to delight him. As if it gave him some perverse pleasure.

'Sorry, George, I didn't realise you're a doctor now. Did you do a medical degree without me realising? Night school, perhaps? Is that what you were doing night after night after I lost the baby? Just give me my bag. I know when I need my medication. And I could do without the lecture.'

Suzie regretted her tirade almost as soon as she'd said it, wishing she'd kept her thoughts to herself. She watched as her husband pressed his lips together, avoiding her gaze. And this time she thought he looked more upset than angry. Or was it disinterest? It could be disinterest. He had one of those faces that could be hard to read. One emotion or another. It was sometimes hard to tell. Come on, George, get your act together. Why wasn't he moving? Why not do as she'd asked?

She lowered her pitch and tone now, persuasive, keen to elicit his cooperation, actively quelling her heightened emotion to get her own way. 'The handbag, George, it's under the seat. It's easier for you to reach it than me. Please don't be difficult. You know my anxiety can get to me when not following my usual routine. If I didn't need a tablet I wouldn't be taking one. It's nothing to worry about. My body's used to them by now.'

George reached down, sighing but then smiling as the people at the front of the standing debarkation queue finally started moving forward, the plane's doors open, daylight pouring in. Suzie thought she heard George mumble, 'About fucking time,' but she chose to ignore it, glad when he finally rose to his feet.

She accepted her bag gratefully, the relief almost palpable, reaching in, taking out the brown plastic medicine bottle, quickly removing the white top, and urgently popping a small pill into her open mouth. There was comfort in the familiar process, almost a therapy in itself. She swallowed hard, once, then again, for the lack of water. She sucked her tongue, rapidly moving it back and forth against the roof of her mouth, creating saliva, forcing the medication further down her throat towards her gut. And as she swallowed, she felt better almost immediately, in an instant, as if a switch had been flicked, despite the drug not yet having entered her bloodstream. She knew that made little sense. She was fully aware the medication had become a crutch of sorts. The fact that it had lifted her mood so quickly meant its effects were at least partly psychological. But she was no less glad of it for that. And she told herself the chemical benefits would come later as she and George negotiated the busy airport, then made their way to the hotel. That was something to look forward to. Travelling could prove stressful. And arrival for her was preferable to the journey. A metaphoric light in the dark.

Suzie looked up at a flawless blue sky dotted with white marble clouds as she left the plane, pleased to feel the warmth of the Canary Island sun on her face, caressing her skin. It was in the low twenties centigrade, as the online forecast predicted. The captain had said as much in an onboard announcement. And the sudden warmth raised Suzie's spirits further still as she keenly anticipated her break. She briefly forgot about her many troubles as she descended the gleaming metal steps towards the ground, her handbag in one hand, the other on a guard rail in the interest of safety. For once, for just a minute or two, she lived in the moment. And it felt good; it really did. But even then, she knew it wouldn't last. It never did for very long. She silently noted she was a worrier as she prepared to head to the arrival terminal. Always had been and probably always would be, despite a strong religious faith. Her mother was no different, and her maternal grandmother, too. It was probably inherited, genetic. Such was life. She just had to ensure those worries didn't overwhelm her. Stay strong, pray, look to the positives whenever possible, and of course, take the tablets, follow her doctor's advice. Those were the keys to survival, whatever her husband thought. Life was far from perfect. But it could be worse. And George wasn't really so bad, was he? We all have our flaws. The loss of the babies must have been hard for him, too, however well he hid it. He wasn't a man to show his emotion. Though it was almost as if he hadn't grieved at all.

Within half an hour or so, the couple had passed through customs, collected their large silver-coloured plastic case from one of several carousels, and made their way through arrivals towards the taxi rank, just a few minutes' brisk walk away. It was well sign-posted, and they found the long, waiting queue of other holiday-makers with relative ease. They stood beside each other in the long line of people, saying very little until they finally reached the front about fifteen minutes later. Suzie looked behind her at one point as George lifted their luggage into the spacious boot of a cream-coloured Mercedes E Class saloon car, to see the beauty waiting alone with her single, small, red bag at her feet. And this time, Suzie briefly acknowledged her, nodding and smiling, glad of the woman's friendly reciprocation before quickly looking away. Suzie felt more certain now that she had misjudged the beauty all along. The woman had won the looks lottery. Lucky her. But that didn't mean she was a bad person. And it seemed George hadn't even noticed her at all this time, an unexpected bonus. Hopefully, thought Suzie, the beauty wouldn't be staying at the same hotel, God forbid. She didn't want George drooling like a dog on heat. Because he would be. She was certain of that.

For goodness' sake, stop obsessing, Suzie said to herself. She did it all too often, overthinking, working herself up about something that might never happen. But life could be so horribly unreliable. Bad things happened when you least expected them. One minute you were reasonably happy, or, at least, coping, and the next, sad, as events took an unexpected turn, tearing your life apart. Even her strong Catholic faith wasn't always enough to protect her from the ravages of fate. The miscarriages had taught her that. Her priest had told her to try to see hardship as an opportunity for growth. To better understand the suffering of Jesus, to get closer to her saviour. But what could a priest know of the loss of a child? It sometimes seemed God could be cruel as well as kind.

Suzie pushed her dark, melancholic thoughts from her mind as she climbed into the car, sitting next to George, who was already seated in the back.

'Does the driver know where we're going?' she asked.

'Yeah, I've told him,' George replied. 'He only lives about twenty minutes from the resort. Anything you want to ask, he's your man.'

Suzie smiled, thinking that for once things were going well. And George's mood had improved. He was almost cheerful. Here was hoping it would stay that way.

The heavily built, dark-haired driver started the car's diesel engine, glanced in his mirrors, signalled, waited for a vehicle to pass and pulled out, leaving the airport terminal within minutes and heading north.

The driver seemed keen to chat as he negotiated the busy road, and Suzie was surprised to find that she was, too. The driver was local and knew the island well, as George had said, so it seemed the ideal opportunity to ask any questions that came to mind.

'About how long will it take us to reach the resort?' Suzie asked, her first question, although she already had others in mind. She spoke loudly enough for the driver to realise she was addressing him.

The driver glanced in his rear-view mirror before increasing his speed. He had a strong Spanish accent when he replied. 'It should take us about an hour along the main coast road, but it's been very busy today. So maybe a little longer.'

'Is there a Catholic church in the resort?' she then asked, as soon as the driver stopped speaking. 'I'm hoping to go while I'm here.'

She could sense George tense momentarily as she awaited the driver's reply.

The driver spoke loudly over the sound of the engine. 'There's at least three I can think of. My family go to the Iglesia de Nuestra Señora de la Peña de Francia though, which is near the commercial district and sea. You'd like it. It's very beautiful.'

Suzie nodded with a smile, but her husband had swivelled in his seat, turning his back to her. She politely replied to the driver, thinking it might have been better if she hadn't asked anything at all. 'Ah, okay, thanks. I might see you there.'

George sighed now, loudly, and Suzie suspected she knew what was coming next. There was a hard edge to his tone when he spoke. A manner she sometimes thought he reserved for her. As if he wanted to hurt her. As if he wanted his words to sting. 'Church, here, really? We're only on holiday for a week. Surely you can do without seeing a priest for that long. God knows, you go often enough at home.'

She swallowed then took a breath, speaking in hushed tones as if she could somehow retain a degree of privacy despite the confined space. A part of her wanted to stay silent, not to say another word until at the hotel. But her emotions were bubbling up, too strong for that.

'I was hoping... I was hoping you'd come with me,' she said.

George let out a harsh laugh that grated. 'Me? Go back to church?'

Should she persevere? Here, with a stranger driving, hearing everything she said, as if it was his business. She really wasn't sure.

But it seemed the right thing to do, one more attempt. If anyone could do with the confessional, George could. His conscience must weigh heavy. She moved her hand, making the sign of the cross. 'Well, yes, it's been months since we went together. You used to go. You were brought up a Catholic, just like I was. And the faith meant so very much to your mum. If it wasn't for church, we would never have met. We both used to go back then.'

George shook his head.

'I lost my faith long ago,' he said, seemingly without an ounce of regret. 'Because of all the shit I went through. And think about it, you've had two miscarriages. You, a good religious woman who rarely misses a service. For all your good works, worship, volunteering and charity work, our children died before they were even born. Don't you feel let down, Suzie? Where was your God in that?'

'Shush, please, quiet, not here,' she said, covering her mouth with a hand.

'Okay, I'll shut up. But you know exactly what I'm saying.'

Suzie started to cry now, tears running down her face, finding a home on her collar. Were they really having this conversation? Here? In a taxi, of all places. It seemed, yes. And it had been a long time coming. At least George was engaging, not storming off, slamming a door like he usually did. How could he? Maybe God was giving her this opportunity. Stranger things happened in heaven and earth.

Suzie was glad when the driver switched on the radio, Spanish music, turning up the volume. She turned her head, placing her mouth close to George's ear as she had on the plane. She could not have contained her feelings now, even if she wanted to. Some things had to be said. Maybe then he'd believe without question. Maybe his doubts would melt away.

'I have to believe my babies are in a better place,' she said, tears flowing freely. 'They were too good for this world.'

'Believe what you want to but don't drag me into it.'

She shook her head to left and right, shoulders slumped, then lowered her chin to her chest. Such a harsh thing to say, so dismissive, so unthinking.

'Please, George,' she implored. 'Come to church with me here just once. If you do, I really do believe you'll have a change of heart. And your mother would be so pleased. I know she's looking down from heaven. She prayed you'd rediscover your faith every single night before the cancer finally took her. She told me that herself.'

George was silent for a few minutes after that while Suzie sat there quietly weeping, dabbing at her eyes with a paper tissue taken from her handbag. She waited for George to speak again for what felt like an age, thinking he might be deep in contemplative thought, considering her carefully chosen words. But in the end, she could wait no longer, speaking through her tears. 'Come on, George, please say something. Will you come? It would mean so much to me if we could go together.'

He pressed the palms of his hands together in front of him, rubbing them up and down, speaking slowly and deliberately, clearly enunciating each word.

'I'll tell you what,' he began. 'I'll do you a deal. If you pay off the remainder of my debt. And if you agree to all our finances being joint, including your investments. And you make a will leaving everything to me, in the event of your death, *then* I'll go to your church. If you want me to, I'll participate in the service, take communion, and even pray to your God. That's all I can offer. Take it or leave it. It's up to you.'

Suzie felt her jaw tense above a corded neck, her muscles jumping under her skin. But then she thought, maybe a will wasn't such a bad idea. A way of reaching out to him. A gesture without any short-term commitment. And it had to be done sometime.

'Would you make a will, too?' she asked. 'Saying the same thing, leaving everything to me?'

He laughed scornfully.

'Well, I haven't got much, have I? And what I have got isn't worth having.'

His bits and pieces didn't matter to her; she had plenty of her own. It was the principle of the thing. A mutual commitment.

'There's your life insurance,' she said.

George nodded, seemingly still oblivious to her distress. 'Yeah, yeah, fair point. Okay, we'll see a solicitor, make the wills when we get home. But what about the rest?'

Suzie felt herself shiver and said a quick, silent prayer for strength. She suspected she knew exactly what was coming next.

'The rest?' she asked.

'Your investments, a joint account.'

Not again, she thought, so predictable. At every opportunity, always on the make.

'I'm sorry, George, but that's a step too far. You know why. I've explained more times than I care to recall. And I have to do the right thing. It's not easy for either of us. But it's so important that you remember I'm doing it for you.'

George spat his words as the driver turned up the volume of the music. 'I thought good Catholic wives were supposed to love, honour and obey.'

'That's not fair.'

'Isn't it?'

She shook her head. 'No, George, no it's not.'

'It seems to me you can choose which rules to follow just to suit yourself.'

Suzie let out a heavy sigh. Sometimes, she thought, George was so very unreasonable. Provocative, so ready to argue even when so obviously in the wrong. 'I've talked to my father,' she said, 'asked his advice. I've talked to my priest. And I've prayed alone for hours contemplating God's word both at church and at home when you're out or asleep. It would be all too easy to give in to your requests. So very easy. But I have to do the right thing for you, for me, and for our marriage. Please try to understand that. You'll benefit in the long term. I promise you will. And when you do, I'll be so very proud of you. And you'll be proud of yourself. You'll be the man you always should have been. I have to stay strong for us both.'

George folded his arms across his chest, moving a few inches away from her, sliding sideways on the black leather seat. 'Well, in that case,' he said with feeling, 'if you think I'm coming to church with you while we're here, you're very sadly mistaken. And that's your doing, Suzie. Things could have been very different. But they're not going to be, because of you. You'll be going on your own, and I'll be sunning myself by the pool.'

Suzie considered a response, something that went right to the heart of the matter. But she quickly decided that silence was best. Because anything she could say would fall on deaf ears. So frustrating, so very disappointing, and much as expected from a man like George.

The couple sat without speaking for the rest of the journey; with an atmosphere you could almost cut with a knife. The driver likewise stayed quiet, until they finally reached the hotel, set back from the street, the traffic no less busy than he'd anticipated.

Suzie paid in cash, counting out the new notes from her brown faux leather purse, before George retrieved the luggage from the boot with the aid of the driver, who did the heavy lifting. Nothing more was said by the couple. All was silence.

A tall, smartly dressed doorman assisted Suzie and George through the large, smoked glass double doors that led into an impressive, spacious lobby with a high ceiling, a wide, sweeping, carpeted staircase and plenty of light.

Suzie told herself that at least the hotel was as pleasant and impressive as she'd hoped, as she crossed the marble floor, approaching a polished wood reception counter to her right. She could feel her husband's eyes on her as she completed the necessary formalities, filling forms, handing over passports, accepting keys, booking in.

Please, God, not another argument, she thought when the process was complete. She didn't have the strength. And George still had a scowl on his face. It wasn't exactly the start to the holiday she'd hoped for or dreamed of. But things could improve, couldn't they? Yes, yes, of course, they could. The bad start didn't have to continue. It needn't set the scene for the entire trip. Say a little prayer, Suzie. Reach out to God. That's what Dad would do, and he knew best. Hopefully, things would get better from here.

**4**

There was no more talk of money as the couple travelled to the hotel's second floor by lift and then walked silently down a wide, well-lit corridor to their room at the back of the four-storey building. Suzie entered first as George held the door open. He followed to see a luxurious double deluxe bedroom with a Mount Teide view, the room she'd chosen without ever consulting him. But he had to admit that it was probably the most excellent hotel room he'd ever been in. First impressions, he had to admit to himself, were good. Although, of course, he was never going to tell Suzie that. Why would he?

George turned in a small circle, taking in and appreciating the elegance, comfort and peaceful surroundings. At the same time, Suzie visited the bathroom, closing and locking the door with a metallic click. Their luggage was already in the room, to one side of the king-size bed, close to a three-doored mirrored wardrobe offering ample storage. Not that that mattered a great deal to George. He had other things on his mind. Something he thought far more critical. Like persuading his mean bitch of a wife to approach their relationship with a more generous spirit. Yes, she'd paid for the holiday, and the room was nice enough. But they could have had a large suite. Why didn't she book a suite? It wasn't like she couldn't afford it. If he had ready access to the money, he would have. They'd be living the dream. Relaxing in the lap of luxury. Shit, if it wasn't for the money, he wouldn't stay with Suzie at all.

George walked out onto the private balcony to breathe the warm air and take in the view, which he had to admit was spectacular. There was a large pool surrounded by sub-tropical greenery, and the high mountain beyond that, topped by snow, stood out dramatically against a deep blue sky that seemed to go on forever. Such a lovely vista, he pondered, could almost rekindle his faith in an all-powerful creator. Nature's majesty at its very best. Almost – but not quite. He'd come to see his religious upbringing as a moral straitjacket. Something he'd come to resent. A belief system that limited his joy. And he'd seen far too much of life to think the world was good. People were selfish. He was selfish. He wanted the best, to suck the juice out of life, to live every minute to the maximum. And, as he felt the bright autumn sun on his face, he told himself there was nothing wrong with that. Yes, he was a sinner if sin was anything more than a human construct. But no one was perfect, not even his mother, whatever she'd thought before death. She'd sometimes been somewhat overenthusiastic with the corporal punishment she'd inflicted, beating him black and blue while quoting the Bible: spare the rod and spoil the child, and all that. And what about the priests? What about the many horrors inflicted on the innocent by the Catholic Church? He'd met a priest like that, a right bastard. Sin? George knew he was a virtual saint by comparison. Why couldn't Suzie see that? God knows, he'd tried to explain often enough. Why couldn't she trust and value him for the man he was? There was only so long he could wait. She was so unreasonable. Expecting too much. Things had to change in the interest of his sanity. And they had to change soon. Time was running out.

George was panting slightly now, sweating as he stepped back into the room, his thought process suddenly stopping as he heard the toilet flush and a tap turn on. And then, only seconds later, Suzie appeared, smiling as if she was in the right and he was in the wrong. He was sure he hadn't misread the signals. Everything about her seemed to imply criticism, like his mother and that priest who haunted his dreams. That leering monster of a man. That demon from the darkest corner of hell.

Look at how Suzie stood as she faced him, George thought. Hands on her hips, a grin on her stupid face, focussed only on him, with those accusing eyes. His mother used to stand like that, just like that, and then he'd suffer. He'd always suffer, bruises where they didn't show. His mother was tight with money, too. Nothing unless he earned it, not a penny. Exactly like Suzie, just like her.

'What do you think?' Suzie asked, turning away towards the balcony.

George wondered what to say in response. What to say? What the hell to say? Had she read his thoughts? Or was she simply asking about the room? The room she'd chosen.

George pictured himself throwing her off the balcony, watching her tumble, arms flailing as if trying to fly before she hit the ground, splat, dead and gone. If only it were true. There'd be no more criticisms, accusing looks, or snide remarks.

'Think about what?' he asked, genuinely unsure what she'd meant. Thinking she must have some unspoken hidden agenda. It seemed she often had. Something else he'd come to despise.

Suzie turned her head with another smile he considered mocking. As if he was too stupid to understand the simplest of questions. As if he was below her. A lesser form of life.

'The room,' she said with a smile. 'What do you think of the room?'

He avoided her gaze and sat at the end of the bed. Was that all she really wanted to know? Or was a reminder of the cost coming next? The cost to her. Probably!

'Um, yeah,' he said, 'it's nice, great view.' Should he add something, say more? Yes, yes, of course, he should. 'I can't wait to get in that pool.'

She crossed the floor to face him and what she said surprised him. 'I thought we could walk down to the seafront once we've settled in. You could show me where you stayed as a child. There'll be plenty of time for swimming. We've got all week.'

He sucked in the air and blew it out slowly, his heart beating so loudly he thought she might hear it. With her, he told himself, it was all about control.

'If we take our stuff, we can use the saltwater pool on the front,' he said with enthusiasm. 'It's right next to the sea, fantastic location. I'm sure you'd love it.' He wasn't sure of anything of the kind. But he thought it sounded right. She sometimes enjoyed a pool despite being unable to swim, staying in the shallow end, relaxing. So why not now?

Suzie checked the time on her phone before returning it to her handbag.

'Oh, I don't think so, not today, George, not after all the travelling. I thought, after the seafront, we could look for that church the taxi driver mentioned. I'd like to light candles for the babies.'

Not a church again, he thought. And lighting more candles, always candles. What good would they do? It wouldn't bring the babies back.

'Yes, okay, if you like,' he said, thinking a walk by the sea might be nice, even with her. And maybe he could avoid the church all together, stay outside.

Suzie smiled again before replying.

'I think I'll unpack before we head off, if that's all right with you. I'd like to hang the clothes up, stop them from getting creased. It'll only take five minutes.'

He rose easily to his feet.

'Okay, yeah, no worries, I'll take a quick look around the hotel and be back with you before you know it.'

'What, now?'

Again, there was that accusatory tone, he thought, as he looked back at her. Unmistakable, dismissive, as if he'd suggested the most ridiculous thing she'd ever heard. She really was a mean-spirited shrew.

'You always take longer to unpack than you expect,' he said, keen to escape if only for a time. 'And I can ask for directions to the church at reception if that helps?'

Her face took on a sour expression. 'Maybe we should leave the church until tomorrow morning,' she said. 'The hotel's got a nice choice of restaurants. I could ring down and book for about seven. We could take it easy for a couple of hours before eating. Maybe read our books and relax.'

George felt his entire body tense. Stuck in a room with her, he thought. Lying around. Doing not very much at all. There'd been no sex since the party. Not since those photos. Not with Suzie, anyway. Stay in the room? She had to be kidding. He couldn't think of anything worse.

'I might go for a run,' he said. Another escape route he sometimes used.

'What?'

Had she gone deaf all of a sudden? 'A run. I brought my kit; I might go for a run. It's a lovely day for it.'

'Now?'

He grinned despite his agitation, thinking she'd be a great

interrogator. She should be a police officer, a pig, not work in a bank. She'd missed her calling. Escape, he had to escape.

'Yeah, why not?' he said after a brief silence, considering his choice of words, what best to say? 'You know I'm working hard to keep fit. And you can do whatever you want to here, book whichever restaurant you fancy, and I'll be back in plenty of time to freshen up. It's a win for both of us.'

She screwed up her face, her brow furrowed, eyes narrowed. Like a serpent, he thought, just like a snake. A poisonous, slithery snake out to get him.

'I quite fancy the Asian restaurant if there's a table available,' she said. 'It looks amazingly atmospheric and there's some fantastic online reviews. Is that okay for you?'

Like his opinion mattered.

'Yeah, lovely, whatever you want, that'll be fine,' he replied, glad he was about to get out of there. 'You know I'm happy with anything spicy. I'll, er, I'll just get my kit and be on my way.'

'Your trainers are wrapped in an orange plastic bag in one corner of the case. I didn't want them dirtying any of our clothes. They were in a right state before I cleaned them off. They weren't cheap either. You really should look after them better.'

More criticism, always criticism, and another reminder of her expense, no surprises there. What had she paid for them, 100 quid, 120 maybe? A pittance compared to her fortune. No more than that.

He bit his tongue, deciding not to comment as he lifted the heavy case onto the bed, unzipped it and retrieved what he needed, the recently purchased training shoes, blue shorts, cotton socks, and a sleeveless white vest he thought showed off his muscular arms to their best advantage.

Within minutes, George had changed and was heading for the door as Suzie held the room's phone to her ear, talking to reception. She called after him as he went to turn the door handle.

'The table's booked for forty minutes' time. They're busy, but they fitted us in when I said we were celebrating our anniversary. And the daylight is going to be going soon. Please be back in plenty of time. It's good of them to accommodate us at such short notice. I really don't want us to be late.'

George pondered why she was always so desperate to please other people but not him, more an observation than a genuine question. He really was at the bottom of the pile. Always was, always had been. Her father came first, then her mother, then her priest, then her sister, with him last, always last.

He pushed his dark thoughts from his mind as he stepped out into the corridor, his spirits raised by the simple act of leaving. And at that moment, life seemed momentarily sweeter. If he could get all her money and make it his, he'd never feel sorrow again.

He smiled and said a cheery hello to two attractive young women in the lift, thinking it likely they were either Spanish or Italian, with their long, shiny black hair and come-to-bed doe-brown eyes. Just as he liked them, so very beautiful, he thought. And he knew they'd flirted with him because he was irresistibly handsome. He had, he silently observed, always been a looker. A girl once told him he resembled a young Sean Connery, and she wasn't far wrong. Although, he was probably better looking than the star. So, how could he not take advantage of that? How could he stay tied and loyal to one miserable woman who kept so much to herself? It was a contradiction of nature. Almost a sin in itself. There were so many girls and so little time.

Time passed all too quickly after that, before George returned to the room at the allocated time to be met by Suzie, resplendent in a new floral dress he barely noticed, staring at him with a puzzled expression that said a thousand words.

'Did you go for a run?' she asked.

George shifted his weight from one foot to the other as if the floor was too hot to stand on. He asked himself if Suzie was suspicious, staring at her face, studying her expressions and body language, trying to read her thoughts, anything to gain an advantage. Had she seen through him? Or were her questions and demeanour simply a fishing exercise? Her way of snooping, sticking her nose in. That could be it. She had that tendency. Was he worrying about nothing for once? Maybe she was just making conversation like a normal person. Someone without a hidden agenda. Even that wasn't entirely beyond the bounds of possibility. Life could be stranger than fiction.

Suzie slightly shook her head as he stared at her, lost in his thoughts. He thought she might be looking at his neck. 'Are you going to say something, George? I asked you a question. You seem in a world of your own.'

'Running? Well yeah, of course I have, you know that,' he said. 'Where the hell else do you think I've been? I told you what I was doing before I went out.'

Her expression darkened, her voice faltering as she spoke. She was either angry, upset, or both; he wasn't sure. But he thought it was more likely irritation when she spoke. As if she felt that was somehow justified. As if she owned him. Like a pet.

'Please calm down, George; I was only asking. It's just that you look so fresh. You don't look as if you've run at all. It's still warm out, even now. You haven't even been sweating.'

She was right, of course. Something he should have thought of. A clue, a dead giveaway. What to say? He forced a laugh.

'I must be getting fitter,' he said. 'I could have run for miles. I may even do a marathon next year. London, perhaps, if it's not too late to apply.'

She stepped towards him and reached up, looking far from persuaded.

'What's that red mark on your neck?' she asked.

George took a backward step, turned away.

Would she ever let up? Questions, questions, always questions. He thought about his response for a second or two, deciding to play the innocent, go on the attack.

'What on earth are you talking about now?' he asked, hands held wide. 'I've only just got back to the room, and it's one thing after another. I sometimes think you don't trust me at all.'

She stepped forward, reached up, touched the side of his neck with a finger.

'There's, there's a red mark,' she said.

A sudden flash of inspiration made him smile.

'Something bit me. Maybe a mosquito. I felt a sting when I was running back to the hotel.'

She lifted her eyebrows, head tilted at an angle, shoulders sloping to the left.

'It, er, it doesn't look like a mosquito bite,' she said. 'And I don't even think they're a problem here at this time of year. I haven't seen a single one.'

He thought it would feel so good to shut her up once and for all. To tape her mouth shut, anything to silence her.

'Stop fussing,' he said. 'Something bit me. I don't know what. I'm not David Attenborough. I need a wash if we're going down for food. Can't we leave it at that?'

She reached out a hand, touching the mark again. 'Do you want me to put some cream on it for you?'

No, I just want you to shut up, he thought. Change the subject, distraction, that was best. 'I'm fine, thanks. A shower, get dressed, and I'll be ready. I had a quick look at the restaurant. It looks ace. I'm sure the food will be delicious.'

She seemed to relax now, and he felt a warm glow of satisfaction for the moment. But how long would it last?

'Thanks for being on time,' she said, stepping back with a smile that looked strangely out of place. 'I want this evening to be special for both of us. We've been through some tough times. I want this to be the start of something better.'

He asked himself how any evening could be good with her. They'd sit there searching for something to say. He'd have to put up with whatever crap she came out with. And then, as if that wasn't bad enough, she'd pay at the end, use a gold card, make a big deal of it, give a generous cash tip, and make him feel small. And she'd expect him to be grateful, as if he didn't have as much right to the money as her. The bitch! Always the same.

'I'm sure it's going to be fine,' he said with faux enthusiasm as he turned towards the bathroom.

'I do love you, George,' she called after him as he entered the marble-tiled room. 'You know that, don't you?'

Strange way of showing it, he thought. Maybe he'd loved her once. Perhaps, but probably not. He'd been hooked by her initial pregnancy. That was the truth of it. And now *his* needs had to come first. That he was certain of. Whatever it took. Her fault, never his.

George began stripping off, dropping his running kit to the white marble floor, thinking he'd never loathed anyone more. Except for maybe the abusive priest. That devil disguised as a man. Yes, probably him.

'Thanks,' George called out as he switched on the water. 'I love you too.'

# 5

George hurried to keep up with Suzie half an hour or so after breakfast the following day as she rushed towards the entrance of an ancient Catholic church that apparently dated back to 1637, and which faced beautiful sub-tropical landscaped gardens close to the sea. She burst into the volcanic stone-built building with its striking wooden Mudejar ceiling, with what, to George, seemed an utterly unjustified sense of relief and enthusiasm. As if just by entering the building, being in that space, with its naves, alter, and physical depiction of Christ, Mary and the saints, she was somehow brought closer to her lost babies. As if rather than blame an unseen God for their untimely deaths, she found solace in His presence.

George felt very different as he stood there in the building, having finally decided to enter despite his misgivings. For him, there was a mix of memories, of childhood, of his mother, and a priest he wished he'd never met. His experience, he pondered, was one thing and Suzie's entirely another. It was as if they were in different worlds and living separate lives.

George could see the growing sense of peace in his wife's eyes as she lit two candles, slotted a few euros into a collection box, then prayed, eyes closed and hands pressed together, now on her knees close to the altar. And as George watched his wife in pensive silence, lost in deep and serious thought, he reminisced that he too had once found comfort in such a familiar religious ritual. He considered that now as the memories flooded back, an irresistible tide far too powerful to resist.

At his mother's insistence, he'd attended church services weekly as a child. It had been a big part of his life. And in some way, it had shaped him, made him the man he was. He'd listened to the Bible stories, sung hymns, and even prayed to a God whose existence he sometimes doubted. And for a time, he felt relatively safe; his fear of hell apart. As if God was looking out for him. As if everything was as it should be and made sense in the world. And he could trust the adults in his life, who'd tell him the truth and do the right thing. Even the priest... as if he could trust the priest. That dirty bastard! So far from the truth. How very wrong he was.

George looked around the church again, first one way, then another, his eyes now adapted to the dim light. He rubbed the back of his neck as his head began to ache, putting it down to stress. The building was indeed beautiful. There was a time he'd have appreciated that. He may even have wanted to spend time there. But all that had changed. Oh, how it had changed. Now all he saw was bitterness, the abuse of power, manipulation and control. And he believed that was the reality. That he'd seen through the subterfuge. Cynical, yes, but for good reason. Not that Suzie would ever see that. He'd tried to explain his issues with the religion, with passion and forethought. But she didn't want to hear it. She was brainwashed to the point of delusion; whatever cruel hand her life dealt her. Suzie would never understand.

Enough, enough, thought George, no more. He couldn't stand it, not for another second. He had to escape.

George dry-gagged once, then again, as vivid childhood memories flooded back, flashbacks all too real. He ran for the door, out into the warm sunshine, looking up at the perfect blue sky. He threw his arms up, raging at whatever force lay behind creation. Why him? Of all people, him, a victim, a survivor! That bastard priest had spotted his vulnerability, had been drawn to it like a moth to the flame. That curse on all that was good. That destroyer of innocence.

George dabbed at his eyes now, frustrated by the strength of his emotion but unable to silence his mind. Why were the memories so strong? Yes, his childhood abuser had changed so much. The bastard, the complete and utter bastard! A man who presented as a force for good was nothing but evil, poisoning everything he touched.

George sat on a convenient, low wall now, the past still surrounding him mercilessly, beating him down. He'd told his mother what had happened when he and the priest were alone. Not an easy thing to do, but he'd done it. And yes, she'd complained to the church authorities and demanded explanations, appropriate action. He'd rarely seen her so angry, full of indignation, very much on his side, once finally persuaded his allegations were true.

'Don't lie to me, Georgie.' She always called him Georgie. 'I want the truth and nothing but the truth. Swear it on the Bible.'

And he had, he'd sworn it, convinced her in the end. He'd given her the sordid details as she held her head in her hands, covering her eyes, peering through her fingers as if she couldn't bring herself to look at him. And he never saw the priest again. Not as a child, not back then. He'd naively thought that was it. That the man had been punished for his sins and would never pose a risk to any child again. But, no, it didn't work out that way, not even close.

George recalled his gut twisting, the crushing disappointment and burning sense of injustice he'd felt when reading an online article only three years ago. There was a black and white photo of a man he recognised immediately, big and bright, on his computer screen, staring back at him with unblinking eyes. The man looked older and greyer than he appeared in George's nightmares. But it was him all right; it was definitely him. How could he forget that face, the priest's dark satanic look, his lying mouth? And the article named the priest too, gave details of his offences and told a story. A tale of horrors that was hard to read.

George dropped his head, looking at the ground, and reminded himself he'd thought about those caustic events so many times before. Whatever he was doing, the memories were always some-where in the background, ready to resurface without warning and pounce. And once his thought process began, it was almost impos-sible to stop. Think about something else, George. Come on, anything but that. Thinking didn't change anything. Not a fucking thing! What happened, happened. Now all he could do was make the best of the life he had left. There was no undoing the past. And especially not with a millstone like Suzie hanging around his neck.

It seemed that after his mother's complaint, the priest had simply been moved on to another church, then on from there, and on from there. No doubt he just repented, then reoffended, moving from one place to the subsequent, spawning destruction as he went. What a horrendous failure of the system. What warped morality and misplaced loyalty. Why hadn't the church been able to see that? And Suzie, why couldn't she? He'd explained; he'd told her everything. But all she could talk of was forgiveness. How little she understood. Where was her empathy, her loyalty? Yet another way of letting him down. No wonder he'd strayed, looking for other women. That was Suzie's fault, it was all down to her. She wasn't even very good in bed.

George wiped away a tear as he continued his rumination. The priest had finally been charged, photos had been found, and videos of his many crimes, yes, videos, too. As if the doing wasn't enough. As if the priest needed to relive his vile crimes, feeding his grotesque fantasies until he could do it all again. And because of all that evidence, the priest had finally paid the price for his sins, pleading guilty to numerous sexual offences committed over many years, resulting in a lengthy prison sentence that wasn't nearly long enough. What were eighteen years for all those ruined lives? And the hypocritical bastard would only serve half. Nine fucking years, shit. At least thirty victims, and probably more. He'd be let out, forgiven, and undoubtedly welcomed back by the church as if saved, like the prodigal son. And he'd be a danger forever, always a danger; no child would ever be safe, not from him. If the bastard felt genuine remorse, he wouldn't have been able to stand to live.

George wanted to scream, to stamp and shout like a petulant child as he sat on the wall in the sunshine, but then a young woman strolled past, catching his eye. He focussed on her bubble-shaped backside as she walked on by, just the distraction he needed. And in that instant, he was back in the present, the memories quickly fading. What did it matter if he'd screwed a few girls? Compared to the priest, he was a saint. No wonder he'd lost his faith. No wonder he had no time for religion. No wonder he could no longer trust. People were so unreliable, so untrustworthy. And Suzie, bleeding heart Suzie, so full of contradictions. Keeping her riches to herself. It sometimes felt like she was the worst of them all.

He looked back towards the church's door as Suzie suddenly

appeared, repeatedly blinking when the bright morning sun caught her face.

'Thank you so much for coming, George. I'm feeling so much better after that,' she said, a look of contentment on her face as she approached him, still seated on the wall. 'I do realise it isn't always easy for you. But I really do believe if you keep trying, you will find your faith again.'

Faith? In a creator, the Catholic Church, with its nuns and priests? There was the reality right there in those words she uttered with such misplaced belief. The crazy bitch really didn't have any idea at all. What to say? Change the subject, George; she was never going to listen.

'Do you fancy a coffee?' he asked. 'And then maybe the pool? We've done the church thing. It's time to focus on other things.'

Suzie held his hand as he stood, gripping it tight. 'You do realise what happened to you had nothing to do with God, don't you?'

*Oh, shut up, woman, please shut your stupid mouth*, he thought. It was always the same mindless crap. 'We passed a nice café close to that small beach with the surfers,' he said. 'How about calling there?'

'I dearly wish those awful things hadn't happened to you, George. If I could undo the past, I would. But the priest was one bad apple. You can't condemn the entire priesthood because of one misguided man.'

*One? What?* Who was she trying to kid? The woman was deluded. There was a plague of the bastards all over the world. Did she ever watch the news? George began walking in the direction of the café, keen to get as far away from the church as possible, wishing he'd never visited at all. 'I did this for you because I know it matters to you,' he said. 'You do realise that, right? You lit the candles, put money in the collection box, it's done. And now it's my turn. You need to do something for me. I thought we could sit down at the café, relax, have a coffee, maybe a piece of cake, and then talk again about the joint account. If we can't arrange one immediately, let's at least agree on a date not too far in the future. It would show me you trust me and give me something to look forward to. I've served my time. It's been long enough. I need to know we're a team.'

Suzie let go of his hand as he finished his final sentence, sighed, looked away, and he was sure he knew what was coming next. He'd have bet on it if he could. 'Let's not talk about that now, George. Let's think about that when we get back home; now isn't the time.'

He felt his face redden, his heart beating hard in his chest. Everything was one way, he thought to himself, digging his nails into the sweaty palms of his hands, picturing himself slapping her face hard. He'd made a generous gesture, and what did he get in return? Nothing, fuck all, that was what. She really was a selfish cow. No wonder he was thinking ill of her. She really did deserve all she got.

'Well, can I at least email the solicitor to arrange an appoint-ment to make the wills?' he asked. 'Will you do that for me? My mum died intestate and it caused all sorts of problems. Not that she had much to leave me.'

'We've already talked about this, George. We're young and we're on holiday. What's the rush? Surely it can wait until we're back home?'

*Screw you*, he thought. Had she realised he wanted her money above all else? Maybe she wasn't so stupid after all. 'It's the grownup thing to do, Suzie,' he said. 'It's been playing on my mind.'

'Doesn't the sea look wonderful crashing against the black rocks?' Suzie asked. 'That dramatic contrast between the white foam and the dark volcanic lava.'

So, thought George, it seemed she could change the subject, too, when it suited her. All he could do was move things along as quickly as he possibly could. He'd prise the cash from her cold, dead hands if he had to. If it came to that. And if it did, it would be *her* fault, all her fault, not his. Anything was possible if she drove him to it. There was only so much any man could tolerate. Nothing could be ruled out. And who could blame him for that?

## 6

The couple ate a late lunch by the hotel's main pool after a brief café visit, choosing tuna with a salad dressed with dark, sweet Italian balsamic vinegar; an ideal accompaniment. They didn't have much in common aside from their taste in food.

Suzie sipped chilled sparkling water with ice and a large slice of lemon while George drank Spanish wine, enjoying a bottle of local red to himself and getting gradually louder as the alcohol had its inevitable effect.

Suzie checked her watch once, then again, then looked at him across the table with a disappointed expression she couldn't have hidden even if she wanted to. Some people, she thought, became increasingly jovial when drunk, entertaining even. But George, well, he was different. He became more argumentative than usual, even more ill-tempered and morose. And that, she said to herself, was the last thing she wanted on a warm Tenerife afternoon when she badly needed to relax. Just look at him. He was so prone to excess, whether gambling, drinking himself into a gradual stupor, or indulging in any other selfish activity that took his fancy. Why on earth was he pouring the damn liquid down his throat as if he feared someone might snatch it off him at any second? Didn't the man have even the slightest semblance of self-control?

Suzie took a gulp of water, washing down a mouthful of green salad she'd been chewing for almost a minute. She sighed loudly once her mouth was empty, more a groan than a breath.

'Don't you think you've had enough of that, George?' She pointed at his glass. 'You've drunk well over half the bottle. And it's not even two o'clock. You'll be next to useless for the rest of the day if you drink more.'

He tilted his head back, emptied his glass down his throat, a dribble of wine running down his slightly stubbled chin.

'Oh, give it a rest,' he said while wiping his face with a paper serviette, crunching it up, and throwing it on the table beside his plate. 'It was a stressful morning,' he continued, his voice raising in pitch. 'Or, at least, it was for me. I went to that church for you. Do you get that? For you! You know I struggle with those places. Surely, you're not going to deny me a drink?'

Suzie let out a long, deep audible breath. 'Have some wine by all means,' she began, trying to be understanding because she felt she should, dredging up some empathy from deep inside her. 'But please don't get drunk. I thought we could go on the mountain trip tomorrow morning. It would mean an early start. You don't want to wake up with a hangover. It would ruin the day.'

He made a face, turned his head, looked up at the high volcano dominating the vista.

'It does look good,' he said. 'There's no denying that. But are you sure you can afford a trip? I wouldn't want you wasting your money on me. Perhaps it would be better if you went on your own. What do you think? It would save you a few euros. Maybe keep those investments to yourself.'

Oh, no, she thought, not this again. Always same: money, money, money. And was there really a need for the sarcasm? It would be so easy to give in. So very easy. But she had to stay strong. What if she capitulated? What if he blew her money on an orgy of ridiculous bets? A frenzy of insane gambling he couldn't control until every penny was gone. It wasn't beyond the bounds of possibility. Past behaviour was the best predictor of the future, wasn't it? That's what her dad had said. All her security would be gone. Where would that leave them? Living from one monthly paycheque to the next.

'Not this again, please, George,' she said, almost pleading, elbows on the table, hands tightly linked. 'Let's not go down that road. It never gets us anywhere. And particularly when you've had a drink.'

A sheen of sweat was on his cheeks, chin and forehead as he snapped back his reply, growing agitation painted all over his face. 'What road's that? Perhaps you could enlighten me?'

Suzie rose to her feet on unsteady legs as George refilled his glass almost to the brim. Enough, she thought, more than enough, the stress getting to her, feeling a little faint, everything around her momentarily becoming an impressionist blur. Best change the subject, she told herself insistently, as she swallowed her words, resisting the temptation to say precisely what she thought of him, in unequivocal language he couldn't fail to understand. How she hated arguments. Appeasement was best, anything to soften his mood. Would he ever change? She had so much to put up with. But for better or worse, he was her cross to bear, as her mother would say.

'Oh, isn't that the woman who sat alongside us on the plane?' she asked, pointing, controlling her breathing as her chest rose and fell; the threat of fainting now passed. 'The one lying on the sunbed next to the tall palm tree, wearing a white bikini? I'm sure it's her. She was standing behind us in the taxi queue.'

George looked up, took a large gulp of wine, narrowed his eyes.

'Um, maybe,' he said. 'I think so, yes. I wouldn't have thought about it unless you'd said.'

Suzie didn't know whether to laugh or cry, and in the end, she smiled, thinking, *like hell, he wouldn't have noticed*. The beauty was even more stunning with her clothes off than when dressed. She could be a model, a film star.

'I'll, er, I'll sort out our bill and then find us a couple of sunbeds,' Suzie said, relieved the quarrel seemed to be over, at least for the moment, the distraction working better than she could have hoped. But she suspected, soon enough, George would find something to moan about. He had that look about him, a disagreeable, drunken glower. Any excuse for an argument. God knows, it didn't take much these days. George really had changed so much.

Suzie pointed. 'Maybe those two beds over there. That's one thing I like about this place; it's never crowded, there's always plenty spare.'

George refilled his glass yet again, this time emptying the bottle.

'What, in all that shade?' he said. 'I'd prefer to be in the sun; I want to go home with a tan. What's the point of coming here if we don't take advantage of the weather? It's a big part of the holiday for me.'

Complaints, complaints, always complaints, she thought.

'Just put the umbrella down or move your bed forward, George; you'll be fine.'

He shook his head, seeming far from persuaded. Suzie noticed him looking up, glancing at the skimpily white-clad beauty on the other side of the pool as she lay there reading her Kindle. And again, despite acknowledging unwelcome feelings of jealousy, Suzie hoped the distraction might be enough to silence him. But no such luck. He drained what was left in his glass with one greedy gulp before speaking.

'Have you got 20 euros?' George asked. 'I fancy another bottle of red, just the house stuff, nothing expensive for you to worry about.' He gave a little bow and a wave of his hand. 'Or I could sign it to the room if your imperial majesty consents.'

Suzie asked herself if there was really a need for yet more sarcasm.

'No, George,' she said, a tear in her eye. 'Please, no more wine. You know what you get like. Come and sit in the sun. You can always have another drink tonight at dinner if you really want to. I might even join you then. We could share a bottle together.'

His tense body language portrayed his mood before he even spoke.

'Who the fuck do you think you are?' he asked with an angry glower. 'I'm a grown man, not a child. You're not my mother.'

She pulled her head back. 'Please calm down, George. I'm worried about you, that's all. And please don't swear, not here in public. There's no need for bad language. You know I don't like it.'

George's expression darkened further still, his face suddenly contorting as he jumped to his feet with such force he knocked the table back, sending the empty wine bottle and two glasses crashing to the tiled floor.

Suzie looked around her, shuddering, acutely aware of people staring, as George yelled, pointing at her with a jabbing digit, his eyes wide, showing the whites, spittle forming at the corners of his mouth. 'You're not my boss, money or not,' he shouted. 'I wish I'd never come on this fucking holiday. You're an absolute nightmare. I went to your church. I made that sacrifice. But nothing is ever good enough for you. It's pretty clear to me you should have married somebody else. Maybe then you wouldn't be such a miserable, killjoy cow.'

Suzie slumped into the nearest seat as George turned his back on her, storming off toward the hotel building, mumbling crude obscenities as he went. She curled her shoulders over her chest, making herself smaller, covering her mouth with a hand as a smartly dressed, black-haired waiter who looked in his thirties began carefully collecting the broken glass without a word, placing it on a tin tray. Suzie had never felt so self-aware. As if sitting in a spotlight on a stage. As if the whole world was now watching her, not just a few fellow holidaymakers and staff around a luxury hotel pool. My goodness, it was awful, she thought to herself, the embarrassment was crushing. Had the ground opened, she'd have jumped right in.

Suzie closed her eyes for a beat, head in her hands, wishing she was anywhere else but there. And she was surprised and a little disconcerted to see the white bikini-clad beauty rushing towards her when she opened her eyes moments later. As if there hadn't been enough drama for one day. *Not me, please go away, don't talk to me.*

Suzie looked up, blinking away her warm, salty tears as the young woman stood just feet away, a concerned look on her beautiful face. 'Are you all right, lovely?' the beauty asked in an accent similar to Suzie's, the vowels stretched out, the pitch going from high to low. 'I couldn't help but see and overhear what happened. Men, eh? Poor you! I had a boyfriend like that, Adam. I'd had enough in the end. Got rid of him. That's why I'm here on my own.'

Suzie felt a flush creep across her face. 'I'm er, I'm okay, thanks,' she stuttered, still wishing the beauty hadn't approached her at all. 'Nice, nice of you to ask. But my husband's not usually nearly so, so bad. I think it must be the sun. And he'd had, he'd had too much to drink.'

The beauty smiled, reached out her manicured hand. 'It's all right, no need to make excuses for him. I saw what happened. My name's Amelia. Good to meet you. Shame about the circumstances.'

Suzie forced a thin smile, lips pressed together, then shook Amelia's hand ever so briefly, just fingers to fingers, thinking the beauty such an unexpected good Samaritan, standing there smiling in her revealing swimsuit. 'Um, I'm, er, I'm Suzie; nice to meet you, too,' she said, thinking there was no choice but to reply. But once she'd started speaking, all the pent-up emotion poured out of her. And to some extent, the telling was a relief. It felt good.

'Oh, gosh,' Suzie began. 'George can be such a prat sometimes. This is all so very embarrassing; everyone's looking. I hate this sort of thing. I'm such a private person. And it's such a nice, quiet hotel.'

'Don't you worry about it,' Amelia said insistently. 'Let them look. They'll lose interest soon enough. Most of them already have. And you should have seen what mine was like. He was so much worse than yours. He even hit me once, the jealous bastard, and left bruising on my ribs. He couldn't stand me getting any male attention, however innocent. And I never cheated on him, not even once. It's not my way. It got his back up if a bloke even looked at me.'

'Oh, I'm so sorry, that's terrible,' Suzie replied, a little taken aback by Amelia's candour. 'George would never do anything like that. He's never been in the least bit physical.'

Amelia was quiet for a moment, hands on shapely hips, then broke the silence. 'Anyway, enough of men, useless gits. How about a coffee or a nice French brandy for the shock, my treat? My gran used to swear by it. She always used to keep a small bottle in her handbag for emergencies, any excuse.'

Suzie laughed despite herself, thinking her own maternal grandmother had done the same, although, in her case, it was Scotch. Suzie felt inclined to refuse what seemed to be Amelia's kind offer but then had a sudden change of heart. She was surprised to find herself liking the beauty with her open, friendly personality. And it seemed they had much in common, more than she could ever have imagined. Who'd have thought it?

'Maybe an Irish coffee, just a splash of malt with coffee and fresh cream.'

Amelia gave a broad smile, her gleaming, moist, overly white teeth standing out against the dark red of her lipstick. 'That's the spirit,' she said. 'Us girls have got to stick together; great suggestion, sounds good to me.'

Suzie reached for her bag, thinking maybe Amelia was a little older than she seemed on first sight. Botox maybe? A lot of women were using it. Her forehead didn't seem to move at all. 'Are you sure I can't give you something towards the drinks?' Suzie asked. 'You've already been so kind.'

Amelia shook her head with what seemed a sympathetic look. 'I wouldn't dream of it. Like I said, my treat. It's nice to talk to someone from home. When two Welsh girls meet on holiday, they become instant friends.'

'Thank you, it's appreciated.' And it was; Suzie felt genuine appreciation; they weren't empty words.

A nod of Amelia's lovely head this time, her large breasts bouncing ever so slightly with each movement of her body. 'You're very welcome,' she said.

Amelia strolled off towards the nearby bar with a wiggle, returning a minute or two later with the order, an Irish whisky for Suzie and the same for herself. She sat herself down close to Suzie with a smile, teeth gleaming in the afternoon sun, too perfect to be real.

'I saw you on the plane, you know,' Amelia said. 'Where in Wales are you from?'

Suzie realised she was staring at those teeth before lowering her gaze, focussing on her drink rather than Amelia's face. Amelia was indeed lovely. But there was effort involved. She might even have had work done other than dentistry.

'Um, we, er, we live in Ferryside, in west Wales,' Suzie replied.

'It's about eight miles from Carmarthen, a small village on the coast with a view of Llansteffan Castle across the estuary.'

Amelia took a slurp of her hot drink, leaving a milky moustache above her top lip.

'Oh, yeah, I know it,' she said. 'I've passed through there on the train. Nice quiet beach, it looks great. Must be lovely in the summer.'

Suzie handed Amelia a tissue, pointing at her mouth, waiting while she wiped it.

'Do you live in Wales?' Suzie asked, feeling the need to reciprocate.

Amelia smiled as the same thirty-something waiter walked past, unable to take his eyes off her, looking her up and down, head to foot, mouth hanging open.

'I grew up near Llanelli, but it's Aberystwyth these days,' Amelia said. 'I study plant medicine. I work as a medical herbalist. Helping people with their health issues. And I love it. I've always been fascinated by science.'

'Wow.' That's all Suzie could think to say. And it was a genuine reaction, nothing faked. A medical herbalist? Didn't that take years of study, a degree? And after all her earlier assumptions. Those first impressions really were badly awry. It was the last thing she'd been expecting to hear.

'What about you?' Amelia asked as Suzie brought her musings to a close.

'Oh, I just work in a boring old bank. It's in Carmarthen, King Street, not far from the old post office.'

'Nothing boring about it; we all need money.'

Suzie nodded once, looking far from convinced, her mind going off on a tangent. 'I guess so... Do you know, it's strange, my George went to university in Aberystwyth... small world.'

An apparent look of recognition dawned on Amelia's lovely

face. 'Ah, yeah,' she said. 'That makes sense. I must have seen him around. Aber's a small town. I thought his face looked somehow familiar. How long ago was he there?'

'Um, he'd, er, he'd have left about seven or eight years ago. He lived in digs in Queen's Road.'

Amelia jerked her head back. 'Never! That's a crazy coincidence, so did I back then. I've bought somewhere on the front now though, a flat with a sea view, not far from the pier.'

Suzie made a face. 'Strange George didn't say something. He must remember you. You're not an easy girl to forget.'

Amelia laughed, ran a hand through her long hair, and looked down. 'Oh, I've had a bit of a makeover since Adam left. Or rather, since I kicked the idiot out. I've lost over a stone, dyed my hair, Turkish veneers, focussed more on myself. The bastard always used to put me down, crush my self-esteem.'

'Well, good for you, you look absolutely marvellous.'

'Thank you,' Amelia replied.

'And there's no new man in your life?' Suzie asked, already thinking the answer was likely no.

Amelia shook her head.

'Forget men, screw them. Let's talk about something else.'

Suzie took a slurp of fast-cooling Irish coffee, appreciating the rich, sweet, nutty taste as she swilled the warm liquid around her mouth before finally swallowing. She checked her watch.

'Oh, no,' she began. 'I can't believe how much time's passed. I'd better go and look for George. Hopefully, he'll have calmed down a bit by now.'

Amelia sat back and crossed her long legs, right over left. 'If you're sure?' she said.

Suzie drained her glass, taking several sips to reach the bottom, and then went to stand. 'Yes, better had. But thanks so much for coming over. You've been so very kind. And it really did help. I'm not usually nearly so talkative.'

'How long are you here for?' Amelia asked with another beaming smile.

'Just a week.'

'Me too. Hopefully, we'll see each other around. And if you need to talk or just need some female company, I'm in room 134. Don't hesitate to say hello.'

Suzie allowed the table to support her weight. 'He's really not that bad, you know, George, not usually. He's been going through a tough time.'

'I'm sure you have, too. But it wasn't you behaving like an idiot.'

Suzie sighed, thinking never a truer word had been said.

'I'd better go.'

'It's room 134. And don't be a stranger. You know where I am if you need me.'

## 7

When Suzie eventually found him about half an hour after she'd left the pool area, George was lying prone on the king-size bed, snoring intermittently, propped up on three plump feather pillows with a line of drool running from one corner of his mouth. She'd looked in the bar, the lounge, the gym, the hotel gardens and even the spa before finally heading back to their room, tired and full of despondency. And now, there he was, lying in his black, bulging, too-tight underpants, lost to his dreams, clothes thrown to the floor for her to collect like some hotel skivvy. As if she existed only to serve him. An inferior creation. As if he didn't have a care in the world. Amelia was right. Men could be gits. And George was no different.

Suzie stood stock-still, looking down at her sleeping husband, slowly shaking her head as he rolled over, letting out an explosive snort, the air forced from his nose. Like a pig, she thought, just like a muscular boar, all pink and hairy. Should she wake him? Disturb his slumber? Look for an apology? Or should she fetch her book, sit on the balcony in a shady spot, and enjoy the peace for as long as it lasted?

Suzie was still standing there, deep in thought, swaying slowly
from one foot to the next, one arm holding the other at the elbow,
oblivious to her involuntary dance when the decision was made for
her. George slowly opened his eyes, red, bleary, first one, then the
other, then yawned and stretched, arms above his head, hands
against the padded headboard. A half-empty bottle of Spanish red
wine was next to him on the bedside cabinet, a cork on the floor
next to his shorts and T-shirt.

'What, er, what time is it?' he asked, then yawned again. 'How
long have I been asleep?'

Suzie crossed her arms, shoulders drooping.

'Almost an hour.'

He blew out the air, scratched his balls. 'Oh, shit, feels like
longer. I think the travelling must have caught up with me.'

Suzie stared down at him shaking her head, thinking his
contention ridiculous. 'Haven't you got something to say to me?'
she asked.

He screwed up his face. 'Such as?'

'You shouted at me, George, in public; you swore in front of all
those people. And you broke two glasses, smashed them on the
ground when you jumped up. It was all so very embarrassing,
totally humiliating. And I had to apologise for your behaviour after
you stormed off. And over what? Another bottle of wine. Was it
really worth all the unpleasantness? I don't think so. Have some
respect. The least you can do is say you're sorry.'

He yawned for a third time, made a show of it as if already
bored by the conversation. As if her impassioned pleas hadn't regis-
tered. A reaction she thought contrived, soon confirmed by his
words. 'Is the lecture over?' he asked. 'You know I've got a low
boredom threshold. And I've heard it all before.'

She sent him a long, pained look, asking herself if he was still
drunk. And it seemed he was. Yes, of course, he was. 'I thought

you'd want to make up,' she said, suddenly close to weeping. 'But I can see you've had more to drink. Over half a bottle! And in case you hadn't noticed, you spilt some. For goodness' sake, you've stained the carpet. Two broken glasses and now this. What will people think of us?'

He smirked a silly, seemingly smug smile, conceited, as if her distress only amused him. 'Me, drunk? Me?'

Her eyes narrowed. 'Yes, George, you.'

'Well, aren't you the clever one, Little Miss Perfect? You don't miss a thing. It's like being in a relationship with a detective. Anything else you want to point out while you're at it? Best get it over with. Maybe then I'll get some peace.'

Suzie started crying now, the emotion too much. Was there any point in arguing with him when influenced by alcohol? Why do it? What possible good could it do? He probably wouldn't even remember their conversation when sober. Maybe just leave, get out of there. Yes, that was best.

She was about to go, retreat from the room, but then had a change of mind, her father's words recalled. *Stay strong, Suzie, stay strong, for your sake and for the sake of your marriage. Don't give in to him. Don't let him bully you.*

Suzie found strength in her father's advice, a new energy, as she heard the words as if whispered in her ear. Yes, do as Dad said, she thought, and perhaps change tack, turning George's drunken inhibition to her advantage. He was prone to spouting off when inebriated, letting the truth slip out, saying things he might later regret. *Yes, ask away, Suzie, ask away.* Some things needed clarification for her peace of mind. And maybe he wasn't so clever after all.

'Does the name Amelia mean anything to you?' she asked calmly, lowering her tone.

George shook his head, rubbed his crotch, and burped at full volume, not covering his mouth.

'Should it mean something?' he asked. 'I'm sure you'll tell me if it should.'

Suzie chose to ignore his blatant antagonism, slowing her breathing, taking deep breaths, and focusing on the task at hand. Another question, ask away.

'The girl in the white bikini,' she said, consciously relaxing the contours of her face. 'I talked to her. She lives in Aberystwyth.'

His eyes narrowed. 'You talked to her?'

'Yes, George, she was living in Queen's Road at the same time as you.'

He cleared his throat and gave a disinterested look she found far from convincing. A look she'd seen before.

'Was she?' That's all he said; just two words.

'Yes, she was. She said she'd seen you there. She recognised your face. Do you remember her?'

He shrugged, his shoulders rising and falling after he sat up.

'What does it matter?'

'I just can't understand why you didn't say something, that's all. She was sitting close to us on the plane, and we've seen her twice since.'

George laughed as Suzie mumbled under her breath. *Could he be any more infuriating?*

'Well, of course she remembers me with my looks,' he replied. 'And I might have seen her in Aber. Who knows? It's a small town. There's always that possibility. But what's the big deal? It's so like you to make a fuss about nothing. I don't think I can remember her at all.'

Another deep breath. 'I think she might be older than she looks.'

'Good for her, so what?' he replied, open hands held wide.

'She works as a medical herbalist.'

'Does she? Am I supposed to care?'

Suzie paused before speaking again, only for a second, maybe two at most. She looked at her husband closely, studying his face, weighing up his reactions. 'I was thinking when I was looking for you,' she said, 'didn't you see a herbalist for your hay fever in your third year at Aber? I remember you saying there was a time when the antihistamines you'd bought didn't agree with you?'

George shook his head, no longer laughing, perhaps saying more than he wanted to. 'No, no, I don't think so.'

Suzie took a slight step back, rocking on her heels. 'I know you did, you told me. We were in a café in Carmarthen. The one in Merlin's Lane, the veggie place. I can clearly remember our conversation. You said the tablets made you feel nauseous.'

A look of recognition dawned, but Suzie doubted its sincerity. Something else that seemed contrived, less than natural. 'Ah, yeah,' he said, 'I remember. I arranged an appointment with someone, then cancelled when I didn't have the cash. You must be thinking about that.'

A part of her wished she'd never addressed the subject at all. But only a part. The more he said, the more she doubted his sincerity. Was he even capable of the truth? Lying had almost become the norm, his immediate fall-back position whenever challenged, like a politician; a greedy, conniving, dishonest MP out for everything he could get. Why on earth was he talking in riddles? Suzie drew breath, releasing it before speaking, rushing her words as her frustration mounted.

'Why can't you just be honest with me, George?' she asked, again using his name, as was her custom, much more so than the norm, as if he needed reminding who he was. 'You told me the herbal medicine tasted terrible. I clearly remember you saying it. You had to boil the herbs, making a drink.'

He reached for the wine bottle, held it to his mouth and took a swig.

'For fuck's sake, what's all this about? If I saw a herbalist, so what? I might have done. But I don't think so. And if I did, it wasn't her. You're not getting paranoid again, are you? Because of those stupid photos that idiot of a girl posted online. I've told you there was nothing to it. It was just some stupid drunken messing about. The sort of thing that happens at all work Christmas parties. You'd know that if you weren't so uptight. Take a chill pill and relax. This is supposed to be a holiday. I could do with some more sleep.'

She glanced at her watch.

'Anxiety and depression are nothing to joke about,' she said. 'My medication isn't due for another twenty minutes. And your attitude really isn't helping. I wonder what goes on in your head sometimes. You say the most inappropriate things.'

He looked her up and down, feet to face, licking first his top lip and then the bottom before laughing.

'You can look rather hot and sexy when you're angry, all that righteous indignation, quite a turn-on after a few glasses of vino.'

'What?' she asked, sure he was simply trying to upset her, throwing one verbal grenade after another into the conversation because it amused him to do so.

'Oh, you heard me,' he said with a wide grin, touching his cock, now semi-erect. 'Come on, come to bed? It's been a while. And you know the booze makes me horny. Do a strip tease; give me a bit of a show. Get your boobs out; wiggle that arse.'

You have got to be kidding, she thought, taking another backward step. Sex! After everything he'd said, all he'd done. He was so crude, so unpleasant. Alcohol really did bring out the worst in him. If it wasn't for the church's teachings, divorce might be an option. It wasn't the first time she'd thought it. But, no, she had to stay strong, make him a better man. And, one day, perhaps forgive him. Her cross to bear.

'For goodness' sake, sleep it off, George. And maybe say a

prayer. You're not very nice after a drink, that's the truth of it. I'll wake you in time for dinner.'

He looked her in the eye, statue-like, unblinking. 'I sent that email we talked about.'

Suzie gave a puzzled expression, wondering if she should continue the conversation at all. 'What email?' she asked.

'To the solicitor.'

She shook her head. 'I still don't know what you're talking about.'

'The wills, an appointment to sort out the wills. Me to you, you to me, all our worldly possessions. As we said.'

'What, you sent an email from here?'

He made a face. 'Duh, that's what I said, didn't I?'

'We're on holiday, George. Surely, it could have waited.'

He rubbed his balls again. 'Well, it's done.'

It seemed to Suzie there was little, if any, point in further discussing it. She decided she'd said enough. And certainly heard enough. 'I'm going to read my book downstairs in the lounge,' she said, her tone betraying her irritation despite her best intentions. 'I'll wake you at seven for a shower. And please, please, please, don't drink more.' She stepped forward, reaching down before continuing. 'I'm going to take this bottle and pour what's left away. And before you make a fuss, I'm doing that as much for your sake as mine.'

He raised an open hand to the side of his head, mockingly saluting. Not the first time he'd done it in recent weeks. Something she found a lot less amusing than him.

'Yes, ma'am, anything you say, ma'am, your wish is my command,' he said. 'I am here only to please. Even if I'm not going to get a shag.'

She walked toward the bathroom, the bottle in one hand and a charity shop paperback in the other. A lucky find. Book two in a cosy crime series she was particularly enjoying.

'I'll see you later, George,' she said. 'And please sober up. No more alcohol.'

He blew her a kiss, then slipped the same hand into his underpants, moving his fingers as if kneading dough. Just to annoy her, she thought, anything to upset her, all part of his show. And all because he wanted her money. Her money! What part of that didn't he get? He wasn't entitled. It was hers.

'Missing you already,' he called out with a grin.

Suzie poured the wine into the toilet bowl, flushed it away with a heady sense of relief, then left the empty green bottle on a white tiled shelf, a testament to her small triumph. A reminder not only to herself but to him that she'd done the right thing. The moral thing. Like a good Catholic woman should. She thought it and believed it. Someone had to retain a sense of propriety, whatever the circumstances, conforming to acceptable norms, and within their relationship, that was her. Maybe that was God's plan all along.

Suzie wiped a tear from her eye, her mind racing, one thought after another. What was it Father O'Shaughnessy had advised when she'd discussed her marital difficulties? Have a baby and become a mother as soon as possible, without delay! The priest seemed to think a baby would solve everything, like some magic bullet. As if motherhood was her only purpose in life. As if nothing else mattered. And as if parenthood would somehow bring her and George closer together, more like it had been before his disillusionment with the faith. And she'd tried, she'd really tried, time and again before seeing the photos, before her husband's betrayal. But not since, not after that.

Because how could she even think to ever trust George again with things as they were? And he hadn't mentioned wanting a child, not even once. Did he even want a baby? Was he even capable of being a decent father, placing someone else's needs above his own? He sometimes seemed hostile to the idea of parenthood. At the very least, a lot less enthusiastic than her. Everyone had their flaws; no one was perfect, not even her. But her sins were so much more forgivable than his. No man would ever truly understand a woman's plight, least of all her husband, with his selfish sexual wants. He'd put so much pressure on her before marriage. Pressure to lose her virginity. And she'd finally given in. Not an easy thing to do. Not without regret. Physical intimacy was, she acknowledged, more of a challenge for her, an activity inevitably accompanied by guilt. But it seemed so very different for him. He seemed to see sex as much a form of recreation as a means of procreation. What was the point in even thinking about it all? It didn't change a thing. It didn't change George. He was what he was. And she was, too.

Within a minute or two, Suzie had left the bedroom and was in the corridor, glad to have found George but even more so to escape. Sometimes, she ruminated, her husband was just too much. She made the sign of the cross, suspecting he'd be stripped naked and masturbating before she even reached the lift, sins against chastity, an intrinsically and gravely disordered action, another certain sign of his moral decay. Her mother had warned her all about men as she grew up, warned of their dirty ways.

Suzie shuddered at the thought despite the building's ambient warmth, still deep in contemplative thought as she strode towards the lift, gradually increasing her pace. Maybe when she finally found the God-given strength to forgive George, she should make more effort, try to tolerate his advances a little more often and try not to tense up. Another pregnancy wouldn't come along by magic, an immaculate conception. And sex, after all, had unitive as well as procreative purposes within marriage. The church itself taught that. Her priest had said as much, so it must be right. Sex wasn't all filthy and disgusting, as her mum had said, that awful day when she caught her touching herself as a teenager. Oh, it was so terrible. If only it was possible to erase that awful memory from her mind, press rewind, delete. Never to think of it again.

Suzie felt herself flush now, sweat patches forming under both her arms, her gut twisting as she thought back to that day, one thought after another, an irresistible tide. Her mum had walked into her small bedroom at the back of the house without knocking on the door, a horrified look on her face, as if she'd seen the worst thing in the world, an abomination, a thing to cause disgust and loathing.

Suzie winced now as the memories flooded back, colour images playing behind her eyes as if in real-time. As if she was back there, lying on top of her summer quilt in the soft evening light of the window, her homework book on the bed next to her, still half done. She'd moved her hand quickly, but not nearly quickly enough, as her mother stood to stare, her face contorting.

All hell was released as her mother yelled, stamped her feet, and finally stormed off after what felt like an age, slamming the bedroom door behind her so very hard it shook in its wooden frame.

Suzie recalled being left in her childhood bedroom with its sky-blue painted walls and bright yellow half-open curtains, alone again, but with her mother's anguished angry words ringing in her ears, repeated time and again like some crazed Eastern mantra she already knew she'd never forget until her dying day. As if hearing those damning words only once wasn't enough to drive home her plight. She'd felt so small, so dirty, as if she'd let herself, her family, God and the church down in the worst possible way. As if she wasn't good enough to live in a world with decent people who knew the difference between right and wrong.

'May God forgive you,' her mother had shouted, the pitch and tone so different from her usual sing-song voice, eyes narrowed almost to slits, wringing her hands, almost spitting her words, hateful. 'What will your poor father say when I tell him what you've done?' she continued, looking Suzie in the eye, never looking away. 'And the priest, oh, no, what about him? Can you imagine? Picture it, hang your head in shame. A man of God shouldn't have to hear of such unnatural things.'

'I'm, I'm, so sorry, Mum. Please don't tell anyone. I promise, I'll, I'll never do it again.'

But her mother had shaken her head. 'If only it were that simple,' she said, as if she meant it. 'But it's not, Suzie, it's not. Get on your knees. Come on, pull up your clothes, off that bed, down on the carpet. Pray for your soul, young lady. Pray harder than you've ever prayed before. Ask the Almighty to teach you the wisdom and control you so obviously lack. Believe me, you don't want to spend an eternity in hell. Not burning forever. That would be a terrible fate.'

And then, after all that, alone again, when she'd finally found the courage to leave her bedroom, the silent treatment for days. That and disapproving looks sent her way. School had been an escape. But the fear was always there. Her mother's voice was never far away. And God saw everything, He heard everything, read her thoughts, knew her dreams. So, there was no real hiding place, not even in sleep. Not for any minute of the day or night.

And then, days later, worst of all, her confession. She'd had so long to think about it. So long to consider her choice of words.

Suzie shuddered now at the thought of it, the memory of events stinging still as they had that day. Oh, entering the confessional was so very hard, her entire body trembling, sitting in that stall, at church, behind that screen, telling the priest what she'd done, just sixteen years old. And he asked for detail, because he had to.

Because it was for her own good, her salvation. She had to tell the whole story, all of it. All that stress, all that shame, and the guilt, the predominant emotion, followed finally by absolution, until the next time she sinned in one way or another. There were so many ways to get things wrong.

She'd wanted to touch herself again, of course, as the days passed, as she lay alone in bed at night, temptation calling, the devil whispering in her ear. But she resisted; she stayed strong, just as the priest had said she had to. No one was free of sin. Not her, not even her parents, and certainly not George. Like everyone else, he was flesh and blood, susceptible to the desire to do wrong. So, perhaps she should forget those party photos, push them from her mind, although more easily thought about than done.

And did George even deserve forgiveness? Or was he beyond redemption? He hadn't confessed. Was she her punishment for her teenage failings, her flesh getting the better of her not so very long ago? Maybe, that could be true. Only time would tell if she could save him. Perhaps he'd return to the church one day, or maybe he wouldn't, blaming that one priest, that one bad apple in the barrel. She resolved that she'd continue to offer what encouragement she could, out of duty, as a good wife should. All she could do was try.

## 8

George woke to find himself alone in the hotel bedroom early the following day, the bright morning sun pouring through a gap in the rich, heavy red curtains, filling the space with light. He checked his watch, eyes narrowed against the glare, his head pounding and mouth parched. It was just after 7 a.m., so it seemed Suzie had let him sleep through rather than wake him for dinner the evening before, as she'd said she would. No wonder he felt so flaming hungry; all her fault, the stupid cow.

George called out Suzie's name once, then again, louder the second time, intending to ask for a glass of water to quench a burning thirst. But all was silent. He asked himself if she was in the bathroom and ignoring him. It wouldn't be the first time. Or, if, for some inexplicable reason, she was already out and about at such an early hour. He reminded himself that she'd been behaving even more unreasonably than usual in recent days, so maybe she was. Anything was possible where his wife was concerned. So much to put up with. Such a burden.

George rose from the bed, stretched, farted, and headed to the spacious bathroom. He emptied his bladder with a satisfied sigh before drinking from the cold tap, greedily gulping down mouthful after mouthful until his thirst was finally quenched. He raised his aching head, studying his features closely in the illuminated mirror above the white porcelain sink, his nose only three inches from the glass.

George stood there naked, staring with bleary eyes, turning his head slowly first one way, then the other, focussing on every part of his face in turn, never looking away. He acknowledged he was looking a little jaded. That was true. There was no denying the alcohol had taken its inevitable toll. But such things were temporary. A nice hot shower, a bit of much-needed breakfast, a full English, the works, strong, sweet coffee and a slice or two of brown toast, and he'd be looking his usual handsome self again. A man at the very top of the evolutionary tree. A vision of muscular alpha male perfection, irresistible and charming. A magnet for the girls. Sex on legs.

He turned away from the mirror, his mind still in overdrive. Where the hell was Suzie so early in the morning? Was she trying to annoy him? Wind him up again? Probably! She really was getting worse by the day. A whirlpool dragging him down. How much longer could he stand it? That was the real question. A week, a month, a year, maybe? Certainly no longer, whatever the situation. He had to find a means of escape. The plan had to work. And if not, surely, anything was justified. How much could any man take?

George entered the shower cubicle, pushing thoughts of Suzie from his mind, sliding the glass door shut, turning on the water and taking sensual pleasure in the hot flow warming his skin.

He stood there washing himself from head to foot with scented soap, his headache slightly lifting and his mood more positive, at least for a time. But his thoughts soon returned to Suzie as he stepped from the cubicle, drying himself with a large fluffy white cotton bath towel. How to play it? Should he ask her about the money again whenever she finally made an unwelcome appearance? Or should he give her a day or two to calm down after the events of the day before? Yeah, that was probably best.

George first saw the handwritten note resting on the small polished wooden cabinet to Suzie's side of the bed when he was balanced on one leg, pulling on a pair of dark blue linen shorts. What the hell was that? A letter on hotel paper, written in black ink? What the hell did the woman have to say for herself now? As if he didn't have enough to put up with without her endless nonsense.

George picked up the single sheet of watermarked, ivory-coloured paper, holding it close to his eyes with a slightly trembling hand, rather than fetch his reading glasses, a red plastic-framed pair he never wore in public for fear of ridicule. He repeatedly blinked away what was left of his headache as he prepared to read, asking himself why on earth Suzie hadn't just used her phone and texted like a normal person?

He shook his head, feeling nothing but disdain as he answered his own question. Because a letter was more dramatic, that was why. She really was pretentious, so full of herself, so uptight. Right, this was it, brace yourself, George. Let's see what the silly cow has to say for herself.

*Dear George,*

*You looked so peaceful when I returned to the room yesterday evening. I thought I'd better let you sleep. I hope I did the right thing. You'd drunk so much, and well, the truth is, I couldn't face another argument. And I very much hope we can both make a new start today, enjoying what's left of our holiday together.*

*I do understand that visiting the church wasn't easy for you.*

*So, I'm sure you'll be glad to know I've forgiven you for all you said and did. I won't mention any of it again, promise!*

*After much thought, I finally decided to go on the mountain trip this morning without you. You didn't seem that keen when we talked about it, so I thought a few hours without me, when you can do what you like, visiting the pool or the spa, would do you some good and be very welcome.*

George paused, a little irritated but mainly relieved as he turned over the sheet of paper, reading what was written on the back.

*I saw Amelia sitting alone in the hotel restaurant last night and joined her for dinner. We get on surprisingly well. She really is a pleasant person, so easy to talk to. She's not Catholic, not religious at all. But I like her, nonetheless. We've exchanged contact details. And she agreed to share a taxi with me this morning, so we will go up the mountain together.*

*I'll give you a ring as soon as I'm back in the resort. I thought we could meet near the harbour for lunch. There are some beautiful old historic buildings there, classic Tenerife, and some lovely-looking restaurants I found online.*

*Bye for now. And PLEASE don't drink today. It would mean so much to me if you could stay sober. I left ten euros in the pocket of your blue shorts in case you decide on a taxi. See you soon.*

*Love, Suzie. x*

George screwed up the sheet of writing paper into a tight ball, tossed it into the nearby wastepaper bin with a sneer, and imagined talking to Suzie, as if she was in the room, a one-way conversation with him speaking and her listening.

An x, of all things an x, as if a kiss means anything. And you had to go and mention my drinking, didn't you? You couldn't let it go. And ten measly euros. You have got to be kidding me. I'm a man, not a child. I don't want pocket money. I want to be treated as an equal. No, no, I'm the man of the home, the head, more than an equal. Isn't that what your church teaches? I'm starting to loath you, Suzie, like I've never loathed anyone before. Not even the priest. And I'd kill him if I could. Tear him limb from limb. Be careful, or I might fancy doing the same to you.

George continued indulging the fantasy, starting to enjoy himself, picturing himself slapping Suzie's face hard and feeling slightly aroused as his anger slowly subsided to be replaced by a train of thought that further raised his spirits.

He grinned to himself as he picked up an item of clothing from a nearby chair, pulling on a T-shirt most would think was too tight.

George punched the air, picturing what he saw as a better future, his mind racing. He wasn't doomed to a life of drudgery. No, there were exciting times ahead, when he'd have all the money, every single penny, and be free of her. He just had to bide his time. Amelia and Suzie were now friends. And hurrah for that. That had to be a good thing. There could be advantages. It was a sign he was on the right track, thinking straight, moving towards his goal. Yes, this development was, without a doubt, a much-needed win when he needed it most.

He laughed now, a belly laugh, head back, Adam's apple bobbing as he reflected on events. A trip up the mountain with Amelia! Miss Beautiful and Mrs Dowdy sitting together in a taxi. And all at Suzie's instigation. The first welcome thing she'd done in ages, perhaps ever. And she didn't even know it. What a strange world. He'd best keep that to himself, his little secret.

# 9

Suzie rang George at just before twelve that afternoon when he was sunning himself by the hotel's smaller spa pool. A stylish, comfortable relaxation area at the far side of the sub-tropical gardens. He'd already enjoyed a steaming hot sauna, followed by twenty glorious minutes in a heated jacuzzi, chatting to a lovely young Polish woman, whose large bobbing breasts he'd repeatedly focussed on as they moved with the bubbles.

He thought of the woman now as he picked up his phone, taking it from a pocket of his shorts on the floor next to the sunbed. He let the phone ring another three times before answering, in no rush to speak, wishing he could spend the day alone, that Suzie had never rung at all. And then he heard her voice, that grating sound he'd come to hate so much, like a dentist's drill, he thought, or a knife scraping against a glass bottle. If anything, Suzie's voice was even worse than those things. The most aggravating sound in the world.

'Hello, George, I'm back in the resort. We had a wonderful time. You missed a treat. The views were absolutely stunning. You could see for miles. And there was even a cable car that took us to the summit.'

George could hear the enthusiasm in her voice, and he hated that. Suzie enjoying herself, having a good time, and spending money which by rights should be his. He'd like to crush her like a bug, shut her stupid mouth forever, and would, if there were no negative consequences, if he could get away with it. She wouldn't enjoy herself then.

'Glad you had a good time,' he said. 'I've just spent a couple of hours reading by the pool. Is Amelia still with you? That's her name, isn't it?'

'She stayed in the taxi for a trip to Garachico, a pretty, small town in an unspoilt part of the island further down the coast.'

George laughed to himself. Who the hell did Suzie think she was, a travel correspondent? Like he was interested. Too much detail.

'You didn't fancy going with her?' he asked, wishing she had.

'Um, well, yeah, it would be nice to see the place, but I thought we could go together, you and me.'

Oh, joy, he thought. A day trip with Suzie, could anything be worse? Another day in hell.

'Yeah, maybe, if we have the time. Are you coming back here for lunch? I'm not sure I fancy the resort. The food here is so good. That tuna we had was the best.'

Suzie paused before responding, a second, maybe two at most. He could hear the disappointment in her voice when she finally replied, which pleased him. 'I've er, I've found a lovely little restaurant with a view of the harbour. It's perfect. I was incredibly fortunate to get a table. And the menu looks fantastic, lots of local dishes at very reasonable prices.'

He gave a little laugh. The price, money... With her, it always came down to money. It would feel so good to tell her where to stick her restaurant, but best keep her onside. One day he'd say to her what he thought of her. That day would come.

'I'll walk down,' he said. 'Order me a glass of red. I fancy the exercise. I should be with you in fifteen minutes.'

'You don't want to get a cab?'

He'd spent the ten euros on a generously proportioned vodka with tonic, thinking the spirit less likely to show on his breath.

'Like I said, I could do with the walk. Where exactly are you?'

She gave him the name of the restaurant, followed by the street.

'You really can't miss it. Just walk down into the resort, to the seafront, then turn left and head for the harbour. You'll see me sitting at a pavement table for two. There's a large blue sun umbrella with yellow writing. But please be quick. I told the waiter you're already on the way. Other people are waiting for tables.'

Other people! Why the hell was she always so eager to please other people rather than him, the one she should have been pleasing all along?

'Order that wine; I'll be with you before you know it. I might even put on my trainers and jog.'

He heard a predictable sigh at the other end of the line and pictured a look of disapproval. A look he'd both seen and imagined more times than he cared to count.

'Don't you think a soft drink would be better?' she asked. 'I'm having sparkling water with ice and lemon. I've already bought a large bottle, plenty for two. You don't want another hangover, another ruined day.'

He stood, formed his hands into tight fists, gritted his teeth, grinding them together, loathed to continue the conversation. Didn't she always have water? Like it needed saying. Control, control, always control. Who the fuck did she think she was? She wouldn't know a good time if it sneaked up and bit her on her fat arse. Didn't she understand the concept of powering through?

'Are you still there, George?'

'Yeah, still here,' he replied.

'I thought you'd gone, for a minute.'

If only he had. *Escape, glorious escape*, he thought.

'I'll have whatever you think best,' he said. 'I wanted to talk to you about our finances again. I've got a few ideas. Lunch seems the ideal opportunity. I'm on my way.'

## 10

Within twenty minutes or so, George had joined Suzie at her restaurant table, resenting the shade of the blue umbrella, desperate to sit in the Canary Island sun. He gulped his chilled water without enthusiasm, then picked up one of two menus, already having decided on a medium rare steak with salted potatoes in their skins. He needed red meat, had a hankering for it, something to give him strength. It was going to be a difficult day.

George glanced up appreciatively as two giggling girls of about sixteen or seventeen strolled past wearing short skirts and skimpy tops. He smiled, his spirits lifted, but then quickly returned his attention to Suzie, who seemed focussed on him.

'Are you ready to order?' she asked, seemingly unaware of the distraction. 'Have anything you fancy, my treat.'

Wasn't it always? George thought to himself. Her money, her bank cards, always hers, like he was some charity case. Not the head of the family, not someone to be respected. He should be in charge. Wasn't that what her precious church taught? It seemed she chose which teaching to believe as it suited her, like they all did. Couldn't she see the contradiction in that?

'Have you chosen, George? You look as if you're in a world of your own.'

He pushed his resentments from his mind and told her what he wanted, pointing to his particular steak of choice on the menu.

'Are you sure you want it medium rare?' she asked, eyebrows furrowing before releasing, another look he'd seen before.

George nodded. 'Yes, I'm sure. I couldn't be more certain. I'm a big boy now. I can choose my own food, thank you very much. I don't need you mothering me. I got more than enough of that from Mum. All that pressure she put on us to get married. I wouldn't be sitting here now if it wasn't for her.'

Suzie opened her mouth as if to speak but then closed it again as if unable to find the words. For the briefest of moments, he thought she might start weeping. 'Come on, George, there's no need for that. Please try to relax.'

He pushed the menu away. 'There's no need for what, exactly? Perhaps you could enlighten me.'

'It's nothing, forget it; I'm being oversensitive, that's all.'

'Ah, time of the month. That explains it.'

She glared at him. 'No, no, it's not! Why do you always assume that?'

He was silent for a second or two. 'Is there something else you want to say?' he asked. 'I can see you're still irritated. Spit it out. You have my attention. I'm all ears. Now's your chance.'

She slowly lowered her eyes, avoiding his angry gaze. 'Let's j-just order and en-enjoy our food, please, George,' she stuttered as a pencil-thin waiter, wearing an immaculate white shirt and slightly flared black fitted trousers, approached them with a friendly smile, looking from one to the other.

Suzie cleared her throat, a slight cough, then gave their order as George looked on. He waited for the waiter to walk away, then counted in his head, one to three, before speaking, carefully choosing his words, regretting the antagonism he'd created because it didn't serve his purpose. 'Sorry, love, it's just that things get on top of me sometimes. Everything that's happened, it's just too much.'

Suzie nodded, her expression softening. 'It hasn't been easy for me, either,' she said, touching his hand across the table. 'But there's a lot of good things in our lives. Try to focus on the positives and pray; that's what I do.'

He gave her his best smile, thinking the time was right. This was it. *Go for it, George*. It was now or never. 'I had a lot of time to think this morning when you were, er, when you were on your trip with that woman you met, your new friend.'

Suzie looked at him across the table, seemingly interested, giving him the confidence to continue.

'Now, please hear me out before responding. I've been looking online,' he said. 'Zoopla. There's a really nice flat for sale in Narberth that looks ideal for renting. It's close to the centre of town, with on-street permit parking, two bedrooms, a lounge, kitchen and bathroom. Why don't you buy it, put it in both our names? It needs a bit of work, but that wouldn't take me long. You know I'm pretty handy when I put my mind to it. And there's a long lease, I rang and asked, over 900 years. So, there's no worry there. And the annual charges are very reasonable.'

'I don't want to move to Narberth,' she replied. 'I'm happy where we are. I like being near my parents and the church.'

He shook his head, still hopeful of a positive outcome but beginning to think she'd use any excuse to shoot down his initiative. She almost always did. He'd mentioned renting clearly enough.

'No, no, you're not listening to me,' he said. 'I'm not talking about us moving. The flat would provide an excellent rental income. A friend at work is doing it in Carmarthen, renting to students, making a fortune. Your money is dead as it is, doing nothing. You get hardly any interest at the bank. Inflation's eating it away.'

Suzie leant away, sucking in her cheeks. 'Do we have to talk about this now?'

Hold it together, George. Keep trying. Avoidance, avoidance, constantly avoidance. Don't let her get away with it. 'Why *not* now?' he asked, trying to dampen his anger. 'I've found us a great opportunity, something for our future. And it would give me a fairer share. Cement our partnership. That has to be a good thing, doesn't it?'

Suzie made a face, crumbling the complimentary bread.

'Can you even own a property with your debts?' she asked. 'Wouldn't the recovery company take it from you? And imagine the complications if that happened. It would affect my credit rating, too. Neither of us would be in a good place financially. I can't take that risk; sorry, it's out of the question.'

George swallowed hard. This was it, the whole point of the conversation. The proposition he had in mind all along. But would she listen? Did she ever? Maybe this time. 'Yeah, but there's a way around all that,' he said, trying to sound encouraging; confident and assured. 'Think about it. We've just got to be creative, think outside the box. That's what really successful people do. People who've made themselves rich. You could pay off what's left of my debt first. That's the key. Then we buy the flat for cash. It's only £140,000, a real bargain. You could afford all that with no problem at all.'

George watched his wife closely as she shifted in her seat, her body language crushing his hopes before she uttered another word. She was silent for a few seconds before speaking. There were tears in her eyes. But all George felt was loathing.

'This isn't easy for me, George. I do love you. And I can see this means a lot. I can see and hear your enthusiasm. But I have to do the right thing. I'll talk to my dad when we get home. Let's see what he thinks. But I have to be honest with you; as of now, I don't think it's a good idea, for all the reasons we've talked about before.'

George imagined himself punching her in the face time and again, breaking her nose, dark blood flowing from her nostrils, another powerful blow cracking her jaw. And then stamping down as she lay on the ground, shutting her up forever. He forced a PR smile, not ready to give up quite yet. Her money was calling. He could see piles of notes in his mind's eye.

'What if I started to go to church with you again?' he asked in a quiet voice, playing what he thought was his best card, the ace in his pack.

Suzie's eyes lit up but her tone suggested an element of doubt. 'Would you really do that for me?'

He nodded frantically, thinking he was finally winning. Reel her in, George, reel her in. You've got her this time. 'Yeah, yeah, I would,' he began, looking her in the eye. 'If you pay off my debts, open a joint account and put the flat and our house in both our names. Then, I definitely would. I give you my word.' And then a phrase intended to lighten the mood. 'Scout's honour! And I'll never gamble again.'

Suzie dropped her head, a hunched posture, shoulders slumped like a slowly deflating blow-up beach toy. And in that instant, George knew his initiative was failing despite his best efforts. He hated her for that, even more so than before. What a waste of time and effort.

'I'll pray and ask for God's guidance,' she said. 'But I really don't think so, George. You've made so many promises and broken them. I know you believe what you're saying now, and you mean well. But you have an addictive personality. Come to church every Sunday for a few months, talk to Father O'Shaughnessy, ask for his support, go to confession, and then maybe we can talk about this again. I need more than words, however well-intentioned. It would be so easy for me to give in to you, so very easy. But I have to stay strong, for you and me, too. Anything else, and I'd be letting us both down.'

'Have you finished?'

She nodded. 'I've said all I want to say.'

He held his hands wide, knife in one, fork in the other as the food arrived and the waiter walked away. 'What good has all that money done for you? I thought being rich was against your principles. Matthew, isn't it? "It's easier for a camel to go through the eye of a needle than for a rich man to enter the kingdom of God." That's what Jesus said, isn't it? And I'm sure that means women as well as men. Share the money with me. Be charitable. All it's done is make you miserable.'

'Perhaps I should give more to the diocese and charity than the amount recommended.'

He felt himself shake at the extremities. 'Charity begins at home. You need to remember that.'

She was silent for a beat. 'I think we've both said enough, George. It's not something we're going to agree on. I've told you what I think. And that's not going to change, not now, not here. Let's eat our food, then go for a walk around the harbour. When we're back at home, there'll be plenty of time for money talk. This week is supposed to be a break from all that.'

George felt inclined to bite back but quickly decided there was little, if any, point. The bitch, he contemplated, seemed as entrenched as ever, a tight-fisted Scrooge. And maybe a walk wouldn't be such a bad thing, get some sun, burn some calories, just a shame it had to be with her. If only she were Amelia. How good would that be? Now, that would be a walk worth taking.

Suzie waved the same waiter over about fifteen minutes later, paying the bill with her gold credit card, the balance of which she always made a point of clearing in full each month to avoid interest. She reached out on standing, trying to hold George's hand as he went to walk away, crossing the road towards the harbour. But he increased his pace, pulling away, thinking just being in Suzie's company was bad enough without physical contact. Was that really beyond her comprehension?

As she hurried after him, reaching for his hand again, he decided that it was. She was the most ridiculous and utterly stupid woman he'd ever encountered.

George did his best to ignore his wife, further increasing his pace and pretending she wasn't there. But then he slowed to a stroll, staring at the peachy backside of a middle-aged woman with a tangle of curly brown hair, bending over to fasten a sandal.

At first, he was oblivious to Suzie. Still, she touched his shoulder as she caught up, panting slightly from the effort as she approached the harbour's edge, an approximately ten-to-twelve-foot drop leading to the choppy, salty water below.

There were multi-coloured boats of various descriptions and sizes, both fishing and pleasure craft. And grey-white seabirds swooped and cried in the azure-blue sky, not a cloud in sight. But George barely noticed any of it as the sun shone down, warming his angular face. He looked away from the woman as she walked away, her bright green kaftan blowing in the warm breeze. And then it happened, Suzie tripped on the uneven cobblestone surface; she fell with a loud shriek, not to the ground, but over the harbour's edge, tumbling towards the sea, her arms flailing almost in slow motion, as if trying to fly.

George was reminded that Suzie couldn't swim as she hit the Atlantic water headfirst, splashing around for a second or two but then slowly sinking down between two tethered boats. He thought about her will, that it hadn't been made, and then about the complimentary holiday insurance that came with her bank account, which would pay out a hefty sum in the case of an accidental death. He asked himself if this was the break he'd prayed for, if he should let her drown. He would get the insurance money, wouldn't he? Even without a will? They were married, after all. Yes, of course he would. It had to be worth a try. But the woman in the kaftan was shouting, pointing, and a harbour swimmer was rushing quickly in Suzie's direction from about forty to fifty feet away, adopting an efficient front crawl, one powerful stroke after another.

George took his phone from a shorts pocket, placed it on the ground at the harbour's edge, and then jumped, feeling he had no other choice, fearing onlookers' criticism and that of the wider world, being labelled a coward, or worse still, a killer, a trained lifeguard who'd stood by watching his wife drown. The shame would be too much, too damning, whatever the potential reward.

George hit the cold Atlantic water feet first, gasping, catching his breath with a wide-open mouth, his hands spread wide to avoid his lithe body sinking too far under the murk. He was still acutely aware of a growing group of strangers looking on as he quickly reached the surface, suddenly wanting to be seen as a hero as he dived down, eyes wide open though he was seeing very little at all.

He thought he'd probably done enough as he resurfaced, that he could let Suzie drown after all. She'd been under the water for two, maybe three minutes. A little longer and he'd be free of her. But the swimmer was close, watching, just seconds away, so George dived again, kicking his legs. He felt Suzie's arm first, then her limp hand in his. He grasped her tightly, out of breath, swimming slowly to the surface, turning her on her back, lying under her, supporting her head, keeping her nose and mouth above the water by her chin because people were watching. He thought she might be dead, that he'd timed it just right, as several onlookers shouted their enthusiastic encouragement.

George resisted the impulse to laugh as he manoeuvred Suzie's seemingly lifeless body towards a nearby flight of barnacle-encrusted stone steps. And he thought that fortune had finally smiled on him at the most unlikely time and in the most unexpected way. He was free of her and would be seen as a hero. He might even get some coverage in the papers, maybe even on the TV news. How good would that be? What would Suzie's parents say then? There'd be no more criticism, no spiteful remarks putting him down, crushing his self-esteem. He'd be seen as a man who was nothing but selfless, who'd risked his life to try to save his wife. Come on, George, nearly there – a few more strokes.

As George reached the steps, still deep in thought, panting, adrenalin flooding his system, two men rushed down, urgently taking Suzie from him and carrying her up to the cobblestone ground bordering the harbour's edge. Oh my God, he thought, they'd try to save her – the worst possible outcome. Maybe there was still life in her. Perhaps he wasn't free of her after all. What a crushing realisation. Please let her be dead. Come on, George, one step at a time; up you go. All he could do was hope. Things might still work out for the best.

By the time George reached the top of the slippery, wet stone steps less than a minute later, Suzie was on her side in the recovery position, coughing and spluttering as she spewed out water, one mouthful, then another. He picked up his phone, glad it was still there. And then Suzie slowly turned her head, looked up at him, eyes red, filled with tears, and he'd never felt lower or more despondent. He resisted the impulse to scream out his angst, thinking she couldn't even die with good grace, choking back his tears. The bitch couldn't even get that right. Just look at her clinging onto her worthless life to spite him and crush his hopes. To make his existence even more miserable.

An older man with thinning grey hair and gold-coloured metal-framed glasses that looked too big for his gaunt face patted George on the back, congratulating him in a strong Spanish accent, and then offering him a towel, as he stood there shivering despite the sun's warming rays. And then there was the sound of a siren, getting gradually louder as it got nearer, several onlookers still standing to stare but others walking away, seemingly losing interest.

'She will live. You did well, young man,' the old man said, still standing at George's side. 'You may keep the towel, my gift to you. Is she your wife?'

George nodded once, then lowered himself slowly to the hard ground, sitting next to Suzie, placing the towel under her head as she rested it on the stones, feeling he had to. People were still watching. Some were taking photos, others videos, using their phones. He had to keep up the show. It would be all over social media soon enough. He could share it. Milk the inevitable praise. Women liked heroes; they admired them. Yes, best focus on the positives. It wasn't all doom and gloom. There'd be a torrent of pussy coming his way.

Suzie was breathing more deeply now, greedily sucking in the warm air, gulping. George thought it ugly, like a fish in need of water. Okay, she could breathe. But she still hadn't said anything, not a single word. Not a thank you, no praise at all. What an ungrateful cow, George observed, as a white ambulance festooned with several red crosses arrived, stopping just a few feet away.

George had a sinking feeling deep in his core as two paramedics walked towards him, the siren now off. That was it. The final act. A good chance was gone. A dream had ended before it truly began. Such a terrible shame. One of the saddest times of his life. Something else to resent her for. Was God punishing him, taunting him for amusement, pulling his strings like some mocking puppet master in the sky? Or was it random chance, just bad luck, like an unwelcome throw of the dice? He really wasn't sure.

A little over two hours later, George had returned to the hotel room, showered, changed into dry clothes, and was now at the private hospital, sitting at Suzie's bedside as she slept propped up on pillows, quietly snoring, a look of peace on her face, as if the earlier events hadn't happened at all. He'd asked an attractive, young, dark-haired nurse why Suzie had been admitted. It seemed as she'd swallowed a lot of seawater and had lost consciousness, it was simply a precaution, no more than that.

George looked at his wife with what he could only describe as disgust. All that effort to get there, and she couldn't even be bothered to stay awake to greet him. Still no thanks, still no praise. The shame of it. She should be falling at his feet, begging his forgiveness for the misery she'd made his life. But despite all that, for the first time since her fall, he was glad she hadn't died. Not because he felt any love for her. But because of the will. The lack of it. And the complications that could entail despite their marriage. Maybe, he pondered, he wouldn't have got her money at all, not even the insurance, a travesty, a disaster. Letting her drown, acting impulsively, however seemingly advantageous in the moment, could have ruined everything. Far better to play the long game for as long as it took. That way, if everything worked out, one way or another, he was sure of getting his due, even if she didn't give in to his persuasions. And that's what mattered most – winning in the end.

George waited at Suzie's bedside for another ten minutes or so, repeatedly cracking his knuckles and tapping a foot against the floor until he decided he could take no more. Why waste his time sitting inside a depressing hospital ward when he could be lounging by the hotel pool with a drink in hand, enjoying what was left of the day's sun? If the stupid bitch hadn't been daft enough to fall in the water, he wouldn't be there at all. All her fault. Seconds seemed like minutes, minutes like hours.

He checked the time, reached out, grabbed Suzie's arm just above the right elbow, roughly shook her awake, then sat back, looking up and smiling warmly as a full-figured white-uniformed nurse hurried on by carrying a bedpan.

'Hello, George,' Suzie said, her voice slightly croaky, as if the effort of speaking hurt her throat. It seemed the salt water had stung.

He looked at her with a frown.

'Is that it, "hello"? After everything I've done? Is that really the best you can do?'

Suzie reached out to touch his knee for a beat before withdrawing her hand. 'Thank you, George,' she said, tears welling in her still-red eyes. 'Thank you so very much. I'm very grateful.'

George sat back in his chair, one leg over the other, arms folded across his chest. His left eye was twitching ever so slightly. He blinked in an effort to stop it. 'What exactly are you grateful for?' he asked. 'Perhaps you could expand on that for me. I'm keen to know your thoughts.'

He wasn't sure if she was upset or confused, maybe both. She averted her eyes to the wall. 'Thank you for saving my life. I, I very nearly died.'

He quickly replied, thinking her fragile mood may be to his advantage. 'So, hopefully, you know you can trust me now.'

'I really thought I was going to die. I looked up through the water, sinking down, and then everything went black.'

He nodded slowly, deliberately, once, then a second time, letting her dwell on events, giving her time to think. 'You were drowning, gone; I jumped in, risking my own life to save yours. You owe me; you owe me big time. That is *your* debt. You're only breathing because of me.'

'I've... I've said a prayer of thanks. And I've asked God to bless you.'

George raised his eyebrows, head tilted back, looking at the ceiling. 'It wasn't God who saved you. It was me. Perhaps you could give me some credit for that. Or is that beyond you?'

She touched her face, wiped away a tear.

'I've s-said th-thank you, George,' she stuttered. 'And I think what you did w-was wonderful, I really do. I don't kn-know what else I can say. You're my hero.'

He looked her in the eye, his face blank, showing zero emotion. 'Are they keeping you here?' he asked. 'Have the doctors said anything?'

Suzie seemed relieved to change the subject. He could see her face relax. 'Just for the one night,' she said, no longer stuttering. 'They want to keep an eye on me. All being well, I'll be discharged in the morning. We'll, er, we'll be able to get on with our holiday. Put all this behind us.'

'Do you want me to tell your parents what happened? I could give them a ring if you like. Who knows? They might even think better of me then. After saving their little girl.'

Suzie shook her head. 'No, George, please, I don't want to worry them. Not with my dad's heart problems. I can tell them when we get home. Or perhaps keep it to ourselves. I don't want him having another attack.'

Good luck with that, he thought, amused more than anything. It would be all over the net soon enough if it wasn't already. And people talked in the village. Everyone was going to know, whether she liked it or not. Not everything was within her control.

'I'll need money,' he said, blurting out the words as if he couldn't wait to expel them from his mouth. And then he repeated himself, using the exact same words as before, just to drive home his point.

This time Suzie's look was definitely one of confusion. George was sure of it. It seemed talk of cash always unnerved her, and it had again now, even now, after all he'd done, saving her worthless life.

'Money? What, er, what for?' she asked.

He felt his pulse quicken. 'I had to walk here. And it's a long way. It took me almost an hour. Did you even think about that? Surely you'll not deny me a few miserable euros after I saved your life?'

She shook her head frantically.

'No, no, of course not. There are still about two hundred euros at the hotel, in the safe in the wardrobe. The code is 3377. Take as much as you need.'

George swallowed hard, silent for a second or two before finally speaking again, his tone conveying his irritation. 'What use is that? I'm going to need money for a taxi back. You're not the only one who had a shock this afternoon. It wasn't nice for me either. And I've had enough of walking for one day. I shouldn't have to ask. It shouldn't be this hard. I'm beginning to think you're not grateful at all.'

Her eyes widened.

'Don't be so silly; of course I am. Don't think that way, please.'

'So, what are you going to do about it?'

She sighed, blew out the air, and held her hands to the side of her head as if surrendering at gunpoint. 'My credit card was in my shorts when I fell in the harbour. It was still there when I arrived at the ward. It's in the drawer in the cabinet next to the bed.' She pointed. 'In there. It should still work fine.'

He stood, opened the drawer, and took out the card, clutching it tightly in one hand. And it felt so good, just plastic but full of possibilities.

'What's the number?' he asked.

'8437,' she whispered, leaning her head towards him. 'Spend what you need; you're welcome. But please, no gambling. Don't give in to temptation. I want you to promise me. Maybe avoid going online at all.'

George felt a tightness in his chest, his temperature rising to a savage high. 'I did a rehabilitation course, remember? I went every week for months. I was humiliated to make you happy. And I passed. I got a certificate. It's on our wall at home. So, what the hell are you worried about? You never stop banging on. You nearly died. I saved you. All that happened just a few hours ago, and you said you're grateful; empty words. You're still the same old mean Suzie you always were. It doesn't seem you've changed at all.'

She covered her face, speaking through her fingers, and then made the sign of the cross. 'You lost thousands of pounds, George, *thousands*. If the house wasn't in my name, that would be gone, too. That's not an easy thing to forget. You very nearly brought us to ruin.'

He drew his arm back and threw the card on the bed, suddenly oblivious to other nearby patients as a red mist clouded his thinking. His eyes were wide, bulging, showing the whites as his nostrils flared. He so wanted to hit her. Something he'd never done. But it would feel so good. 'You can stuff your fucking card,' he yelled. 'Stick it where the sun doesn't shine. I'd rather crawl back to the hotel on my hands and knees than use your card. I wouldn't use it if you begged me. Not if my life depended on it.'

Suzie called after him, sobbing, as he rushed towards the ward door. 'Take the card, please, George; there's no need to be upset. I'm sorry, I didn't mean anything.'

George laughed as he entered the corridor, his anger subsiding as quickly as it appeared. It seemed the worm was turning. Maybe he was winning at last. And it felt so good to get out of there. So good to hear her weeping. A quick jog back to the hotel, get the money from the safe, maybe a swim, and then a few drinks, see where that took him. Who knew? Perhaps he'd see the lovely Amelia, tell her the story, and make himself a hero. Or maybe another girl. Someone just as hot. A beauty to flirt with and cash to spend. How good would that be? His cock was getting hard now, even at the thought of it. Swelling in his pants.

George smiled, then frowned hard as he approached the lift, rechecking his watch, still deep in thought. Time was rushing on, tick-tock, the second hand moving faster now. He'd have to make the most of his opportunities while they lasted. Grasp the mettle. Shame Suzie wasn't staying in the hospital for longer. Hopefully they'd keep her in. He could say a little prayer for that.

## 11

Suzie rang Isobel half an hour or so after George had left the ward, amazed that her phone was still working after its time in the sea. It seemed the protective case had done its job remarkably well. In truth, Suzie was ringing more to pass the time than anything else. Although, she wanted to share her story. And she only had to wait a few seconds before hearing her sister's familiar voice at the other end of the line.

'How's the holiday going?' Isobel asked.

'Hi, I, er, I thought I'd better let you know I'm in hospital.'

Isobel's concern was evident from her tone. 'Hospital? What on earth is wrong?'

'Oh, it's nothing to worry about. I'm fine. But I had a fall. Off the harbour and into the sea. I very nearly drowned.'

A quick response. 'Are you sure you're okay now?'

'Yes, absolutely, I'm as good as new.'

'You would tell me if you weren't, wouldn't you?'

'Of course I would.'

'Do you want me to fly over? I can if you want me to, it's no bother.'

Suzie shook her head as if her sister could see her, picturing a concerned look on Isobel's pretty face. 'No, no, there's no need for that. I told you, I'm fine.'

'If you're sure?'

Suzie hesitated for a second or two. 'George will look after me. He saved me.'

'*George*?'

Suzie gripped the phone a little tighter. 'Yes, George, why is that such a surprise? He was an absolute hero. Risking his life to save mine.'

Isobel sounded less than persuaded. 'Well, he was a lifeguard as a teenager. In Tenby in the summer holidays. I remember him banging on about it. I can imagine him posing, parading up and down the beach. Saving you would have been easy for him. And it was in a harbour, not the open sea. You said that yourself. How dangerous could it have been for him?'

Suzie shook her head, exasperated but unsurprised by her younger sister's dismissive response. 'Look, Izzy, I know you don't like George. You've told me often enough. And I know he can be a prat. But give him a break – credit where credit is due. I'm alive because of him. I'm beginning to think I shouldn't have rung at all.'

'Don't be like that.'

Suzie felt a pang of guilt. 'Sorry. I know you've got my best interests at heart.'

'I suppose you're paying for everything as usual?'

Suzie shifted in the bed, struggling to get comfortable. 'How's Mum and Dad?' she asked. 'Have you seen them?'

'Are you changing the subject?'

'So what if I am?'

Isobel gave a little laugh. 'I haven't visited, but I saw Mum in Tesco. They're fine. I won't tell them about your fall unless you want me to. You know what they're like.'

'Yeah, I've been thinking the same thing.'

There was a second or two's silence before Isobel spoke again. And when she did, her tone was reluctant. As if she was unsure if she should share what she was about to say. 'I hear what you said about George, his saving you and all that. But I still think you could do so much better. He's never going to make you happy. You know what I think. He's selfish. And he's not to be trusted. He's not the man for you.'

Suzie silently observed that there was some truth in what her sister had said. Happiness seemed beyond her. 'Marriage is for life.'

'It doesn't have to be.'

Suzie lowered her chin to her chest. 'It does for me,' she said, wiping away a tear. 'I made my vows. Now I have to make the best of it.'

'But why?'

Suzie shook her head. They'd had the conversation before. It never changed anything. And it didn't now. 'I'll give you a ring when I'm back in Wales,' she said. 'Sending love.'

Isobel emitted what sounded like an exasperated sigh.

'Well, I suppose that's it then. Love you, too.'

## 12

A stunning young woman of colour wearing a tight, silver jumpsuit that sparkled under the lights was singing an uplifting medley of classic American soul songs when George entered the hotel's main lounge just after seven that evening, heading for the well-stocked bar at the approximate centre of the room. An otherwise unremarkable middle-aged couple were dancing, almost to a professional standard, thought George, as the man took the lead, whirling his partner around a polished wood floor bordered by thick blue carpet. But, as impressive as they were, neither the singer nor the dancers captured George's attention for very long. He had other things on his mind as he spotted the lovely Amelia on a large purple three-seater sofa, one long, slightly tanned leg crossed over the other, her tight black skirt raised enticingly above one knee, almost to the centre of her shapely thigh.

George smiled at Amelia, raised a hand, waved, then continued to the bar, just a few quick steps away, where he ordered a bottle of French red wine, one of the most expensive on the menu, and two glasses, before paying in cash taken from the safe. He poured himself half a glass, lifted it to his mouth and drank greedily, savouring the smooth, bold, dry flavour, swilling it around his mouth for a second or two before finally swallowing with a satisfied sigh. He took a second mouthful, swallowing almost immediately this time, then took the bottle in one hand, empty glasses in the other, and strode towards Amelia with growing confidence, looking her up and down, making no effort to hide his interest. Like a hunter, he thought, spotting his prey and ready to pounce, a predator at the very top of his game. Yes, the sight of her was utterly intoxicating, even more so than the wine, that glorious liquid he loved so much. And he silently acknowledged that reality as he got nearer, one step, then another, quickening his pace, his senses heightened, soaring, already thinking of sex.

George placed the bottle and glasses on the table and sat beside Amelia, a beaming smile on his fine-looking face, their legs almost touching. He filled both glasses, his first, then hers. Not because hers was any less important but because he needed another drink. The alcohol was calling out to him, seductive, pulling him in.

'Well, fancy meeting you here,' he said with a grin. 'And with you looking so very hot, too. Wow, that dress, fabulous. I was hoping to see you this evening. And now, here you are. The most beautiful woman I've ever seen. A vision of feminine perfection.'

Amelia shuffled a few inches away from him, then turned her head, meeting his eyes with a frown. She picked up her glass but didn't drink, cradling it with both hands, then looked around her, eyes darting from one part of the room to another.

'Yeah, thanks, George, always with the flattery. You're nothing if not predictable. But, more importantly, where's Suzie? This is all a bit risky, don't you think?'

He let out a short laugh. 'She's in hospital.'

Amelia pulled her head back. 'What?'

'Hospital, she's in hospital. Will be overnight. Won't be back until sometime tomorrow. You can relax. She's not going to see us together. Nothing to worry about at all.'

But Amelia didn't relax. George could see the tension in her face, worry lines around her eyes. 'What the hell is she doing in a hospital? It isn't something you've done, is it?' she asked, her concern still evident.

George's grin became a full-blown laugh as he inched towards her, moving sideways. 'The silly cow fell in the harbour. Nothing to do with me. She tripped, stumbled, and over she went. You should have seen it; hilarious. And people were watching. Loads of them, locals, other tourists. I had to jump in, save her. It's already all over social media. I'm quite the hero.'

'Is she okay?'

He nodded, more serious now, his expression changing. 'Yeah, she is, more's the pity. We've got one night, and then she's back. Like a bad smell.'

Amelia sipped her wine, wetting her full lips. 'Then we'd better make the most of our time together.'

'I was hoping you'd say that,' he replied.

Amelia touched his knee, her manicured nails painted red, then quickly withdrew her hand. 'I can't wait for us to be together,' she said. 'Properly, I mean, not like this. There's only so long I'll wait, George. All this scheming, it doesn't sit comfortably. Money isn't everything. I sometimes wonder if it's all worth it.'

He sighed, thinking it was something she'd said before. Perhaps not with such intensity of feeling and not using the exact same words, but the meaning was much the same. Shit, not her, too. The one potential flaw in his plan. The unreliability of females, however desirable.

Come on, George, he said to himself, keep her onboard, say the right thing. You won't get your hands on her otherwise. 'Oh, come off it, Amelia,' he said with passion. 'You know the score. I've had to live with the silly bitch. I've put up with her for years. And now she's rich. Drowning in cash she doesn't want to spend, and certainly not on me. And I'm entitled to at least half. That's only fair. The natural way of things. We've got to play the game. We've gone this far and made progress; we've just got to stick to the plan. It'll all be over soon enough.'

Amelia shook her head, looking less than persuaded. 'Not quickly enough for me. All this cloak and dagger stuff, well, it's just horrendous. I sometimes think you enjoy it. But I don't, George, I don't.'

He tried to sound understanding, empathetic, to hide his irritation as best he could. Manipulation was a game to him. Something he'd worked at, practised to get his own way. What did Amelia's feelings matter? It was all about him.

'Look, I know this is tough,' he began. 'It's far from ideal. I do realise that. But Suzie didn't give me any other choice. I've explained all that. It's her fault, not mine, so blame her. And now we're so very close to success, so very close. I know we are. I can feel it in my bones.'

Amelia sipped her wine, her throat moving only slightly as she swallowed. 'I suppose you're right,' she replied, with an insufficient conviction for his liking.

'There's one thing I've been meaning to ask you,' he said. 'Why the hell did you tell Suzie about the Aberystwyth connection? It had her asking me all sorts of awkward questions I'd have preferred not to answer.'

Amelia made a face. 'I run a business, George; I advertise. She'd have found out easily enough if she'd looked online. And anyway, a bit of honesty amongst all the lies isn't such a bad thing. What better way to get her to trust me?'

He nodded.

'Yeah, good point, clever.'

'I thought so. But don't ever go thinking I liked doing it. I'm doing this for you. That's it, only for you. Conning another woman isn't in my nature. If it wasn't for everything you've told me, I'd actually think Suzie's okay. In different circumstances, we might even be genuine friends.'

'Well, she's not okay. She's so far from that,' he replied. 'Don't ever feel sorry for her. She doesn't deserve that.'

'It's crazy, George, mad, the whole thing. Why can't you divorce her like a normal person? Thousands of people do it. So why not you?'

George drained his glass, shook his head, and sighed. Why the hell did he have to repeat himself? 'I've explained all this,' he said, then paused for effect. 'It's a church thing. She believes God doesn't recognise divorce, whatever a court says. And that's a problem. I remember telling her about a couple I know at work. They weren't getting on; they split up and made it legal. And Suzie said she'd rather give all her money to charity than share it in similar circumstances, every single penny. And she would, I'm certain of it; as soon as she got even the slightest hint I was planning something, all the money would be gone. I'm not even sure I'd get a share of the house. She'd find some way around that, too. I think she'd rather burn the thing down than give me half.'

'I very much doubt that.'

'You don't know her like I do,' he replied with feeling. 'The woman is crazy. You've got no idea what she's capable of.'

Amelia shook her head, then reached down, fingering the gold chain around her slender ankle. 'Yeah, I know, you've told me. But it all seems insane in today's world. And she seemed so normal when I spoke to her, nice even. We're not in the dark ages. I wish it was different, that's all.'

George refilled his glass and topped up hers, which was still half-full. 'She's a good actor, that's all. Only I see the real Suzie, only me.'

'I guess that must be true.'

'It is true,' he said insistently. 'Of course it's true. You do trust me, don't you?'

Amelia touched his knee. 'Of course I do.'

His relief was almost palpable. 'Good, good, that's good. And you know what we're doing,' he said in a reassuring tone, squeezing her hand. 'The plan's going well. You've befriended her. You've already made a good start with that. And next, when she trusts you completely, after however long that takes, you persuade her that it's best for her if she and me permanently separate. You tell her it's the only option in the circumstances. To sell the house, give me half of everything she's got and cut ties. Not a divorce, that's crucial, that's never going to happen; she'd never agree to that. We'd stay married, just like she wants, but live apart. That's got to be our best chance. And now isn't the time to give up on it. I really think this can work. You've done the hard bit. She told me she likes you. Now for the rest.'

Amelia uncrossed her legs, sitting with them slightly apart, looking down at the floor, straw-yellow hair falling forward.

'But what if the plan doesn't work?' she asked. 'What then?'

He took another swig of wine, feeling the need for it to feed his confidence, to blunt his anxieties, a chemical cosh of sorts.

'Let's cross that bridge if we come to it.'

She sat back up. 'What's that supposed to mean? I don't know how much more of this I can stand. I sometimes wonder if you've thought this through at all.'

He was silent for a few seconds, listening to the music, watching the dancers, glad of the distraction, trying to think about anything but Suzie. And then he glanced at Amelia's legs, her full breasts and wine-red lips. And all his anxieties melted away. Suddenly, there was only one thing on his mind.

'Can we please forget about my bitch of a wife for one night?' he asked, touching Amelia's bare knee, appreciating the warmth of her skin. 'Let's pretend Suzie doesn't exist, and we're here together as a couple. Here for a sexy holiday. I do love you. You know that, don't you? I wish we'd got together when we first met. Long before I married her. We'd have been living the dream. I'm so glad we got back in touch online.'

Amelia smiled, then giggled, girlish. 'Ooh, a sexy holiday, eh?' she said.

'No one is as sexy as you. Not even close.'

Another white smile. 'Do you want to dance?' she asked.

'Ah, I'm the worst dancer in the world, two left feet.'

She stood, swaying seductively in front of him on her three-inch heels. 'Oh, come on, just this once, for me. I love this song. And there's no one watching us. I don't think anyone cares. Don't worry about Suzie. Who's going to tell her? Nobody is, that's who.'

He rose to his feet and whispered in her ear.

'What underwear are you wearing?' he asked, his imagination running riot.

Amelia pecked him on the right cheek, poking out her pink, wet tongue, lingering for a second or two, leaving a lipstick smudge and warm saliva on his face, her heady perfume filling his nostrils. 'A black satin thong and no bra,' she replied, looking him in the eye, batting her long lashes, smoky eyeshadow framing her pretty eyes.

He blew out the air, imagining himself touching her, tasting her, caressing her with his tongue. 'I want to take your thong off with my teeth,' he said, salivating.

Amelia placed an open hand on each of his shoulders. 'And you will, lover boy. You can lick me all over. But first, the dance. You can wait that long.'

George felt his cock swell. 'I'm not sure I can.'

She took his hand, squeezed it, and led him onto the dance floor. 'Put your arms around me,' she said. 'Come on, hold me close. Tonight, you're mine. No one else exists. There's just you, me and the music.'

'Where are we going to go?' he asked. 'To make love. My room or yours?'

Amelia paused for a beat, then kissed him full on the lips, once, then again. 'Um, yours, I think,' she said. 'I want you to fuck me in Suzie's bed. Because you don't belong to her. You're on loan. And soon you'll be mine, all mine. She'll be out of our lives forever. I have to believe that. We've got to make it happen. Then we can make love whenever we want.'

## 13

George was enjoying a steaming hot shower when his mobile rang at just after nine the following morning. He'd been thinking about Amelia as he soaped his body, of the time they'd spent together, watching adult entertainment, then exploring each other's bodies, one position after another, all the things he enjoyed the most, visceral, instinctive, almost animalistic, some of the best sex of his life.

Amelia, he pondered, was so uninhibited, so ready to indulge his fantasies. She was hot, so very hot. But she was never going to be enough, not her alone. There were so many other women in the world, so much temptation. How could he ever resist? But wow, she came close. What a lover, and what a great night!

But now, as his phone rang out, filling the white-tiled bathroom with sound, all his happy thoughts were brought to a sudden and morale-sapping end as he stepped out of the glass cubicle, grabbing a large towel from the heated rail. He guessed he'd hear Suzie's grating voice at the other end of the line before he even answered. It was just like her to ruin his morning, he thought, as he switched on the phone's speaker feature with a touch of a finger.

Oh, well, here goes. He couldn't put it off forever. Best get it over with.

'Hello.'

'Hi George, it's Suzie. I'm ready to be collected.'

He began drying himself, bending at the waist, starting with his legs. He noticed he still had a slight erection, but it was fast subsiding, shrinking by the second. Suzie could do that, he observed, like a bucket of cold water, the cock-shrinker extraordinaire.

'Collected?' he said loudly. 'Can't you get a taxi? I was just about to go down for breakfast.'

He heard what sounded like a sigh before she replied. 'I really would appreciate it if you came. I'm still feeling a bit fragile after everything that happened. It scared the life out of me, nearly drowning like that. And my phone's dead. It needs charging. I'm using one belonging to a nurse. Oh, and I need our insurance details for the hospital. They should be in my emails on my iPad. Although, I did bring the policy booklet with me. It's in the big case. Best bring that with you.'

The last thing George wanted was another trip to the hospital. He didn't want to go. And he didn't want to see Suzie. But did he have a choice? 'So, what, er, do you want me to come to you?' he asked, hoping for an escape route.

'Yes, George, have you listened to a word I've said? Come as quickly as you can. Come straight to the ward. And please bring me some dry clothes and sandals. My things are still damp.'

So demanding, he thought, and so damned awkward. No change there. So ready to ruin his day almost before it began. There were so many other things he'd rather be doing. 'Is there anything else madam requires?' he asked in a sour tone. 'A massage, perhaps, or I could feed you some peeled grapes. Would that be to madam's satisfaction?'

'Just come and get me, George. There's no need for sarcasm. Not today of all days. I very nearly died.'

Such a drama queen, he said to himself. 'Yes, I do know. I saved you.'

'And I'm grateful.'

It didn't seem that way, he silently observed. Telling her where to stick her gratitude would feel so good. 'I'll be there within an hour,' he said.

Another sigh, louder this time. 'An *hour*?' she said, placing a heavy emphasis on the second word. 'But it's only ten minutes by car.'

George began towelling his short black hair, enjoying the feel of it, the stimulation of his scalp. 'Yeah, but you know I'm hopeless on an empty stomach. Bacon, eggs and a coffee, and I'll be on my way.'

'I really would like you to come straight away, George. Please, I'm sick of this place. I really don't want to wait longer than I have to. The holiday wasn't cheap, and I really want to make the most of what's left of it.'

There she was, using his name again as if he needed reminding. Driving home her demands. Who did that? Her, only her. And money, she had to mention the expense, her expense.

This time it was his turn to sigh. 'Then can we at least stop at a café on the way back here?' he asked. 'I'm starving.'

'We can eat together at the hotel if you're quick,' she replied. 'The restaurant doesn't close till ten. I haven't had breakfast either.'

Tight cow, he thought, anything to save a few miserable euros. So typical. 'Okay, Suzie, I'll say goodbye for now. Ten minutes and I'm on my way.'

George picked up the phone and headed into the bedroom to get dressed, choosing tailored navy shorts, a white, short-sleeved Egyptian cotton shirt with a collar and buttons, and tan-brown

Italian gladiator sandals he thought suited him well. Such a hand-some man, he thought. Such a sight to behold.

He studied himself in the full-length mirror on the front of the wardrobe door for about thirty seconds, liking what he saw. He considered it advantageous to look smart as he appreciated his reflection. To make a good impression on the ladies, any hottie who might be interested. And maybe he'd meet someone else if he went out alone one fine evening. Another quickie, who knew? Such things were always possible for a good-looking guy like him.

George had just run a comb through his hair for a third time and was about to leave the bedroom for the hospital when he had a sudden thought, stopping him in his tracks. Oh, shit, the bed sheet, he'd almost forgotten the bed sheet. What if Suzie came prying? It would be typical of the cow if she did, sticking her nose in, snoop-ing. What if the maid hadn't changed it by the time they got back? That could give the game away. There'd be no money after that.

He threw back the summer weight quilt, again recalling the night before with a smile, then removed the king-size sheet, turning it over before putting it back in place, tucking in the edges and smoothing the surface with the palms of his hands. He studied the results closely, still deep in thought. Yeah, not bad, all consid-ered. It wasn't perfect. Some staining was still slightly visible if you looked hard enough. But it was undoubtedly a significant improve-ment. And, anyway, he'd done all he could, taken all reasonable precautions. It would have to do.

Within the hour, a silver Toyota hybrid taxi cab had dropped the couple off at the hotel entrance. And to George's huge irritation, it was too late for breakfast. They'd missed the restaurant's closing time by a fraction over ten minutes. Just typical of the woman, he thought, selfish, ruining everything just by drawing breath.

'I'm going to go up to the room, George,' Suzie said. 'Why don't you have something to eat at the pool bar? I think they do sandwiches, maybe even toast. You must have some euros left. Or you can put it on the room if absolutely necessary.'

I'd like to ram your euros down your ugly throat, he thought to himself as he felt a note from his pocket.

'I think I'll come up, too,' he said, thinking he could distract her from the bed if it hadn't been changed. Lie on it, yes, lie on it, on top of the quilt. That would work.

George held the bedroom door open for Suzie to enter first, thinking it less suspicious, an action likely to put her at ease. As if nothing significant had happened there. No wild night of sexual abandon with him coming twice.

George smiled, again reminiscing, feeling a slight stirring in his genitals as Suzie threw her damp clothes into the bath before joining him in the room, saying she'd send them to the laundry later.

'Give me a few minutes,' she continued. 'And I'll be ready to go down. I want to change into my swimming costume. I quite fancy a sauna. I'm still aching a bit after my fall.'

He quickly sat on the bed, which hadn't been changed. Relax, George, she doesn't suspect a damn thing. 'You're not going swimming?'

Suzie smiled, amused as intended. 'Not today,' she said. 'I think I've had enough of water for one holiday.'

'Not surprising.'

She smiled again. 'Having a shower at the hospital this morning was a bit of a challenge.'

Well, fancy that, it seemed she was capable of humour. Who'd have thought it?

'You've got to get back on the horse sometime,' he said.

'Yeah, I know, but not today.'

And then an unwelcome development George hadn't expected or anticipated... Suzie sniffed the air as he stretched out on the bed, thinking of the soiled sheet, believing he'd covered all the bases. 'Can you smell anything?' she asked, a puzzled expression on her face.

He felt himself tense, every muscle, every sinew. Where the hell was this going?

'No, I, er, I don't think so,' he said. And then a thought he considered inspired. 'Unless it's my aftershave. I did splash it on this morning after my shave. It's the one your mum bought me for Christmas.'

Suzie sniffed again, walking slowly around the room, head back, nose in the air, like a bloodhound.

'No, it's a woman's perfume, expensive, floral, Chanel, I think. Lovely! It's the exact same scent Amelia wore when I shared a taxi with her. I'm certain of it. Is, er, is there something you need to tell me?'

What to say? What the hell to say? Calm down, George; hold it together. You need to sound as matter-of-fact as possible. This had to be convincing.

'Oh, yeah, um, I forgot to mention that,' he began, pausing, thinking hard, buying time. 'Amelia knocked on the door at about seven yesterday evening to ask how you were. I asked her in and made her a quick cup of tea before going down for food. You two are friends; you said you liked her, so it seemed like the polite thing to do. She was here for about ten minutes at most, certainly no longer.' He pointed. 'She sat in that chair, the one next to you.'

Suzie looked back at him.

'Why would she ask how I was?'

Think, George, think. This has got to be good. 'It's simple, really. When it all happened, one of the other hotel guests was at the harbour. He saw you falling in and me rescuing you. Everyone is talking about it, apparently. Amelia recognised our descriptions when the man told her what he'd seen.'

'Really?'

Keep it up, George; one more lie. 'Yeah, I said so, didn't I?'

Suzie kept eye contact, never looking away. 'Did you and Amelia go to the restaurant together? You mentioned going down for food. Did the two of you share a meal? Is that what happened?'

He screwed up his face, asking himself when the inquisition would finally be over. She was like a dog with a bone. Questions, always questions. How could he stand it?

'No, of course, we didn't eat together. Why would we? She's your friend, not mine. We hardly know each other.'

Suzie looked less than persuaded. 'If you say so.'

'I do say so. Because it's true. Don't let those stupid party photos confuse your thinking. Paranoia can destroy relationships once it takes hold. For God's sake, let it go. Amelia did a nice thing; she was concerned about you. Don't turn that into something bad.'

'And Amelia will confirm your story if I ask her, will she?'

He'd have to warn Amelia, he thought, a quick text or phone call, he'd need to be fast. The first chance he got.

'Why wouldn't she? It's the truth. Ask her whatever the hell you want to. All this is becoming a little too much, Suzie. I've done nothing wrong. You'd be dead if it wasn't for me. If our relationship is going to survive for very much longer, you really do have to learn to trust and relax.'

Suzie dropped her head, shoulders slumped, and looked away. And in that instant, he knew he was winning, even before she spoke. 'I'm so very sorry, George, I, er, I'm truly sorry. I wonder what's wrong with me sometimes. It's just that I can't bear the thought of you with another woman. All I can do is apologise. I, er, I need, I need to take a tablet. It's, it's well overdue.'

'Yeah, I can see you trembling,' he said. 'Good idea. I'm beginning to think the doctor was right. You need them more than I realised. You worry about the craziest things. You see problems that aren't there. You get so many things out of proportion. And it's not good for you, Suzie. It's not good for either of us. You need to get a grip.'

Her eyes filled with tears. And then a reluctant smile. 'I know I can be a nightmare. I do realise that and will try to do better, I promise. I really do think the tablets are helping.'

George grinned, the victory his. He felt like punching the air, letting out a yelp of triumph, but resisted. She seemed surprisingly vulnerable, on the back foot; an ideal time to take advantage.

'Oh, there is one other thing I wanted to mention before we go downstairs.'

Suzie wiped her face with a hand, then swallowed before speaking.

'What's that?' she asked in a quiet voice resonating with emotion.

*Go for it, George.*

'The, er, the solicitor's appointment I mentioned. You know, to sort out our wills. I've changed it for lunchtime the day after we're back, at ten past one. His office is only a few minutes' walk from the bank, making it easier for you. And you won't need to miss any work. I know how dedicated you are to your job.'

Suzie cleared her throat, slightly coughed, and blew her nose into a paper tissue, still a little tearful. 'Um, okay, yes, I still don't know what the rush is all about. But the appointment works for me. Thank you for being so considerate.'

Naïve in the extreme, he thought, resisting the desire to laugh. For once he'd got his way. 'You're welcome,' he began. 'And perhaps we should increase the life insurance,' he quickly added, wanting to make the most of the opportunity before her mood changed. 'Look what happened yesterday. Just imagine if I hadn't been there. You very nearly died. Life can be so very unpredictable. Maybe next time, it'll be me. I'd hate to think of you losing my monthly income. None of us knows what's around the corner. It would be such a shame if you had to spend your investments just to pay the bills.'

Suzie sat next to him on the bed. 'I'm quite liking this new serious, more responsible George,' she said. 'It's like you've matured all of a sudden. It's usually me that worries about these things. And it's nice that you're thinking of me.'

He smiled, thinking her stupid; the most gullible fool in the world. 'Maybe I have matured,' he said. 'I came very close to losing you yesterday. That's some wakeup call.'

She was silent for a few seconds, hesitant, stalling. 'Maybe now's the right time to try again.'

'Try again?' he asked. 'What do you mean?'

'A baby, perhaps it's time to try again for a baby. Maybe what happened yesterday was God's way of telling us to get on with it. To create a new life. Being a mother would mean so very much to me. You do want to be a father, don't you?'

The sex would be bearable, he thought, but as for the rest of it, no. He'd come to the firm conclusion he didn't want a child at all, not with her or anyone else. Too much hassle, too much responsibility he didn't need. Play the game, George thought, keep her onside.

'I'm not sure either of us could handle another miscarriage,' he said with a solemn expression he thought suitable. 'And especially not you. I'm not even sure you've got over the last one. And our relationship, well, you know the problems we've got. I'm still drinking a little too much when the pressure gets to me; I freely admit that. And you've got your trust issues. All those anxieties that muddle your thinking. Things are far from perfect. You're still in your twenties. I don't think there's any mad rush. But maybe you're right. Perhaps yesterday was a wakeup call for both of us. Let's give it some thought.'

Suzie went to hug him, putting an arm around each muscular shoulder, pulling him close. 'I do love you, George, you do know that, don't you? I realise I don't tell you often enough.'

Should he ask about money again? Was it worth it? Was the time right? Yeah, what the hell? What was there to lose? 'Enough to trust me with joint accounts?'

George felt her body tense, the mood changing in an instant as she pulled away.

'Not now, please,' she said. 'Not that. When we're home, maybe we can discuss it again, but not now.'

It was strange, he thought, suddenly distracted by the faint scent of Amelia's perfume on his pillow, memories of passionate lovemaking flooding back. Suzie could look reasonably attractive if the light was right. She wasn't entirely repugnant. And some other men seemed to fancy her. He'd seen the appreciative glances sent her way from time to time. Particularly when she was in a swimsuit. Hell, he'd once fancied her himself.

'But you are serious about trying for another baby?' he asked, a thin smile on his face.

'Yes, yes, absolutely I am. I was thinking about it in my hospital bed last night when I couldn't sleep. I meant every word I said.'

He touched her thigh, running his hand slowly from knee to groin, picturing the lovely Amelia in his mind's eye. And it was almost as if Suzie's features became hers. 'In that case, fancy a shag?' he asked with a grin.

Suzie let out a laugh. 'What, now?'

George undid the zip of his shorts, already partly erect, the pink tip of his cock poking through the gap as he pushed his underpants aside.

'Yeah, come on, why not? It's been a while. And if we're going to try for a baby again, we've got to start sometime. Now seems as good a time as any. We're on holiday, in a comfortable, big bed with a great mountain view. It couldn't be more romantic. What more do you want?'

He noticed her eyes were blinking fast and repeatedly before she spoke. 'Really? You're up for trying again for a baby after all that happened? You're not just saying it?'

George pulled off her top, unfastened her bra, threw it to the floor, and looked at her erect nipples. They weren't as prominent as Amelia's, not as sexy or suckable, but there was still an attraction to them. And her tits were big and bouncy, that was a plus.

'We only live once,' he said. 'And, for you, yesterday, that very nearly came to an end. If we're not going to try now, then when?'

Suzie lay back on the soft quilt and took off her white cotton knickers. 'It's strange,' she said. 'Even the bedding seems to smell of perfume.'

George placed a hand between her legs, but she pressed them together. Oh, for fuck's sake, he thought, so very typical of her. She never made things easy. Frigid! Think fast; another hurdle to overcome.

'Please don't get paranoid on me again, Suzie,' he said, whispering into her ear at touching distance. 'You're imagining things, girl. Your mind's playing tricks on you. If you really want to try again for a baby, open your legs, we can get this done, and then you can take your medication. Or, if you weren't serious, well, we can forget it, no pressure from me. But don't think I'm ever going to agree again. Emotional rollercoasters aren't my thing. There's only so much upset I can take.'

'Sorry, George,' she said, relaxing her thigh muscles, slowly parting her knees.

'That's okay,' he said. 'As long as I know what you want, that's all.'

Suzie kissed him now, mouth open, then grabbed his stiff cock, moving her hand.

'That's the girl,' he said, thinking of Amelia again, recalling stimulating her clitoris with repeated rapid flicks of his tongue.

He climbed on top of Suzie, not his favourite position, but one that required minimum effort after the exertions of the night before.

George grinned as he entered Suzie, moving his lower body with gradually increasing speed, thrusting into her time and again. He hadn't told her about his vasectomy, only weeks before. He hadn't told anyone, saying he'd suffered a groin strain lifting heavy weights. It was something else he thought wise to keep to himself.

'I do love you, George,' she said as he groaned, close to shooting his load. So, the silly mare had finally spread her legs again, he thought as she hugged him tight; about time. She wasn't much use all round, but at least there was that. 'Did you hear me, George?'

He climbed off her and wiped his wet cock with his discarded underpants. 'Yes, I heard you. Come on, up you get, take that tablet, then time for something to eat. It's amazing how hungry sex makes me. Happens every time.'

'Do you love me, too? Say it, George, please. I need to hear it.'

George realised he couldn't bring himself to say he loved her. He couldn't use the word. Even for him, it was one lie too far. He thought the words might stick in his throat.

'Of course I do,' he said, the best he could offer, almost choking on the sentiment. 'Come on, don't just lie there. I'll fetch you a glass of water. You need that medication. Imagine smelling perfume where it doesn't exist. I had no idea how confused you'd become. You're really starting to worry me. To think I encouraged you to reduce the tablets. How wrong could I have been? You need all the help you can get.'

Suzie sat up and lowered her bare legs to the floor. 'I thought I might ask Amelia if there's a herbal alternative I could try. What do you think? I read a lot of medicines come from plants. She may be able to help.'

'What a great idea,' he quickly replied, with no need to feign enthusiasm. 'Something tells me the two of you are going to be very good friends. If that's the one real benefit that comes from this holiday, it's been more than worth it. All I want is the best for you.'

'And we can try again, for a baby, we can try again?'

He nodded with a smile.

'Of course we can. I wouldn't want it any other way.'

## 14

Two days later, Suzie was back relaxing on a sunbed by the hotel pool in the shade of a carefully positioned, large umbrella when she heard Amelia's familiar voice call out her name.

Suzie looked up from her paperback, a mildly entertaining celebrity bio borrowed from the hotel library, to see Amelia walking towards her, wearing a skimpy bright yellow bikini, no less revealing than the white one she'd worn before.

Suzie smiled as Amelia got nearer, thinking it an ideal time to ask her new friend some questions about things that had been playing on her mind. George had headed into the hotel building needing the toilet moments earlier. And so, Suzie pondered, the timing couldn't be better. What really happened that night Amelia called at the room? She liked to think George had told her nothing but the truth. But, in all honesty, there were still doubts. With George, there always were. Not just because of the party photos, but before. She'd never entirely trusted him, not one hundred per cent. She had no concrete evidence of infidelity, nothing as bad as that, but he'd always had a wandering eye. Even her sister thought so. She'd said as much. And, Suzie thought, Isobel was a good judge of men. So much more worldly than her.

'Oh, I'm so glad to see you,' Amelia said as she pulled up a sunbed, sitting close to Suzie's side, suntan oil glistening on her skin. 'I've been keeping a close eye out for you for a couple of days. I heard what happened at the harbour. How awful! How are you feeling? I do hope you're okay.'

Suzie looked into Amelia's heavily made-up eyes, trying to read her mind.

'Um, I'm all right, thanks. A bit shaken up. It was a scare. There's no denying that. But I'm over it now. I'm here, I'm alive, thank God, so it could have been a lot worse.'

Amelia smiled, beaming, like a Cheshire cat, the expression lighting up her face. And those teeth. Suzie couldn't help but stare at them, so very white. 'Oh, wow, and George,' Amelia said. 'Who'd have thought it? What an absolute hero, jumping right into the water to save you like he did. He deserves a medal. You must be so very proud.'

A part of her was. But only a part. The more Suzie had thought about that day, that evening, the more concern she'd felt. George's story seemed a little unlikely despite his insistence. Had he and Amelia simply had a cup of tea together as he'd claimed? Or was there more to it? Amelia was so beautiful, so alluring, and yet so friendly. Seemingly one of the nicest people she'd ever met. So, even if she couldn't entirely trust George, she could trust Amelia, couldn't she? It seemed so, instinctively. But for all her reasoning, the doubts were still there, not letting go.

'So, when did you find out what happened?' Suzie asked without hesitation, keen to establish the facts.

'One of the other guests told me about your fall. But I had no idea you were in the hospital. Not until George told me. He was so worried about you; bless him. He was very close to tears. So very different to the man I thought he was after his drunken rant.'

Was he concerned? Really? Did that sound like her George? The man she knew? Did that ring true? 'When did you talk to George?'

Amelia was quick to reply. 'I knocked on your bedroom door that evening. I was hoping to see you. To make sure you were fine. But George answered and told me you'd been admitted to the hospital as a precaution. That was the last thing I was expecting. I was almost as upset as he was. And he was good enough to make me a cup of tea. I wish my ex had been half as thoughtful. Not a chance in hell of that. Empathy? The git didn't know the meaning of the word.'

Okay, thought Suzie, relaxing her tight jaw, telling herself Amelia's story fitted so far. George had said much the same. Maybe he had been telling the truth all along. Perhaps he was right; she could be seeing problems where they didn't exist, looking at the dark side as the devil whispered in her ear. Paranoia could be a terrible thing.

'Did the two of you have a meal together?' Suzie said. Another question she needed answering. She was hoping for the best, for further reassurance, but a small part of her still feared the worst. 'I don't mind at all if you did eat together.'

Amelia shook her head, a yellow ribbon in her hair catching the sun. She rubbed the side of her temple, then touched her chin. 'No, he didn't ask, and I wouldn't have said yes even if he had. It wouldn't have felt right. Not without you being there. I don't know him well enough for that. It seems a strange question. Why do you ask?'

Suzie decided she'd heard enough; her worries alleviated at least for a time. For some reason, her ears felt hot. She could imagine them turning red.

'It's, er, not a big deal,' she said, wishing she'd never asked the question in the first place. 'I was wondering, that's all.'

Amelia had a puzzled expression.

'Ah, okay.' That's all she said, just two words.

'Do you fancy a coffee?' Suzie asked, wanting to change the subject, starting to feel a fool. Fearing her paranoia might be getting the better of her.

'Oh, now you're talking,' Amelia replied with another flash of teeth. 'How about another Irish?'

Suzie placed her book down, stood and smiled. 'My turn to pay.'

Amelia nodded, then smiled again. 'That's good of you, thanks.'

'Not at all, it's my turn,' Suzie said. She paused, then added, 'George will be back soon. He's just popped to the toilet. I'd better get him one, too.'

Amelia made a face. 'But maybe without the alcohol? I know it's none of my business, not really, but, you know, after what happened the other day. You don't want a repeat of all that. I wouldn't like to see you upset again.'

Suzie took a deep breath and nodded, a little embarrassed by the memory but still glad of the advice. They seemed like wise words, sensible and balanced. And they came from a good place. That's what Suzie told herself. She thought and believed it, giving her a warm feeling deep inside. It appeared she had a new friend who cared. A rare thing in her life. And that felt good.

'There was something else I've been meaning to ask you,' Suzie said. 'About the plant medicine, nothing to do with George. I've got a bit of a problem.'

Amelia's eyes widened. 'Okay, I'll help if I can.'

'I'll just get the coffees and tell you all about it.'

George still hadn't returned when Suzie re-joined Amelia at the poolside about five minutes later, followed by a handsome young waiter carrying their order on a shining metal tray. And George's continued absence, Suzie decided, wasn't such a bad thing. It wasn't often she made a genuine connection with another woman. In fact, she couldn't remember the last time. And Amelia was so easy to talk to. Someone who seemed keen to help. Why not make the most of it while she could? There was everything to gain and nothing to lose.

Suzie sipped her hot, flavoursome drink, savouring the thick, fresh double cream at the top. It seemed such an indulgent luxury.

'I hope you don't mind me asking you this,' Suzie began after wiping her mouth, 'what with you being on holiday. But it seems too good an opportunity to miss. I'm, er, I'm taking tablets for anxiety. Have been for some time. My, er, my GP prescribed them. George was keen for me to come off them. But more recently, I think he's changed his mind. I was wondering if there's any herbal alternative I could try?'

'Do you know the name of your medication?' Amelia asked with apparent interest, looking Suzie in the eye.

Suzie provided the answer.

'Ah, yeah, okay, I know the ones. They're very common. How long have you been taking them?'

Suzie wondered if honesty was best. Or if she should minimise the reality. 'Um, it's been a few months.'

'Can you be more specific?'

Okay, honesty. Here goes, bite the bullet. 'Actually, I think it's, er, it's been over a year. Close to eighteen months. And, um, I'm taking more than I was. Probably too many.'

Amelia sighed, reaching out, touching Suzie's hand, holding it for a second or two. 'Try not to worry. And don't be too hard on yourself. Life can be tough. And particularly for women. So many demands. So many expectations. I've heard very similar stories so many times from clients. And the tablets aren't always easy to get off. There's an inevitable element of addiction that can be hard to overcome. It's one of those things that need a lot of thought and care. You can't just stop them dead.'

Suzie looked away. 'No, no, I know. I read a magazine article. And my doctor said something when he first prescribed them. I didn't take it too seriously at the time.'

Amelia paused for a time, about ten seconds, slow to reply. 'Let me give it some thought. It's not something I want to rush. How about we get together for a catch-up a week or two after we're back in Wales?'

Suzie gave a wide grin.

'In Aberystwyth?'

Amelia nodded with a smile. 'Yes, if you like. Although, I'll be down your way around that time. I'm actually thinking of moving my clinic to Carmarthen. I've been looking for suitable premises. I've got a younger brother in Cardiff. Ben. He went to university there, met a local girl and stayed. Same old story. I'd like to see more of him. I'm going to be a first-time auntie. There's a baby on the way. Living and working somewhere in Carmarthen town or the immediate area would give me better access to rail and the M4. Getting anywhere from Aber is a bit of a trek, as beautiful as it is.'

'Oh, congratulations! And if we could meet in Carmarthen, that would be fantastic. That seems ideal. Thank you, I really do appreciate it.'

Amelia took a sip of coffee and then licked her lips, first the top, then the bottom.

'Great, that's a date, then. I'll contact you as soon as I know when I'm coming. A text would probably be best. Although, I might give you a ring for a chat. And I'll definitely be coming on a Saturday, so you don't need to worry about work.'

'Perfect. I do sometimes work on a Saturday morning, but hardly ever. I really couldn't be happier. You're an absolute star.'

Amelia reached out to touch Suzie's hand again with seeming affection.

'You're very welcome.'

Suzie felt close to weeping, her eyes moistening. But they were tears of relief, not sadness or regret.

'I'm so very glad I met you, Amelia,' she said while dabbing at her eyes. 'I'm sure it was meant to be. You're God's gift to me, a blessing. And I'm grateful. Our friendship just feels right.'

Amelia looked past Suzie and stood. 'Oh, look out,' she said. 'Here comes George. I'd better leave you two to it. I'll see you on the plane if not before. And everything we've talked about is one hundred per cent confidential if you want it to be. You're in control. He won't hear a word of it from me. That's a guarantee.'

Like a priest, Suzie thought with a smile, just like her priest. Or an angel sent from heaven.

## 15

George found the return flight from Tenerife South to Cardiff a lot less onerous than the outbound journey. Spending a week in Suzie's company without the escape of work had been just as challenging as he'd anticipated, but now it was almost over. And there'd been certain benefits to the week, which he thought about often during the flight. In some ways, he told himself, the holiday had worked out better than he could have hoped. Suzie was grateful to him for one thing – and another. And Amelia had played a blinder. What a great little actress. Exactly as he'd planned. She'd followed the script with aplomb.

Suzie unwrapped a fruit sweet after about an hour and offered him one, which he declined.

'I'm so very glad we went to Tenerife, George,' she said. 'And you've been wonderful. You saved me from drowning. And then... and then you said you were willing to try for a baby again. I can't tell you how much that means to me. It is like a dream come true. I know there are challenges ahead after everything that happened before. Nothing is guaranteed, not in this world. But I'm going to pray so very hard and beg for God's favour. And if I do get pregnant again, give birth, and am blessed with a boy, I'm sure he'll have your good looks. And if it's a girl, I'm certain she'll be beautiful, too.'

A baby? Good luck with that, thought George, resisting the impulse to laugh. The one advantage of a vasectomy was as much sex as he wanted without any danger of responsibility. And now Suzie was up for it again, spreading her legs, an acceptable backup position if Amelia or some other local hottie wasn't available. He could always close his eyes and fantasise. Anything tight, wet and warm was better than nothing.

'Have you thought any more about our financial position?' he asked, thinking it an opportune time.

Suzie paused, silent for a second or two, which George saw as a good thing. It gave him hope. She usually repeated the same predicable rebuffs, snubs and refusals as soon as he asked the question. He listened intently, keenly anticipating her reply, sensing that maybe something had changed.

'Um, yes, yes I have,' Suzie began, speaking slowly and clearly, as if making a statement in court. 'Actually, I've been giving it a lot of thought. And I've decided that, at the very least, you deserve me to give your requests some serious consideration. No promises, but I'm not saying no out of hand.'

It wasn't exactly what George had hoped for, not the unequivocal 'yes'. But it seemed to be progress nonetheless. The bitch, he thought, was softening. Maybe he was finally getting somewhere. About time! Or would she let him down again?

'You said *consideration*. What do you mean by that exactly?'

Suzie popped another sweet into her mouth, talking while sucking, seemingly now more confident in what she was saying. A lot less formal.

'As soon as we get back home, I'm going to speak to my father. And I'll tell him all about everything you've done, all that's

changed. And if he thinks now's the time to trust you with sharing
my money, I will do it. You'll have that joint account you want so
badly, and I'll clear your debts, every penny. And I won't even tell
Dad about your drinking on this holiday. But, if, and only if, you
promise me you won't ever get drunk again. I'd want you to swear it
on the Bible. A pledge of sobriety. Have we got a deal? It all seems
very fair to me.'

Fair, he thought. Who was she kidding? Always caveats, such a
bitch. Nothing was ever simple with her. And her father, such a git,
such a control freak. The chances of him agreeing were close to
zero.

'Why involve your dad? You're a grown-up, not a child. It's your
money, our money, not his. Isn't it a decision you can make alone?'

Suzie visibly tensed. 'Please don't push me, George,' she said.
'You know I've always relied on my father's guidance. He's always
been there for me, whatever my troubles, as a child and adult. I'd
feel better if I had his blessing.'

George sat back in his seat, not in the least bit surprised by her
answer, but disappointed, nonetheless. He'd hoped for better, but
expected no different. And he resented her response. He hated her
and her father, too. The loathing intensified the more he thought of
it, making him twitch. But he told himself all wasn't lost. No, it now
seemed there were two reasonably acceptable possibilities within
limits.

On the one hand, her miserable git of a father might say the
right thing, as unlikely as it seemed. Miracles did sometimes
happen. And if not, Amelia could continue doing her thing; that
was already on track. Nothing was guaranteed. But in some ways, it
was a win-win. The cash was almost his.

'Do you really think your father will understand how much our
relationship has changed?' George asked, pushing his thoughts
from his mind.

She nodded.

'I do, George. I think he will. He's a wise man, my Solomon. And no one wants you to overcome your demons more than Dad.'

Was she deluded? It seemed so. That didn't sound like her father at all.

'Okay, so, when will this conversation take place?' he asked.

Suzie beamed whilst unwrapping another sweet. 'I've arranged to see him at my parents' place after work tomorrow evening, at six.'

At least it was happening quickly, thought George. Something to be thankful for, small mercies. 'Do you want me to be there with you for a bit of morale support? I can be if you like. I'd be pleased to.'

Suzie's face paled despite the faint hint of a tan. She began rocking back and forth with a pained stare. 'Oh, no, no, I don't think that's a good idea, not at all. Just me and Dad, that's best.'

No surprise there, thought George. Two demented peas in a pod. 'But you are going to try your best to convince him, yeah? To do the right thing.'

She nodded twice. 'Of course. I'll try. Why see him otherwise?'

George shook his head, still far from satisfied. 'I can't understand why you need the man's approval for everything you do. But, you do, so, okay, let's see what he says.'

'I love you, George.'

There she was with the George again, George this, George that, silly bitch. 'I know you do.'

'Do you love me?' she asked.

He closed his eyes, said he was tired, and pretended to go to sleep. And as he sat there, time passing slowly, his initial positive thoughts regarding developments gradually changed. So, what was the best he could hope for even if her git of a father agreed, or if he didn't, and Amelia did her thing? What would he get? Half the money at best? Okay, so he'd be well off, some would say, rich. But was that enough? Shouldn't he have all of it, every penny? He could make use of the money so much better than Suzie. Perhaps live in the sun, girls in bikinis, even topless, a place on the right beach. It was almost a sin to leave Suzie any cash at all. What a waste! There had to be a way. Get the wills sorted, increase the life insurance, and hopefully, she'd die. Maye she'd get ill or get knocked over, fingers crossed. Or, perhaps someone would kill her, bringing her miserable life to a timely end. Brilliant!

George smiled as he pictured his wife lying cold, blue and mottled on a mortuary slab. If only it came true, he thought, if only. He could jack in work, become a wealthy man of leisure. How good would that be? He could tour the world's red-light districts; strippers, whores, drugs, the lot. More sex than he knew what to do with. And he could go to Vegas, high stakes, so exciting. That would be really living. The best times of his life.

But for all that, he couldn't bring himself to seriously consider murder. He toyed with the idea fleetingly, briefly indulging the fantasy, but no more than that. *Thou shalt not kill.* The sixth commandment had been drilled into him as a child. And a part of him still believed in hell.

And anyway, if he did kill her, he might not get away with it. He could end up arrested, prosecuted and imprisoned, losing the best years of his life. What use would the cash be then? And prison, nothing but men, a sexual desert. It was unthinkable. He had to be free to enjoy spending. Half the money would have to do unless some fortuitous unseen event changed things. Getting locked up was never a part of the plan.

## 16

Suzie felt unexpectedly nervous as she left the bank at the end of her working day, her anxiety threatening to overwhelm her entirely as she strode down Merlin's Lane, avoiding the many puddles with quick-moving feet, her black, pound-shop umbrella held above her head to avoid the rain. She took another anti-anxiety tablet from her handbag as soon as she got into her car, parked just a five-minute brisk walk away, close to Marks & Spencer.

But it seemed no amount of medication helped that day. Not as it usually did. Maybe, she thought, it had damped down her over-active emotions to some extent, but nothing like enough. She was shaking, her entire body trembling as if frozen. Because talking to her father weighed heavier on her mind than she'd anticipated. Visits to her parents' house were usually such a positive thing, joyous even, something she looked forward to. But not now. It was so very different today. Not at all as she'd pictured in her mind's eye. But at least, the wills were done. That had been easy enough. One less thing worry about. And George seemed so pleased. One small thing she'd done for him at very little cost to herself.

Suzie thought about her situation some more as she started the

German saloon car's engine with a single press of a button, reversed with the help of a rear-view camera, and left the car park for the adjoining street.

And after much thought, she concluded she was as nervous as she was because her meeting with Dad really mattered. Her perspective had changed, and quickly, too. George had done so very well on holiday. He'd risked his life to save her. And they were planning a family again, the baby she wanted so very much. George seemed to have grown, matured, almost like he was a different man. And that was worthy of reward, wasn't it? Maybe her dreams were coming true, all her prayers answered at once. Yes, it seemed George had finally re-earned her trust. It seemed the only logical conclusion she could reach based on the facts. But could she convince her dad of all that? Would she get his much-needed blessing? Would he agree?

Suzie blew out the air as she negotiated the busy junction at the bottom of Castle Hill close to County Hall, then drove over the bridge, crossing the River Towy. She started singing along to a particularly catchy pop song from the 1970s as she drove past the petrol station on her left and towards the roundabout, the car's wipers battling with an increasingly heavy downpour, the rain seemingly coming from every direction at once.

All she could do, she pondered, was to tell her father precisely what happened and then let him be the judge. Dad was cleverer than her, probably more intelligent and certainly more objective, a good Catholic voice of reason even at the most challenging times. Her father would know if she was right about George and if she should help him financially. As he always did, Dad would tell her what to do with clarity and vision. And if she was wrong or had misjudged the situation in any way, Dad would tell her that, too. He wouldn't hold back. And he always knew best. A font of knowledge. Wise and unbending, that's the kind of man he was.

Suzie was feeling slightly more optimistic as she drove down the narrow, tree-lined road into Ferryside, past the garage, over the hump-backed bridge, and towards the small housing estate, close to the rugby club and playing fields. She said a quick prayer for strength and clarity after switching off the car's powerful engine and exiting the vehicle, not bothering to lock it because crime in the area was remarkably low.

Suzie's mother opened the front door with a nervous smile just seconds after Suzie knocked. She looked tired. Thinner than she had been. Worn down by life.

'Hello, *cariad*,' her mother said, using the Welsh word for love, as she sometimes had during Suzie's childhood years. 'It's good to see you. And I can see you've got a bit of a tan; lucky you. Come on in. Dad's been waiting for you. Best not keep him waiting.'

Suzie followed her mother into the comfortable, recently decorated lounge to see her father seated in his usual brown leather armchair close to a coal-effect gas fire with blue-yellow flames. There was a clear plastic biro, a single blank piece of A4 paper, and a black, well-thumbed Bible approved by the Catholic Church on the small coffee table in front of him. The Bible was never far away. He always kept it close.

Suzie and her mother stood looking down at the middle-aged man they considered the head of the home and family in reverential silence for about thirty seconds, waiting for him to speak, as they knew he inevitably would. And Suzie felt sure he'd have something so very significant to say as he looked up at her, something that truly mattered. The guidance she so badly needed to still her troubled mind at such an important time as this.

'Welcome, Suzie, welcome! Let's say a prayer of grateful thanks that we're all safely back together again,' he said, speaking with a slow, solemn voice he kept for such occasions. 'And then,' he continued, 'we can have a nice cup of tea and a quick bite to eat before we have our discussion. Your dear mother will leave us alone to speak privately at that stage. I'm sure there's something she can be getting on with. God's work never ends for a busy wife.'

Suzie nodded her agreement, sitting on the comfy sofa opposite her father while her mother remained standing, swaying slightly, first one way, then the other. All three bowed heads and closed their eyes, their hands linked together as Suzie's dad spoke again, dominating proceedings, clearly enunciating each word, speaking louder than was necessary.

'Let us pray,' he began. 'Pour forth, we beseech thee, O Lord, thy Grace into our hearts. Give me the wisdom to advise my daughter in these the most challenging of circumstances. And give her the wisdom to act on my advice, as is your will. We ask this in the name of Jesus, and in the power of the Holy Spirit, Amen.'

Suzie's mother hurried toward the kitchen the second her husband stopped speaking, leaving Suzie sitting in silence, waiting to hear whatever her father said next. She briefly considered breaking the quiet when he finally opened his eyes, but he picked up the Bible, opened it, looked down and started reading. And she knew interrupting him wouldn't be a good idea. Painful experience had taught her that, both as a child and more recently. It never was. Spare the rod and spoil the child. He'd said it often when she was younger. And the punishment stung.

Suzie felt a welcome sense of relief when her mother finally returned to the room about ten minutes later, a large plate piled high with ham and tomato sandwiches in one hand and three matching pottery mugs in the other, held by the handles.

Suzie's father carefully placed the Bible on the arm of his chair and picked up his pen and paper, allowing his wife to use the table, giving her permission with a single nod of his head.

He waited for his wife to pick up a mug and hand it to him just a second after she'd put them down. And then another prayer, this time thanking God for the food they would receive and enjoy. There were no thanks for his wife.

The three of them ate and drank together in virtual silence for what to Suzie felt like an age after that, because her father preferred it that way. If he wasn't talking, praying, or singing a hymn, he preferred his peace. He had for as long as Suzie could remember. It had always been that way unless he gave one of them approval to speak. And her father tended to shout if anyone broke the rules.

He looked up at the Victorian wall clock above the gas fire at just after six, chewing and swallowing the last of the sandwiches. He'd eaten most of them, about eighty per cent. That was usual, too. Suzie noted that not much, if anything, had changed since she'd been away.

'If you could leave us now, Mary,' her father said insistently, looking directly at his wife. 'I think it's time I listened to whatever Suzie has to say for herself. I'm sure you can find something productive to do in the kitchen. Leave the plate and mugs for now. You can clear up later. And close the door on your way out. I don't want any interruptions. This is God's work.'

Suzie spent the next twenty minutes or so telling her father all about the holiday, focussing enthusiastically on the positives and ignoring the negatives. And then explaining her hopes for the future in as much detail as her father allowed. He sat and listened, one hand on the Bible, frowning often, asking the occasional question, sometimes raising a hand to silence her, and not expressing an opinion until she sat back on the sofa with nothing else to say. She'd mentioned George bravely saving her life three times and his willingness to try again for a child twice, so what more could she say? She really had done her best. Now it was up to Dad.

He looked into Suzie's eyes with such intensity that she thought he could see into her very soul. As if he was superhuman, not merely a man. As if he had a direct link to the Almighty, just as he sometimes claimed.

'What do you think I should do, Dad?' Suzie asked when she could take the silence no longer. 'Please tell me; I've been thinking of nothing else. I need to know.'

He took a deep breath as if carefully considering his response. 'Are you still taking those tablets the quack gave you?'

Suzie looked away. She knew her father disapproved of doctors, thinking prayer should be enough to heal any ailment. He'd said as much, shaking his head. And she'd tried, she really had. But it seemed she didn't yet have sufficient faith, unlike Dad. Although, he'd had an operation a few months back.

'Yes, yes, I am, sorry,' she said. 'But I'm thinking of a herbal remedy in future, just until I'm better. I thought you might think that a preferable idea, something more natural from nature.'

He leant his head towards her whilst puffing out his cheeks.

'And I'm correct in thinking your medication affects your mind, yes? Isn't that how that stuff works? I'm sure I'm not mistaken.'

Suzie wiped away a tear and broke eye contact, feeling obliged to answer despite having had the conversation before.

'Well, it's, it's, er, for anxiety, so, yes, I suppose it does.' She so wished she could have said something else. Anything to please the man whose opinion meant so much.

Her father sighed, leaning back, flinching, wrinkling his nose. A disapproving, almost disgusted look she'd seen more times than she cared to remember as a child. As if she was an abomination, a piece of shit on his shoe, a disappointment. He'd often used that word. And it hurt every time.

'Yes, I thought as much,' he began, as she took in every word as if it was the very definition of truth. 'And that's the problem right there. You haven't the capacity to think clearly. Everything you've said is confused and muddled. Which, in all honesty, doesn't surprise me in the least. You're weak, Suzie, always have been. But thankfully, fortunately for you, I'm here to help.'

He was silent again for a few seconds after that, smiling thinly, his eyes wide, as if what he was about to say next was the revelation she was there to hear. He held his hands wide, palms forward, fingers spread. 'God has spoken to me, my child. I clearly heard His voice. And He thinks it would be totally insane for you to share your money with George, a terrible sin of the worst possible kind. I haven't seen your husband in church for months. Give your money to the charity if you want to, or to your mother and me. We could make good use of it. If George gets even a single penny, I'll disown you. And God would, too. He'd cast you aside for eternity. He's told me as much. Pay off that man's debts, and you'd be doomed to hell. I've told you before. It's something George has to do for himself.'

'But, Dad, what, what if—'

He held a hand up as if stopping traffic, shutting her off mid-sentence, shouting now, his face contorting with rage.

'Silence, girl! Get on your knees and pray for forgiveness. Do not ever challenge God's will. There are no what-ifs; I've told you what to do, and that's it. All you've got to do is do it.'

## 17

Suzie sat weeping in her car parked outside her parents' house for almost ten minutes before finally finding the mental strength to start the engine to drive home. She'd never felt more conflicted as she drove slowly through the pleasant estuary village, repeatedly dabbing at her eyes with a tissue as she went. She so wished her father had said something very different. But he hadn't. And that, she told herself, was the reality she had to deal with, however tricky and whatever George's reaction. George had invested so much hope in the evening's meeting. And she had too, hoping it was a turning point, the dawn of a miraculous new age. Because almost anything was possible if you prayed hard enough. And if the time was right. Which clearly it wasn't. She knew that now. Dad had spoken, God had told him. But would George understand that, however badly she pleaded? He lacked the required faith. It seemed unlikely at best.

Suzie pulled up at the side of the road close to the railway crossing rather than drive straight home, asking herself how to play it, what to say, or whether to say anything at all. She closed her eyes tightly shut and tried to picture the scene, her telling George the time wasn't right to help him financially, and him saying that was okay. And then she laughed, a harsh sound so far from humour. *Okay? Not a chance!* He wouldn't understand. His reaction would be so far from that. He'd resent every single word.

Suzie took another tablet from her brown plastic bottle, asked for forgiveness as she swallowed hard, then drove on with a new determination, resigned to telling George what she knew he'd consider as bad news. And she was sure that, as a result, their relationship would suffer, at least in the short term. There'd be more arguments, irritation, and cold shoulders. An inevitable consequence. But, she told herself, for all that, it would be worth it in the end because Dad knew best. There was a light at the end of a very dark tunnel. It was just that she couldn't see it yet. She didn't have that wisdom or sufficient faith. Please don't change your mind about the baby, George, please don't, she said to herself. It means so much to me.

A part of her hoped George wasn't in as she approached home. Maybe he'd gone for one of his evening runs, played squash, or worked late. But the lounge lights were shining brightly through the green cotton curtains, and she could hear the sound of the TV as she slowly approached the front door with the key in hand. She was shaking so badly that she dropped the key when placing it in the lock. She picked it up, tried again but without success, and she was about to knock when the door suddenly opened, creaking on its hinges for lack of oil.

There was an atmosphere you could almost cut with a knife as George stood aside, allowing her to enter. Suzie thought she could smell whisky on his breath, but he didn't appear drunk. And she felt more disappointed than angry, given the stresses of the evening. A part of her understood like never before. How many tablets had she taken that day? More than she should have, that was sure. She had her chemical crutch, too. She had her flaws. No one was perfect, except perhaps for her dad. Yes, probably him.

Suzie thought about what to say and when to say it. Should she blurt out her bad news right there and then as she followed George into the kitchen, or build up to it, choosing her time with care? Oh, crap! Would it make even the slightest difference either way? Very probably not. However she played it, there was a storm coming her way.

Suzie had just resolved to telling George the reality and getting it over with as quickly as possible, when he suddenly turned to face her, the bright light of the fluorescent bulb highlighting his features with an electric glare.

'George, have you been crying?' she asked, taken aback. He gave a sideways glance, keeping his head still. And she thought he looked defeated. As if he'd already anticipated her bad news before she even spoke.

'Did you see the Welsh evening news?' he asked.

Suzie touched his arm, wondering what was coming next.

'Um, no, I've, er, I've been over at Mum and Dad's place. You know that. They never watch TV when I visit. They hardly ever watch it at all.'

George slumped into a pine chair, resting his elbows on the kitchen table. 'That bastard priest who abused me and all those other kids...'

'What about him?'

His voice was stilted, halting when he replied.

'They're letting the dirty bastard out of prison.'

Suzie jerked her head back. And instantly, she knew she couldn't possibly tell George what her father had said that evening. There was only so much bad news her troubled husband could take. She would tell him. But not yet. Now wasn't the time. White lies weren't really lies at all.

'But surely it's far too soon for him to be released?' she said. 'He hasn't served his sentence. There's years to go.'

'Compassionate grounds! Like the bastard had any concern for his victims. There's no justice in the world. It makes me want to puke.'

Suzie tried to hug him but he pulled away. 'But, why's he being released?' she asked, a part of her glad they were talking about this rather than cash.

'He's got cancer. In his brain, lungs and spine. He's got months to live, apparently. He's going to spend the rest of his worthless days in a hospice run by nuns. Like the bastard deserves any sort of care. I'd let him rot in agony if it were up to me. Crying alone in a cell. I might pay him a visit. Tell him he's going to hell. Tell him he's going to burn.'

Suzie suspected she was probably going to say the wrong thing even before she said it. But the words came out anyway, almost on autopilot. She blurted out her thoughts, unable to stop. Almost as if they were programmed into her since childhood.

'I know what he did was awful. But we all sin. And I'm sure he's repented, confessed and asked for forgiveness.'

George's expression said a thousand words, none of them good.

'Oh, for fuck's sake, Suzie. Of course he has. That's what Catholics do. That's how priests make all the terrible things they do okay again. And the bastard might even have been sorry every time he ruined a young life. I accept that possibility. But he did it again. That's the point. He always did it again. He hasn't got my forgiveness. And I want him to know that. Isn't that what counts?'

'I'm so very sorry, George. I know you suffered. I wish none of it had happened to you. God works in mysterious ways.'

George banged the table twice, hard with the palm of his right hand. And she knew she'd said the wrong thing again. 'Okay, enough!' he yelled. 'It's time for you to shut your mouth. You just don't get it. I don't think you're ever going to understand. What that bastard did had nothing do with God. The man's a pervert, that simple. Doing what perverts do. And your church protected him. Right up to the time they locked the bastard up. And now, they're protecting him again. What a moral travesty. A lot of priests hurt children in the worst possible way. I was one of many. The church should focus on that abomination and leave consenting adults alone.'

Suzie could think of nothing more to say. Nothing that would help, not a word. And a small part of her knew he was right. 'I'm so sorry, George. But please don't say any more. You know how much I hate talking about this stuff. Have, have you eaten? Can I... can I make you something? There's some chicken in the fridge. I could cook it up with some pasta sauce. I've got the organic one you like. It was on offer; half price.'

And then, to her surprise, George ignored her question, suddenly changing the subject and asking questions she'd been dreading. He sounded more reasoned now, calmer, as if trying to catch her out, she thought. He did that sometimes, jumping from one emotive, psychologically charged subject to the next, as if a switch had been flicked in his head. Not easy to deal with. Hard to respond to.

'What happened at your parents' place?' he asked first. 'What did your father say? Am I going to get the help I need? Do I get my fair share?'

Suzie took a backward step, wishing the kitchen light wasn't so very bright as it shone down from above. She feared her expressions may betray the truth. That her ploy was written all over her face as clear as a large print book. And lying was hard. It didn't come easy. Never had and never would; already laced with guilt even before she uttered the words. So outside her comfort zone. But something she told herself had to be done because George had had enough upset for one day. And God understood, she had, too.

Suzie swallowed hard before speaking, thinking it had to be the most convincing performance of her life. If she were to sin, to lie, those lies had to stick. 'He, er, Dad wasn't there,' she began, then cleared her throat. 'I'm, I'm going to have to speak to him another time. I'll, er, I'll give him a ring sometime tomorrow and try to arrange something for later in the week. Mum said he's got a lot on. So I can't guarantee it will be this week at all. But I will try.'

George snapped out his reply. 'But I thought he knew you were coming. That's what you told me. You said it was all arranged.'

What on earth to say? More lies, no other choice. She wanted the floor to open. Anything to escape the inquisition. 'Last minute change of plans,' she blurted out a little too loudly for her liking. 'Dad, er, he had to visit someone in the hospital. An old friend from church who had a stroke. He's going to be visiting again tomorrow evening and the one after that.'

George glared at her. 'What's the patient's name?'

Suzie couldn't find the words to reply. She just stood there opening and closing her mouth to no effect.

'Come on, Suzie, it's a simple enough question.'

She knew she had to say something. 'I don't, I don't know, I didn't ask.'

George looked at her for what seemed an age but in reality, was no more than five seconds.

'Sometimes, when I look at your face,' he said, 'I think you're full of secrets. You always seem suspicious of me. But perhaps it's you that's the liar.'

She shook her head, fighting the impulse to panic. 'No, no, not at all. I don't know what you're talking about, George. I've told you what happened. The truth, nothing but the truth.'

'Are you nervous?' he asked. 'Is there something you're not

telling me? You're not usually like this. Something's changed. You're even more uptight than usual. You look nervous to me.'

She felt her chest tighten. More lies. A commandment broken. May God forgive her.

'I'm upset by what you told me, that's all. And what with Dad being out, I feel I've let you down. Not that I could have done anything differently. I could never have predicted he wouldn't be there. I did my best.'

George narrowed his eyes as she resisted the almost over-whelming impulse to avoid his accusing gaze.

'So, if I rang your father right this minute and asked him where he'd been, he'd confirm your story, correct? He'd tell me he'd been to the hospital, just like you said?'

Suzie told herself it was too late for the truth. But what to say? Hold your nerve, Suzie, hold your nerve. It would be over soon. 'He might not be back home yet. He might still be on the ward. Visiting time hasn't finished. Or he could be in the car. Either way, best not to bother him.'

'I could ring his mobile.'

Suzie feared her legs might give way at any moment as she allowed a kitchen unit to support her weight. Please don't ring, please don't do that, don't ring. 'Oh, no, Dad wouldn't like you doing that at all,' she said as calmly as possible. 'It would seem like you were checking up on him. He wouldn't appreciate it. And it really wouldn't help with the whole money thing. If anything, it would make things a great deal worse. You know what he's like. He hates it if he thinks anyone is trying to influence his decision-making.'

George was silent for a beat before replying. When he did speak, there was a hard edge to his voice. Suzie stood there and listened because she felt she had to. 'If we're going to try again for a baby,' he began, 'I have to be able to trust you. That seems obvious.

And I have to believe you'll make the right decision about the money, whatever your father says. No money, no baby, it's that simple. But I won't ring him. Just this once, I'll give you the benefit of the doubt.'

She knew the conversation hadn't resolved anything, not really, not for long. She knew they'd come back to it far too soon for her liking. There was no avoiding that. But at least it was over for now. All those lies. Awful! Something else to confess.

'All I can do is my best, George. And I will. I promise I will. I know this means a lot to you.'

He stood and took a half-full whisky bottle from a cupboard, but to her surprise, he didn't drink. Instead, he poured the entire contents down the sink.

'I'm doing this for you,' he said, close to tears. 'Talk to your father if you have to. Convince him. Get his blessing. And then, maybe we can get on with our lives. But at the end of the day, it's your decision, Suzie. It's your life and your money, not your father's. You're twenty-seven, for God's sake. And whatever decision you make, you'll live with the consequences, not him.'

'I only wish it was that easy.'

'Oh, it is, it is,' he said, looking her in the eye. 'You're a grown-up, and your father's word's not law. You just need to get that into your head. Refuse me and you'll never be a mother. Is that what you want? Because, if not, you'll do the right thing.'

She hoped she might already be pregnant after the sex in Tenerife. But she knew that was unlikely. Pregnancy never came easy. Not for her. There were more challenges ahead. More dilemmas to face and overcome. That always seemed to be the way.

## 18

Suzie struggled to focus on her work at the King Street bank the following day, thoughts of the previous evening's conversation playing constantly on her mind. And the more she thought about it, the more conflicted she felt. On the one hand, her father's instructions were crystal clear: God had spoken, or so he told her, and on the other hand, the thought of telling George that reality seemed an unreasonably heavy burden, the consequences of which could be dire. No baby, that's what George had said. And it seemed he meant it, too.

For the first time in years, as Suzie sat there at her desk, she asked herself if her father was always right. Didn't everyone make mistakes, however clever, however wise, even him? Was he really as infallible as he claimed? Her period had started. She wasn't expecting as she'd hoped. And the consequences of refusing George the money now seemed too terrible to even contemplate. Motherhood meant so very much. It was everything. Her true purpose on Earth. Maybe she could talk to Isobel, get a different perspective, tell her everything just as it happened and see what she thought. Yes, why not? Isobel always had a listening ear. And she had wisdom, too. She understood the ways of the world.

Suzie thought about it some more as the morning progressed, time passing quickly as she advised one busy customer after another. And, by the time the clock struck eleven, the idea of talking to her younger sister was cemented in her mind.

After telling her manager she felt sick and needed fresh air, Suzie rushed out to her car, left in the car park close to the library at the far end of King Street. She sat in the driver's seat, took her mobile from her handbag, and rang her sister's number, hoping for an answer. Isobel was working as a newly qualified staff nurse in the paediatric ward at the local West Wales Hospital, so there was always the possibility her phone was off. Come on, sis, answer, please answer. *I need your help like never before.*

Suzie felt a deep sense of relief when she heard her sister's cheery voice say hello after the fourth ring. Sometimes only family would do.

'Hi, it's Suzie. Have you got time to talk?'

'It's my day off, so as long as you need. How was the rest of your holiday? I bet you enjoyed the sunshine once you left hospital. Lucky you! I was stuck here in the cold and rain.'

'I will tell you all about it. But not now; I need to get back to the bank. I told them I was feeling ill.'

'You're not, are you?'

'Um, more nervous than ill. Lying isn't something I'm proud of.'

'Wow, that's not something I ever expected to hear you say. What's up? You don't sound yourself at all.'

Suzie bit her bottom lip. 'Um, can we meet up? I, er, I could do with some advice.'

There was a quick laugh at the other end of the line. 'What, from me? That's a first. You must be desperate.'

'Please don't joke,' Suzie replied, close to tears. 'This is serious. I really don't know what to do for the best.'

'It's not George again, is it?'

Suzie hesitated.

'Well, sort of, but there's more to it than that.'

'When do you want to meet?'

Oh, thank God, thought Suzie, thank God.

'How about this lunchtime at that nice veggie place in Merlin's Lane? We haven't been there together for ages. The food's great and it's close to my work. I'd need to get back after we've eaten.'

'Sounds good to me. What time?'

'Is one o'clock okay?' Suzie asked.

'Perfect, I'll see you there. It will be good to get together.'

# 19

When Suzie opened the café door a couple of minutes before one that afternoon, entering the orange-painted room with paintings and drawings by local artists covering three of the four walls, she immediately saw her sister. Isobel was seated alone on a two-seater black leather sofa at the back of the busy room close to the serving counter. A shiny metal teapot and two cups were on the low table in front of her. She looked up with a warm smile, waving as Suzie walked towards her.

'Have you ordered?' Suzie asked, sitting on a matching settee immediately opposite her sister.

'Just a pot of tea. I thought I'd wait for you before ordering food.'

Suzie looked at her sister across the table, thinking she was looking well, so full of life. As if she was happy, content, all her dreams coming true. So very different to herself.

'It'll have to be a quick snack for me,' Suzie said with a frown she thought had almost come to define her. 'A toastie, or maybe a bowl of soup with a roll.'

Isobel put a hand in the air as a pretty, young, ginger-haired waitress appeared from the kitchen. 'We're ready to order as soon as you get a chance.'

The waitress poised a yellow plastic biro above a small notepad. She looked tired but was efficient and cheery. 'Okay, nice to see you both again. It's been a while. What are you going to have?'

The sisters gave their orders, freshly made tomato soup with a sourdough roll for Suzie and an organic mushroom burger and salad for Isobel.

Suzie waited for the waitress to walk away with a sway of her hips before speaking. She blew out the air. 'Thanks for coming, sis,' Suzie said. 'I really do appreciate it. Sorry about the circumstances.'

'Don't be so silly. Of course I've come. It's just good to see you. What's up?'

Suzie spent the next ten minutes or so telling her sister the whole story, pausing only briefly when their food arrived at the table. Isobel had listened in interested silence but now seemed ready to comment as she picked up her knife and fork.

Suzie looked at her across the table. 'Well, come on, Izzy, tell me what you think. Don't just sit there. Say something.'

Isobel forked some green salad into her mouth, chewed and swallowed before speaking again. 'You say George is *willing* to try again for a baby *if* you share your wealth with him. I know you're desperate to be a mother. Of course I do. But I don't like what he said. He shouldn't be making those sorts of conditions. It almost sounds like blackmail. You know what I think of Dad and his church. I got disillusioned long ago. But this time, I think Dad's right. George is well out of order. In the circumstances, I wouldn't give him a penny. I'd have told him to sod off long ago. He doesn't make you happy, like I've said before. You could do a lot better than George.'

Suzie rested her spoon on the side of her bowl. 'You know how I feel about marriage. I thought you'd be on my side.'

Isobel took a little too long to answer. 'Of course I'm on your side. But I don't like George, that's the truth of it. You can't trust him. I saw the party photos for myself. And I'm far from convinced he's changed. Men like him never do.'

'But he said what happened at the party was a one off. And that the photos made things look a lot worse than they actually were. I think he *has* changed. I think the holiday was the start of something better.'

Isobel suddenly looked as if she'd like to be anywhere but there. 'Look, there's a couple of things I haven't told you. I just couldn't bring myself to do it. But maybe now's the time.'

All of a sudden Suzie had no appetite at all.

'Okay, I'm listening,' she said, fearing what was coming next, unsure if she wanted to hear it because life was hard enough.

'I'm so sorry,' Isobel said, 'but one of the other nurses told me she saw George in a restaurant with another woman shortly before you went away.'

Suzie shook her head. 'I find that very hard to believe. Maybe it wasn't George.'

'My colleague's a local girl and knows George from school. They were in the same class. She was certain it was him. And the woman he was with was more than a friend. They were holding hands across the table.'

Suzie replied with a carefully controlled tone, drawing in slow, steady breaths with a false smile. 'Perhaps it was someone who looked like George. She must have got it wrong.'

Isobel rested her elbows on the low table with her head in her hands, looking down at what was left of her meal. 'I've been dreading telling you this. But what with all you've said, I think I have to.'

Suzie held herself tight. 'What is it?'

'Do you remember the last time I came to your place for a meal?'

Suzie nodded. 'Well, yeah, of course, my birthday.'

The colour drained from Isobel's pretty face. 'You'd gone to the toilet, and... George tried to kiss me.'

Suzie dry gagged, once, then again, not wanting to believe it. Surely not Isobel, not her sister? 'It must have been a friendly thing, a peck, something innocent.'

Isobel shook her head with a dismissive sneer. 'He tried to put his tongue in my mouth. He touched my bum, really groped it. It was disgusting. I told him to piss off. That I'd tell you if he ever did anything like that again. He backed off then. And that was it. I left as soon as I could.'

Suzie felt as if her entire world had been shattered by those few short sentences. 'I did wonder why you rushed away,' she said, a part of her wishing she'd never met with her sister today.

'Well, now you know. It was truly awful. I couldn't wait to get out of there.'

'Why, why on earth didn't you tell me before now?'

'He was very drunk. I put it down to that. And I didn't want to be the bearer of bad news. I know how you feel about divorce.'

Suzie sat back on the sofa with her arms folded. 'The bastard!'

Isobel grimaced. 'Are you going to leave him?'

Suzie shook her head. 'He's my cross to bear.'

'Mum's words or yours?'

'Mine and hers. I have a duty.'

Isobel looked far from persuaded. 'You should dump the pig. I wouldn't hesitate in your place. I'll even help you pack his bags if you want. It's long overdue.'

Suzie made the sign of the cross.

'I can't do that. You know how important my faith is to me. And

I really do believe marriage is for life, even to someone like George. But if he thinks he's getting any of my money anytime soon, he's very sadly mistaken. I'd rather burn it than let him have it right now. He's not getting a penny until the day I give birth to a healthy baby. That's the deal. I'll tell him tonight.'

## 20

George took a couple of hours off at the end of his working day at the gym, keen to make a good impression when Suzie finally arrived home. After their recent discussion, he felt he was closer to her money than ever before. And he wanted to build on what he saw as his progress while he had the chance. He'd bought her a bunch of slightly wilted petrol station flowers that afternoon at a bargain price. And he was preparing an Italian pasta meal when he heard her key at the front door a little before six. He'd decided to avoid all talk of priests and, hopefully, religion, unless it served his purpose. The evening was about money. No more and no less. That, George told himself, was what mattered most.

George looked up from the range cooker as Suzie entered the kitchen, her coat still on, a new bright red wool scarf around her neck. One he was sure he hadn't seen before.

'What's all this in aid of?' she asked, looking first at the cooker and then at the flowers in a glass vase on the kitchen table. 'I can't remember the last time you made me a meal. It's not my birthday, if that's what you're thinking.'

Keep calm, George, he said to himself. Don't let the sarky bitch get you down. Stick to the plan. He forced a quickly vanishing smile.

'Nice scarf,' he said.

'Thanks.'

'Take your coat off and make yourself comfortable. I'm making Bolognese, your favourite. I even followed an online recipe. Five minutes and it'll be ready. I think you deserve a treat.'

Suzie hung her coat and scarf on the back of a kitchen chair.

'A treat, really? What have I done to deserve that?'

He stirred the contents of a saucepan as it came slowly to a boil. There was something about Suzie's tone that unnerved him. She wasn't reacting as he'd hoped or expected. Just typical, he thought. Where was the gratitude?

'I'm sure you'll agree our relationship has taken a turn for the better,' he said, hoping to raise her mood. 'And I think that's worth celebrating.'

Suzie sat at the table.

'Is that so?'

George sensed the tension. But he had an agenda in mind. The whole point of his efforts. He wasn't willing to let it go.

'Have you had the chance to arrange to speak to your father?' he asked.

'It's done.'

He struggled to retain his composure. Why the attitude? Why the simmering antagonism? It was so very obvious. The woman looked close to exploding.

'Done?' he said. 'What do you mean by that?'

'I've had the conversation. I've done my bit. Just like you wanted me to. But it's not good news. Dad hasn't changed his position. He feels exactly the same now as he did before the holiday. Nothing has changed. Not a thing. And it's not going to anytime soon. You're not to be trusted with money.'

George cursed crudely under his breath. Fuck him! The mean-spirited git. 'But you feel differently to your father, don't you? We can still work something out between the two of us, can't we? For the sake of the baby we're going to have. For our future family.'

Suzie began tapping the table with the fingers of her right hand, rat-a-tat.

'I had lunch with my sister today,' she said, still tapping to a slow rhythm like the beat of a drum.

Oh, shit, thought George. Had Isobel said something? What was coming next? 'That's nice,' he said, avoiding eye contact. 'How is she doing?'

Suzie stopped tapping now, glaring at him when he turned to face her. 'Wouldn't you like to know?'

What was that supposed to mean? He imagined himself slapping her. Wiping the smirk off her stupid face. 'What the hell is this all about, Suzie?' he asked. 'I've bought you flowers; I've come home early especially to cook you a meal. We were planning for a baby. And now this. Please don't let your family get in the way of our future happiness. Focus on us, our relationship. That's what God would want. When we married, two became one.'

'Isobel told me what you did.'

George quickly decided all he had was denial. Not the best hand. But the one he had to play. And maybe throw in a half-truth or two to muddy the waters. 'I've got no idea what you're talking about.'

'My actual birthday. When she came for a meal. Ding, ding, does that ring a bell?'

George switched off the heat, took the pasta saucepan off the ring. 'Of course I remember, so what?'

'You tried to kiss her. And you groped her bum, my little sister. In my home. That's low, even for you.'

George jerked his head back, feigning surprise, forcing a laugh.

He saw the money slipping away in his mind's eye, getting further out of his reach. 'No way,' he said, hands held wide. 'It's crazy talk. You know she's flirty with me. Always has been. You've seen that for yourself. We were just messing around. Having a laugh. There was nothing sexual in it, no way. Not with your sister. I wouldn't dream of it.'

Suzie frowned hard. 'Are you saying Isobel's a liar? Because if you are, I know who I believe. You've got history, George. I sometimes think I can't believe a word you say.'

How the hell could he respond to that? Storm off, slam a door, or keep talking. He decided on the latter. 'I'm saying she's mistaken, that's all. I was just messing about, having a joke, like I said. She must have got the wrong end of the stick. Or maybe her memory is playing tricks on her. I'll apologise the next time I see her if that makes you feel better. Not that I did anything wrong.'

'You're a liar, George. I think we're beyond apologies, don't you?'

'Oh, come on. Give me a break,' he said. 'This is all getting way out of hand. It was a joke. Just a stupid joke after a few drinks. I don't know what else I can say. I don't even fancy her.'

'And what about when you had a meal with another woman in town? You were seen, George. You were holding hands across the table. Was that a joke, too? Or are you a cheating bastard who keeps letting me down?'

He so wanted to slap her as she sat there close to tears. But then he thought that maybe, even now, he could turn the situation to his advantage.

'I'm not perfect. You know that. I think you've always known it. But aren't we all sinners in your eyes? Doesn't that include you?'

She gave him a knowing look.

'You're a cheater, George. You're so much worse than me.'

'Okay, hands up, I confess, I've let you down. So, what happens now? If things are so bad, why don't we split everything fairly, half for me, half for you, and agree to divorce on good terms, make a new start.'

Suzie stood, still trembling slightly as she walked towards him. But he thought there was an unfamiliar strength about her, too. A new determination he hadn't seen before.

'You know that's something I'll never agree to,' she said with a steely glower. 'So, don't get your hopes up. Father O'Shaughnessy once told me God sometimes tests us and gives us challenges to make us better people. And you're my challenge, George. And maybe, now, I'm yours. Because I'll tell you what's going to happen. If you ever mention divorce again, if there's even a hint of it, I'll give you nothing. If you force it via the courts against my wishes, we've been married two years, you'll be lucky to get a few grand at most, and that's if I haven't already given it all to the church. From the look on your face, I'm guessing you didn't know that. Not many people do. I've spoken to a solicitor friend. And I'd change my will, writing you out, which means all the money would be gone forever, the house included, even if I die before you. If you want your share of my wealth, you'll earn every single penny. You'll stay here, change your ways, be a better husband, and we'll try for a baby. And we'll do it on my terms. I'll check my fertile days and ovulation. And I'll tell you when we're going to have sex. And I'll tell you how and where we will do it. And then, if I get pregnant again, go to full term this time, and have a healthy baby, you'll get everything you want. The joint account, half of my investments, your name on the house deeds, the lot. But if you disagree or can't fully commit to those terms, you go with nothing. That's the deal. Take it or leave it. I'll give you twenty-four hours to decide.'

## 21

George left the house in his gym kit later that evening, having eaten alone. Suzie was reading a book of baby names in the lounge when he told her he was going for a run with his phone in hand. She'd shown little interest, nodding twice but not speaking. And he was glad to get out into the fresh air, closing the door behind him and jogging down the quiet road towards the sweeping estuary beach with its pale-yellow sand and wine-dark water.

George stopped at the bus shelter close to the railway crossing about five minutes later, only slightly out of breath. As expected, and to his satisfaction, he was the only person there. It was, he thought, the ideal place to contact Amelia, somewhere he wouldn't be interrupted or overheard.

George dialled with a single touch of his finger and only had to wait a few brief seconds before Amelia answered.

'Oh, thank fuck you're there,' he said as soon as she answered. 'You wouldn't believe what's happened this end. The crazy bitch has gone totally mad. Loop the frigging loop. I don't know how much more I can stand.'

'Okay, I'm listening.'

George then told Amelia all about the evening's events, minimising his behaviour and responsibility and placing a heavy emphasis on what he saw as Suzie's faults.

Amelia was silent for a second or two when he finally stopped speaking. But there was an urgency to her voice when she eventually spoke. 'But that's not what you want, is it? We want the money. That goes without saying. If we're going to buy a lovely new home together, we're going to need it. But even if Suzie does go full term, all a baby is going to do is complicate things. And the time involved, it's just too long. And that's a best-case scenario. She might not even get pregnant, and if she does, she might lose it again. There's far too many uncertainties.'

George reminded himself he still hadn't told Amelia about his vasectomy and didn't plan to. What advantage would there be? Maybe she'd want a child someday. Secrecy was best. 'I'm not having a baby with Suzie,' he said insistently. 'That's not on the agenda. If I'm going to be a father, I want it to be with you.'

'So, what happens now?' she asked.

'Have you been in touch with her at all? Since being back in Wales?'

'Not as yet,' Amelia replied. 'I was waiting to hear from you.'

George jogged up and down on the spot as the autumn chill began to bite. 'Okay, now's the time. We need to get the plan back in action. And the quicker, the better.' He laughed. 'Sometimes, it's as much as I can do to stop myself strangling the tight bitch.'

'I hope you're kidding.'

'Of course, I am. Don't be daft.'

'I'll give her a ring now,' Amelia said. 'She might be more talkative with you out of the house.'

'Arrange to meet her. And make sure you don't say anything you could only have heard from me. If she ever finds out we've been talking, we've blown it.'

Amelia sounded a little put out when she responded, 'How stupid do you think I am?'

'Sorry, love, I'm just anxious we get everything right, that's all. I didn't mean anything by it. I can't wait for us to be together. It's all I live for.'

'Me, too.'

'What are you wearing?' he asked, recalling the last time they slept together, feeling a stirring in his tracksuit trousers.

She laughed. 'Really, you're asking me that now?'

'Indulge me.'

Her tone softened. 'Well, actually, when you rang, I'd just got out of the bath. I was rubbing moisturiser all over my body, slowly massaging it into my soft skin.'

He put a hand into a pocket and touched himself. 'So, you're naked?'

'Except for red lipstick, sweet perfume and my high heels, the black stilettos. I know how much those turn you on.'

He turned his back to the quiet road in the semi-darkness and slowly moved his hand as an owl hooted in the far distance. 'I've got to see you soon,' he said, already close to ejaculating. 'Have you shaved your pussy? Are you touching yourself now?'

'Yes, and yes, just for you. Only for you. Always for you.'

'Oh, that's fantastic.'

Amelia giggled, one of the sexiest sounds he'd ever heard 'Have you come yet?' she asked.

He looked around him, making sure there were no potential onlookers, then increased the speed of his hand. 'Nearly, nearly, ah... there I go. I needed that.'

'I'll let you know as soon as I've spoken to Suzie,' she said.

He was more self-conscious all of a sudden as his erection subsided, glancing all around with darting eyes, searching for curtain twitchers. But all was quiet. Nothing stirred other than a single car that drove by, seemingly taking no interest in him.

'I managed to get Suzie to do the will I told you about,' he said. 'Not that that helps us in the short term.'

A humourless laugh.

'Chances are, it won't help us at all.'

'Unless... unless...' he said, staring into the distance.

'What?' Amelia asked.

George hesitated.

'Oh, nothing, sorry, forget it, I was just being stupid. She does that to me. It's back to the plan. Suzie likes you. She trusts you. If anyone can persuade her to do the right thing, you can.'

He heard what sounded like a sigh. 'Okay, I'll try and set up a meeting with her on Saturday. We could get together afterwards if you like?'

George laughed. 'Try stopping me.'

'Maybe book a room at that nice hotel we went to last time? The one in Spilman Street.'

He paused. 'Do you mind booking it? I'm a bit short of cash.'

Another sigh. 'Aren't you always?'

And now, George thought, Amelia was becoming irritating, too. Just like Suzie, just like her. What was it with women? He loved them and hated them; the bane of his life. Sex, the monkey on his back.

'When we get what's due to me, you'll have everything your little heart desires,' he said with feeling, clenching and unclenching his fists. 'But it's over to you now. You've got to do your bit. I've done everything I can.'

## 22

Amelia decided to text Suzie rather than ring, thinking it gave her more control at such a crucial juncture. Made her less likely to slip up, make a mistake, as she could check her messages before sending them. She felt she'd made good progress in Tenerife, establishing a relationship Suzie saw as friendship, and now it was time to progress matters to her best advantage. And, Amelia told herself, there was nothing wrong with that. It wasn't as if Suzie was doing anything worthwhile with the money. George was right about that. What a waste! Someone had to enjoy the cash. So why not her?

Amelia sat in a comfy armchair close to a warm radiator in her small, rented, Aberystwyth ground-floor flat and began typing, deciding to keep it simple, to show interest, share just enough to encourage Suzie to talk, draw her in, and then pounce.

Hi Suzie. How are things with you?

Amelia only had to wait a minute or two before receiving a reply.

Not bad, all considered, thanks. It could be worse. I'm back at work, still on the tablets. It's nice to hear from you. I was hoping I would.

Amelia sipped her strong black coffee, then read Suzie's response for a second time, thinking she seemed vulnerable, willing to share, and needing a friend. All the things Amelia had hoped for. This was going to be more straightforward than she could have hoped. Maybe reel her in slowly, put her at her ease. Not dive right in.

Winter's on the way. It's colder tonight. I'm missing all that Canary Island sunshine.

A reply in about 30 seconds this time, just two words.

Me too!

Amelia carefully considered what to type next. Convey liking, always a good thing. Reel her in, Amelia, reel her in.

I loved meeting you on holiday. It really made my trip. And our volcano visit was the best time for me. Not just the scenery but the company. It's not often I meet someone I take an immediate liking to. Maybe one day we could do it again.

Aww, that's kind. So nice of you to say. I'm so glad you've got in touch.

Amelia grinned as she considered her choice of words, thinking Suzie was so easily manipulated. She almost deserved to be conned. Brought it on herself. The needy woman was hooked like a fish.

How are things with George?

It took Suzie a little longer to reply this time but that didn't concern Amelia a great deal. The response would come soon enough. Ah, there it was. Suzie was typing again.

He's out running at the moment. And, to be honest, things aren't great.

Couldn't be better, thought Amelia, Suzie was sharing, vulnerable, in need of a friend. More of the same.

Oh, I'm so sorry to hear that. He didn't seem like an easy man when I met him on holiday. He was brave saving you, but all that alcohol and such a temper, never a good combination. You must have the patience of a saint.

A quick reply this time.

My cross to bear.

Amelia crossed then uncrossed her long legs, deciding enough of small talk, and enough talk of George, it was time to move things along. The time seemed right.

I've been thinking more about herbal alternatives to your prescribed medication, by the way. There are a few options we could consider. Is that something you still want to talk about? If you do, I really think I can help.

Really?

Yes, absolutely. I've read some amazing case studies of patients with excellent results in very similar circumstances to yours. Are you up for it? Do you want to give it a go? I'd only charge you for the herbs. Exactly what they cost me. And nothing for my professional services. I'd be helping you as a special friend. It's not often I make a connection with someone as strongly as I have with you.

While awaiting Suzie's response, Amelia wondered if she'd pushed too hard and said too much. But when Suzie did reply a few minutes later, it was precisely what Amelia had hoped for. And this time, she felt relief as well as satisfaction. It seemed she'd pitched it just right.

That's so very kind of you. Although, I'd be more than happy to pay. I'd really like to try your treatment if you're sure it's not too much trouble. I can't keep taking the tablets forever.

Amelia let out a sound of pleasure, feline, almost purring, thinking it really couldn't have been easier. That Suzie didn't suspect a damned thing. Now to drive her advantage home.

You'll pay for the herbs and nothing more, that's the deal. As a friend! And I'll be in Carmarthen this coming Saturday to look at a potential clinic a few doors down from the art gallery on King Street. How about we meet at that nice hotel on Spilman Street? The Ivy Bush. There's convenient parking, and it's got a lovely lounge and bar area. I'm sure we could find a quiet corner where we could chat privately. We could do it over the phone. But I always think it's best to see a patient face to face. Results are usually much better that way. And, anyway, I've missed you. It would be lovely to see you again. We could have a proper catch-up and a bite to eat. What do you think?

Amelia smiled while looking down at the screen, welcoming

another quick reply, as if Suzie was as keen as she was. But, of course, for very different reasons. So gullible, so easy to play.

Yes, great, thanks, I'd like that. What time have you got in mind? I'm free all day. I'll fit in with whatever works best for you.

Amelia began to laugh. It really was so very easy. What a needy woman Suzie was. What a trusting fool. Type away, Amelia, tap away.

I'm looking at the building at half eleven. It shouldn't take more than half an hour at most. So, how about we meet at the hotel for an early lunch at about twelve, my treat?

That would be perfect, thanks. And very kind of you. But you've already done enough. Lunch is on me. I absolutely insist. Shall we meet in the bar?

Amelia began typing her final message with a glowing sense of accomplishment that seemed to swell in her chest.

Perfect! I'm so glad I messaged you now. It will give me something to look forward to. And I'm certain we'll have a productive afternoon. See you at twelve. That's a date. X

## 23

Suzie made an extra effort with her appearance before leaving home for Carmarthen shortly after eleven on Saturday morning, acutely aware of just how attractive Amelia was likely to look when she met her in the three-star Ivy Bush Royal Hotel lounge bar.

Suzie had told herself that comparing herself with a woman of such exceptional beauty was never going to be a good idea as she sat in front of her dressing table mirror applying subtle makeup earlier that morning. But such things still played on her mind, one self-critical thought after another. It had always been her way. Feelings of not quite being good enough, mingled with guilt.

Maybe, Suzie pondered, George wouldn't have such a roving eye if she were as stunning as Amelia. Perhaps then, their relationship wouldn't have gone from bad to worse. Not that her average looks were any excuse. George was weak; that was the truth of it. So easily tempted, like Eve and the apple. She shouldn't ever make excuses for him, never! He really should be a better man. And if he prayed more, he would be. Who knew? Maybe that day would come, if she stuck with it and tried to influence him for the better. He could rediscover his faith, couldn't he? Yes, yes, of course, he could. Nothing was impossible with God's help. Prayers could move mountains if you believed hard enough. That's what her father had said. George was the prodigal son. A lost sheep could return to the fold.

Suzie took almost twenty minutes to choose an outfit she thought suitable for her lunch date, a lot longer than usual. And she discarded three potential dresses and two skirts for one reason or another before finally settling on smart but casual. After much anguished deliberation she chose a pair of loosely fitted tweed wool trousers that were a particular favourite, a white silk blouse bought in a local charity shop, and a navy jumper with a round collar she thought made the best of her figure while retaining a proper degree of modesty. Nothing too flashy, nothing in the slightest bit revealing, no flesh on show, and smart, that was best. It was, she reminded herself, essential to retain an appropriate degree of decorum whatever the circumstances. It wouldn't do for a good Catholic woman to be anything other than modest.

Suzie stood, crossed the bedroom floor, and stared at herself in the full-length mirror on the back of the wardrobe door in the light of a window overlooking the garden. And as she stood there, jaw tense, lips pressed together, she told herself she didn't look nearly as bad as she'd feared she might, despite life's many stresses. She looked tired, that was true. The dark shadows under her eyes were still there. There was no hiding those. But she still looked reasonably presentable in the right light. Some might even say elegant. And, anyway, she'd never been a beauty, a five or six, maybe, certainly not a ten. But God had given her other gifts. She had character, loyalty, principles, and, arguably, charm. That should be good enough for George. Good enough for any man. She repeated her internal argument, wanting to believe it but still far from convinced.

Suzie looked herself up and down for one final time, still deep in thought as the seconds ticked by. Maybe some coloured beads would be a nice finishing touch, drawing attention away from her face. Yes, the amber ones, a gift from her gran. Now, where were they? In her dressing table drawer, that was it. They'd do perfectly.

Suzie checked her watch after fastening the beads around her neck, surprised to see how much time had passed. She really couldn't be late. Not when Amelia had been so very kind. The outfit would have to do. She'd have to do. Maybe another tablet. One more wouldn't do any harm, would it? Just one more to settle her nerves. Then a quick brush of her hair and it was time to go.

Suzie drove a little faster than was sensible as she travelled in the direction of Carmarthen, looking forward to her meeting, thinking good things could come of it, but acknowledging an all too common degree of social anxiety that had haunted her for years. She wasn't entirely sure why she felt so nervous as she switched on BBC Radio Wales, hoping her favourite station would provide a suitable distraction. But within twenty minutes or so, as she approached the busy west Wales market town, driving past Morrison's Supermarket and Starbucks on her right, she decided her feelings of anxiety were entirely justified.

Suzie reminded herself she'd come to rely on her tablets. That they'd become an essential tool to her coping, a much-needed crutch when she needed one most. And that was hardly surprising. George certainly hadn't helped with all the stresses he'd inflicted. Any change to herbal medicine would be challenging. Change always was. But hopefully, Amelia could help lighten the burden. Enable her to function more effectively and even find some happiness in a sometimes dark and foreboding world. Amelia seemed so keen to help, which was half the battle. Surely, their meeting must have happened for good reason. All part of God's great plan. Nerves or not, she should trust. It was good to have someone on her side.

Suzie found a free parking space in the hotel car park, locked the saloon car with the press of a button, checked her watch for the third time in under half an hour, and strode quickly up the slight incline towards the hotel entrance, full of hope and nervous anticipation, and determined not to be even a second late. She entered her number plate in the hotel's computer system in reception, took off the smart, black, knee-length coat she kept for special occasions, and headed for the lounge bar to see Amelia waiting for her at the far end, seated on a sofa below a bright and impressive stained-glass window. Suzie thought it a fitting location: a lovely lady under a beautiful artwork. Almost a glimpse of heaven.

Amelia stood and smiled warmly with a flash of teeth as Suzie approached her. And then to Suzie's surprise, Amelia hugged her close, arms around her back, holding on for just a fraction of a second longer than was comfortable before finally letting go.

'It's great to see you again,' Amelia said, as if she meant it. 'I'm so very glad you've come. Are you ready for some lunch? I've ordered us two Irish coffees. They make them so very well here. I hope that wasn't too presumptuous.'

Both women sat.

'Well, I am driving,' Suzie replied, 'but I'm sure one won't do any harm, not if it's with food.'

Amelia handed her a menu with another engaging white smile. 'I've decided on fish and chips,' Amelia said. 'It's usually a salad for me, something low-calorie. But I thought, why not? A special treat for a special occasion. What about you?'

Suzie glanced at the various meals on offer, already starting to relax. Amelia seemed so friendly, easy to talk to, and non-judgemental, a real friend when she needed one most. And she was dressed more subtly today, still attractive, but classy. Very much the professional woman about town.

Suzie smiled back, momentarily wishing she'd opted for the

veneers a magazine article had recommended. Not that there was anything wrong with her teeth. They weren't perfect, that's all.

'Sounds good to me,' Suzie said, pushing the thought from her mind. 'I can't remember the last time I had fish and chips. But just this once, I'm going to have the same as you.'

Amelia laughed.

'Glad to hear it. Once in a blue moon doesn't do anyone any harm. I might even have some mushy peas and tartar sauce.' She patted her slim belly. 'And, who knows? Maybe even some afters if I've got room.'

Suzie was glad she'd come, already starting to enjoy herself.

Amelia gave their order to a middle-aged male waiter who delivered their drinks with a friendly and efficient demeanour.

'Right, so tell me,' Amelia began after the waiter walked away, 'how serious are you about embracing plant medicine? I want to do my very best for you. And I'm confident I can help. But I need to know it's something you're comfortable with. It's your decision, nobody else's. There'll be no pressure from me. I always tell my clients that. It's your body, not mine. So, it's your opinion that matters most.'

Suzie picked up her glass, appreciating the residual warmth as she cradled it gently in both hands. 'No, I'm, er, I really am interested. I know I'm taking too many tablets. There's no point in denial. I know something has got to be done. And it's so very difficult to see a GP these days. And when I do see one, it's usually a locum with very little time. It seems they can't wait to get me out of there. As if I'm an inconvenience. They never seem to understand.'

Amelia beamed; a broad, white smile dominating her features. 'Okay, I hear you. I know precisely what you're saying. Giving a patient sufficient time is so very important for their recovery. I can do that. And you're open to change. So, that's an excellent starting point. Recognising you've got a problem is key to success. But I won't lie to you. If we do go ahead, it's not going to be an easy process.'

Suzie shifted in her seat, interested, enjoying the attention, a little apprehensive, but wanting to know more. 'What do you mean, exactly?'

Amelia gave her a reassuring look.

'We'd need to gradually increase the herbs while carefully reducing your prescribed medication over time. That stuff's highly addictive with potentially unpleasant withdrawal symptoms. There will be bumps along the way. But – and I can't stress this enough – it will be well worth it in the end. And I'll be with you every step of the way. As a friend, an adviser, and a listening ear whenever you need one. And above all, someone you can trust. I won't ever just say what you want to hear because that's easier for me. If we go ahead, I'll tell you how it is every time, with total honesty. Because that's the best way to help. And that's what I'm here to do. Help; no more, no less.'

Suzie nodded, one part of her pleased, another thinking things were running away from her a little too quickly for comfort. Everything seemed to be moving so very fast. But she reminded herself she was taking far too many tablets. That she'd had to lie to her GP, saying she'd left her medication in Tenerife to get a replacement bottle. Something had to change. It wasn't something she was proud of.

'That's, very kind of you, thanks,' Suzie said with genuine gratitude. 'I'm, er, I'm keen to start, but, um, shouldn't I speak to my doctor first? I'll need another prescription soon. Perhaps that would be the logical time to discuss it all.'

Suzie thought she saw Amelia stiffen for a fraction of a second before she responded. But when she did speak, it was with a calm, reasoned voice which went some way to putting Suzie at her ease. That voice was almost a therapy in itself.

'Well, you could do,' Amelia began, looking Suzie in the eye. 'That's the conventional wisdom. And I'd certainly have no objection if you did. But off the record, I wouldn't advise it. Not many doctors understand alternative treatments in any depth. They don't have the training for it. And as you said yourself, they've got so little time these days. Between you and me, I think we ought to keep it to ourselves. But only if you're comfortable with that. I'd never pressurise you into doing anything you don't want to do. At every stage of the treatment, I want you to remember that you're always in control. At the end of the day, I can advise you and tell you what I think is best. But what you say goes. That's the way I work. You call the shots.'

Suzie unbuttoned the top button of her blouse, wondering why, all of a sudden, she felt so very hot. She could feel damp patches forming under both her arms despite her unscented deodorant. 'Um, yes,' she replied, with hesitation. 'I suppose that all makes sense. And I know you've got my best interests at heart.'

Another flashing smile left Amelia's face as quickly as it appeared. 'Good, good, that's good,' she said with evident enthusiasm. 'I'm glad I've convinced you. If we both believe in what we're doing, that will make all the difference. But what does George think of all this? Has he expressed an opinion?'

'Um, I, I haven't told him. He doesn't even know we're meeting.'

Amelia frowned. 'I completely understand. I've seen for myself how difficult he can be. But it's always good to have a partner onside with these things, if at all possible.'

Suzie dropped her chin to her chest, wondering how much she should say. Sharing details of her relationship issues was never easy. Not even with her priest, let alone someone she'd only known for a relatively short time, however caring. But Amelia had stressed the need for honesty. And maybe the telling would be cathartic. All part of the journey to recovery. Yes, honesty was best.

'Um, things, er, things haven't been great since we got home from Tenerife.'

Amelia reached out to touch Suzie's arm momentarily before withdrawing her hand. 'Oh, I'm so sorry to hear that. Men, eh? Is he drinking again? Any more temper tantrums? I've seen exactly what he's like, poor you.'

A waiter indicated their meals were ready. Suzie delayed her response until she was sitting opposite Amelia at a table in the adjoining restaurant area. 'I hate saying this. It's hard to admit, even to myself. But I've come to realise I can't trust George at all,' Suzie began, her lip trembling, 'I knew he's interested in other women. But it's...' She sighed. 'It's much worse than I ever realised.'

Amelia chewed and swallowed a golden chip. 'Really?' she said, seemingly concerned. 'What on earth has happened to make you think that?'

Suzie took a sip of water. Just enough to wet her mouth. 'I don't know if I can even bring myself to say it. Talking about it seems to make it all the more real.'

Amelia put down her knife and fork, resting them on the side of her plate.

'Come on, you can tell me,' she said, with a sympathetic look. 'It's all part of the healing process. Think of it as purging the poison from your mind and body. Words have power. Don't hold them in. Let them go. Use them to your advantage. You're a strong woman, remember that.'

Another sip of water. A touch of her grandmother's beads. A stifled sob. Maybe sharing would feel good, Suzie thought.

'George, well, he, he made a pass at... at my sister. He tried to kiss her. And, and, if that wasn't bad enough, he was seen out in town with another woman at a restaurant holding her hand. I've been a good wife to him. He's let me down so very badly. I feel so betrayed.'

Amelia's mouth fell open as she emitted a small gasp, three manicured fingers touching parted lips. 'Oh, wow,' she said, 'no wonder you're so upset. What an absolute shit. You so don't deserve to be treated like that. No woman does.'

Suzie laughed despite herself. 'Yeah, what a shit!' she whispered, not wanting to be overheard. 'I've called him a lot worse in my head, God forgive me.'

'Well, that's hardly surprising. I'm amazed you haven't said it to his face.'

Suzie shook her head. 'I could never do that. That's just not my style. But I have made changes. He knows how I feel.'

'Are you certain it's all true?' Amelia asked.

Suzie nodded, her shoulders slumped. 'Oh, yes, there's absolutely no doubt. That's George for you: cheating George; dishonest George; George the gambler; George the pig; George the shit.'

'So, what are you going to do?'

Suzie forked a small piece of toothsome battered cod into her mouth before speaking. 'Do?'

'Surely, after all that, you're not going to stay with him? Men like George don't change. He'll do it again. They always do it again. I know that from bitter experience. One of mine cheated time and again before he died.'

'Died?'

'Oh, long story, he got ill, the doctors couldn't find out what was wrong. I'll tell you more another time. Today is about you. This is your time.'

Suzie blinked away a tear. 'A part of me would like to separate from George. You know, make a new start. Maybe even with somebody else. I do fantasise about it sometimes; God forgive me. But that's all it is or ever will be. A stupid fantasy. Because we're married.'

Amelia was quick to reply. 'Well, then, why not get a divorce? I wouldn't hesitate. I'd be in a solicitor's office before you could blink.'

Suzie shook her head. 'I can't do that.'

'But, why?'

'You wouldn't understand.'

'Try me.'

Suzie sighed. 'It's a faith thing, religion, my church. I should never have given in to sex before marriage. But I did. I was tempted. I got pregnant. There was all sorts of parental pressure. But I played my part. And so, here I am. Marriage is for life. It's that simple. I made an unbreakable commitment.'

'What, even after adultery?'

'Yes, even then. That's the way I see it. And I know my father does, too. It's something I've talked to him about. I've made my bed. Now I've got to lie in it. Till death us do part. I made my vows in the presence of God. And now I've got to honour them for good or bad. That's the way it is, with no exceptions. Not even when a husband is as bad as George. I sometimes wish things were different, but they're not. I have to deal with that reality.'

Amelia was silent for about thirty seconds, back to eating, focusing on her meal, adding a tempting blob of tartar sauce with a small spoon. 'Do you know what I'd do in your circumstances?' she asked when she finally spoke. 'I'd pack the cheating shit's bags, tell him to piss off, and then split everything 50-50 for a clean break. That way, there'd be no likely comebacks, no more friction. You'd have done the right thing. And I'm not talking about divorce. So, you wouldn't be breaking your vows: you'd be living apart but still married. And, this is the most important bit: the change would help you heal. It would be a brand-new start for you. A rebirthing. I'm sure of it. There's only so much any medicine can achieve with things as they are. Your body is in a state of fight or flight with a constant flood of hormones, adrenalin, cortisol. And over time that's bound to have a detrimental effect. I can see the strain on your face. But you can change that. You have the power. Divide all your possessions equally with George and make the split. I wouldn't hesitate if I were you. You could have a much better life. Why put yourself through years of unhappiness when there's an alternative within your reach?'

Suzie shook her head determinedly, tears flowing freely as she repeatedly dabbed at her face with a serviette. 'I know what you're-you're saying. I can see where you're c-coming from,' Suzie stuttered. 'Honestly, I can. In some ways, it-it even makes sense. And I know it's what George would want. He's said as much. But it's never going to h-happen. George and I made a holy commitment. So, I'm in it for the long haul. And if he chooses t-to leave... if he breaks the marriage vows he made in the presence of Almighty God, then he leaves with nothing. Maybe then, he'd learn the value of commitment. He wouldn't get a penny. Not from me. I'd do whatever it took to make that happen. And I do mean, *whatever* it took.'

Amelia frowned hard, her forehead slightly wrinkled and her soft-angled, shaped eyebrows brought together. 'Wow, that's quite a statement. You sound very determined about that.'

Suzie coughed, cleared her throat, and then nodded twice. 'Oh, I am. I even told my priest. I've never been more determined about anything in my life.'

Amelia made a face, pressed her lips together. 'Well, in that case, if you're determined to stay with George, there's one thing I'd like you to do for me. As your friend as well as your herbalist...'

Suzie wondered what was coming next as she blew her nose, the right nostril first and then the left. 'What's that?'

'How much exercise do you do?'

Suzie lent forward with a bent spine, wondering how much to say. Another admission. Something else in her life in need of improvement. She reminded herself that honesty was best. 'Um, not much, to be honest. A bit of gardening in the spring and summer. And I used to go to an exercise class at the leisure centre on a Tuesday evening. But everything else seemed to get in the way. I haven't been for about eighteen months. I keep meaning to start again, but I never get around to it. Someone at work suggested yoga, but I don't think it's my sort of thing.'

Amelia gave a sad smile.

'Ah, okay, very little exercise, that's not ideal. But it is easily remedied. I want you to start going for long walks every single evening after work. For at least an hour. It will provide you with a wonderful physical and mental tonic, complementing the herbal medicine I'm going to give you perfectly. The route doesn't really matter as long as you do it. But if you can build in some hills, all the better. Do you think that's something you can do for me?'

Suzie swallowed the last tasty mouthful of her food before pushing her empty plate away.

'Um, yes, I suppose in spring, once it gets lighter in the evenings and warms up a bit. We're heading into winter though.'

Amelia looked back with a pained expression. 'I want to help you, Suzie, and I will, I promise. But you have to do your bit. You live in a lovely coastal village with quiet country roads. Why not wear some warm, brightly coloured clothing and something reflective, and commit? An hour a day. That's all I'm suggesting. I've got one of those head bands with a light on it, if that helps? I'd be happy to lend it to you. In fact, you can have it as a gift. What do you think? I could put it in the post along with the herbs and treatment plan.'

'Do you really think walking would help?'

Amelia nodded. 'Absolutely, I do, one hundred per cent.'

Suzie shrugged less than enthusiastically. 'Oh, okay, I'll start on Monday if you really think it's a good idea. George said I need to lose a bit of weight. Maybe he's right.'

Amelia carefully wiped the corners of her mouth. 'Well, I wouldn't listen to George. You look pretty good to me. The walking is more to do with dealing with stress and getting your heart pumping than weight. Is there a particular route you've got in mind? I find it's always better to plan these things in advance.'

Suzie thought about it, then described her likely route as Amelia listened with apparent interest, asking more questions than seemed necessary.

Amelia stood, speaking in a bubbly tone when Suzie finally finished. 'That sounds ideal,' Amelia said. 'Now, you've got the idea. Think of this as the start of your recovery. Better times are ahead. And it all starts here. Fancy one last coffee before you head off? Back in the lounge?'

Suzie was feeling more positive now. More optimistic than she'd been in quite some time. As if a dark shadow had lifted. She silently thanked God for her new friend; Amelia was clearly a blessing. 'Go on then, why not? But no whisky for me this time. Not with driving.'

After ordering their hot drinks at the bar, the two women sat back on the same sofa they had earlier.

'Oh, my goodness,' Suzie began with an embarrassed look. 'I've just realised I haven't even asked you how the viewing went. I'm so sorry. I've been so focussed on me and my problems.'

'Yes, it, um, it went pretty well, thanks. I think I'm going to make an offer.'

'Oh, wow, that's great news. It would be brilliant to have you working here in town.'

'Yes, and I'm looking at a house in Johnstown tomorrow morning, about half a mile past the leisure centre. If I'm going to work in Carmarthen, I'll need somewhere to live. And Johnstown seems as nice a place as any. I'd miss the sea. But it's only a short drive away.'

Suzie fiddled with her wedding ring, keeping her hands busy.

'Look, I've had an idea,' she said after a few seconds of silence 'It's hardly worth you driving all the way back to Aber if you've got to be back here in the morning. Why don't you stay at my place tonight? George is away all weekend on some kind of gym-related nutrition course. An NVQ 3 or 4, something like that. I've got the house to myself.'

Amelia emitted a heavy sigh. 'Oh, no, that's such a shame. I've already booked a room here. It's all paid for online.'

'Then, why don't we meet up again this evening? For a curry, perhaps. Or even the cinema. There's a good one here in town. There may be something decent on. I can easily find out.'

Amelia rubbed her upper chest as if pained. 'I'd love to. Really, I would. But there's a load of paperwork I need to catch up with. I see patients all week. So, the weekends and evenings are the only time I get.'

Suzie felt a genuine sense of disappointment. And a little deflated, too.

'Ah, okay, then hopefully another time,' she said. 'What do I owe you for the herbs?'

'Let's not worry about that for now. I'll let you know once they're in the post. And I want a report on how the walking is going. I want you to promise me you're going to do it.'

Suzie nodded slightly dejectedly. 'I'm going to buy some new trainers before going home today.'

'That's my girl,' Amelia said with another flash of teeth. 'And I'd highly recommend something reflective. Something to ensure drivers see you on those dark country roads. We don't want you getting run over just when things are looking up.'

Suzie let out a laugh, thinking it was good to have such a caring and supportive friend. Such a change from her selfish git of a husband. 'I'll get something today,' Suzie said. 'I noticed some of those yellow high-vis jackets with the reflective silver stripes for sale in the market at half-price last time I was there. Hopefully, they're still there. You know, like the ones that guy wore on *Britain's Got Talent*? I think he won in the end. Did you see it?'

Amelia nodded. 'Yeah, I did, sounds ideal.'

Suzie grinned, picturing herself all dressed up and ready for her first walk. 'No one is going to miss me wearing one of those,' she said. 'And thank you. I mean that from the bottom of my heart. I'm so glad I've got you in my life. I'm feeling so much better than when I arrived. You've been an absolute star.'

Amelia gave Suzie another hug, and this time Suzie enjoyed the embrace.

'From now on, we're a team,' Amelia said when the two stepped apart. 'I'll be back and forth to Carmarthen a little more often from now on. Let's get together again soon?'

'I'll look forward to that,' Suzie said, and meant it.

Amelia gave one last beaming smile.

'Good, I'm glad,' she said, 'me, too.'

## 24

That evening, Amelia met George in the same comfortable hotel lounge bar at about seven. But she was dressed very differently now. Her tight, black sleeveless dress, plunging neckline, lace-topped hold-up stockings, and high-heeled scarlet stilettoes intended to seduce. As did her pleasant, sweet, French perfume, which she'd dabbed generously on her slender neck, impressive cleavage and ear lobes, as was her custom. She flashed a smile as George walked towards her, looking as handsome as ever in a single-breasted grey suit that fitted him well.

'How's the "nutrition course" going?' she asked with a little laugh. 'I hope you've been good. I might have to smack your bum for you if you've been a naughty boy.'

He bent at the waist, leant forward, kissed her cheek, and lingered. 'I can't wait. I've been such a bad boy. And you look amazing.'

Amelia handed George her empty glass with an engaging grin. 'I'll have another gin and tonic while you're on your feet. You can put it on the room, 22, and have something yourself. Oh, and I don't want a double. A single will do just fine.'

George returned a minute or two later with her order and a pint of strong German lager for himself. Amelia noticed he'd already drunk about twenty-five per cent of it at the bar, which didn't surprise her at all. She smiled as he sat next to her on the exact same sofa seat Suzie had occupied that morning. Something Amelia found amusing. Like a revolving door, she thought, one in and one out. Now it was his turn.

'I'm looking forward to tonight,' he said after slurping another mouthful of beer, draining the tall glass to the halfway point with what sounded a satisfied sigh.

'Me, too,' Amelia replied with a slight nod of her head. 'But slow down on the beer. Best not to drink too much of that stuff. I want you at your best. I don't want you falling asleep on me again.'

George gave a quickly disappearing smile that she thought less than genuine. She wondered if she'd bruised his ego. Yes, probably. It didn't take much. He could sometimes be so fragile despite all his macho male bluster. For all his selfish, self-serving tendencies, there were vulnerabilities, too.

'Did you look at the place in town?' he asked, clearly changing the subject.

Amelia smirked to herself, deciding to go with it. To play his game. 'It needs more work than I realised, if I'm going to get it how I want it,' she said. 'But other than that, it's perfect. The location is great, and the size. I'm going to have to spend a lot more money than I anticipated. But so be it. I want it. So, I'll have it. I've just got to work out how.'

'That's good. Are you going to sell the place in Aber?'

Amelia shook her head. She hadn't told George her clinic was rented, like her flat. Those were things she'd decided to keep to herself.

'I won't sell unless I have to,' she said with conviction. 'Property is a great investment. In a perfect world, I'd like to own both. It's all down to the money, simple as. Isn't it always?' Amelia watched as George drained his glass without a word of reply. 'You look nervous,' she said as he wiped his mouth with a sleeve. 'What's up? Your hand's shaking. Tell me everything. I'm here to help.'

He stood. 'I'll just get another pint, and we can chat. Room 22, yeah?'

Amelia gave another nod. 'Do you want another G & T?' he asked, to which she shook her head. Sometimes it helped to keep a relatively clear head.

'Just a sparkling water with a slice of lemon, no ice.'

George returned to their sofa with the two drinks and a packet of salted peanuts for himself. He hadn't asked Amelia if she wanted a packet and didn't offer her any of his. Neither of which surprised her a great deal.

'Your tits look fantastic in that dress,' he said with a grin after chewing and swallowing. 'I can see your nipples pressing against the cloth. Lovely.'

Amelia turned in her seat, wagging a finger.

'Down, boy, I know your game. Don't change the subject. Talk now, sex later. We've got all night. Now, tell me, what's up? And I want the truth. I can tell something is worrying you.'

'I can tell you one thing that's up,' he said, looking down at his groin, pointing at the prominent bulge in his grey trousers.

Sometimes, she thought, it was like talking to a teenager. Would the man ever grow up?

'Stop it, I'm serious,' she said with a frown. 'Stop thinking with your dick and start talking.'

George popped a handful of peanuts into his mouth, munched away, then took another slurp of beer before responding. As predictable as night and day, she thought. A slave to his wants and needs. 'It's just all this shit with Suzie,' he said. 'She's such a tight bitch.' He blew out the air. 'I've been wondering how it went with you and her this morning. Did you get anywhere? Please tell me you did. I don't know how much more I can take. I've been sitting here, afraid to ask.'

Amelia paused for a beat. 'Do you want the good news or the bad?'

George tilted his head back and drained his glass to the last drop. 'Oh, for fuck's sake. Tell me the good. Please tell me our plan's working.'

'Well, it is, and it isn't,' Amelia replied, looking him in the eye. 'Suzie trusts me. And I'm pretty sure she likes me. I think she sees me as a friend. She's keen for us to meet up again. Those are the positives.'

George bit at his bottom lip. 'And the bad news?'

'Do you really want to hear this now?'

'Let's get it over with,' he replied. 'Nothing can be worse than what I'm thinking.'

'Okay, you asked for it. So, don't shoot the messenger: there is no way Suzie is ever going to cooperate with a 50-50 divorce. That's never going to happen. She couldn't have been clearer or more vehement. But then, you already knew that. And what you said to me before is right. If you choose to leave, just walk out, she's determined you leave with nothing. As far as she's concerned, the two of you should stay together, living in abject misery until one of you dies. I don't understand it. It makes no sense to me. But I've talked to her. That's what she said. And I believe her. Suzie's not like anyone I've ever met before. It all seems insane. She seems capable of almost anything. I think every word she said to me was true.'

George's eyes narrowed as he spat out his reply. 'I think the crazy bitch enjoys suffering. Can you believe that? She seems to wallow in it. I could be the worst husband in the world, and she'd still want us to stay married.'

Amelia sipped her water, thinking no ice would have been so

much better. Why did George never listen? She chose to ignore his heightened emotions, focussing instead on the task at hand.

'The herbs I'll give her, combined with a reduction in her prescribed medication, should make her more amenable to manipulation for a time. She'll be more emotionally fragile than usual, which I guess could work to our advantage. I'll keep working on her. Of course I will. I'll do all I can to try to persuade her to kick you out and hand over some cash. But, in all honesty, I can't see me getting anywhere. She seems pretty entrenched in her views to me. Much more so than I ever envisaged. I've never encountered anything like it.'

'Tell me about it,' he said with a glower.

Amelia put her almost full glass down and crossed her arms. 'Is that it? "Tell me about it"! Is that all you've got to say? Really? Is that the best you've got?'

She thought he seemed to get smaller as he mumbled his reply, sinking into his seat. 'We've tried, we're still trying,' he began, close to tears. 'What else is there? We stick to the plan.'

Amelia rushed her words, her face tightening. 'And if the plan fails? What then? Because that seems pretty likely to me.'

George shrugged. 'I don't know. What do you want me to say?'

'Oh, come on, George, grow a pair. You need money. I need money. And she's got it. Loads of it. You need to get creative. Think outside the box. We need a backup plan. Because there's only so long I'm going to wait.'

He screwed up his face, a bead of sweat forming on his brow. 'A backup plan?' he said, as if the idea was a revelation.

'Yes, isn't it obvious? Yes!'

'Such as?' George looked exasperated. Like a small boy, she thought, looking for his mother's guidance. A sad, pathetic little boy.

'Do I really need to spell it out for you?' she asked.

'Yes,' he said. 'I think you very probably do.'

Amelia sipped her drink, silent for a few seconds as she considered her choice of words. She lowered her voice to a whisper, speaking directly into his ear almost at touching distance. 'You need to decide how much you want the money. And how badly you want a new life. Because as things are, Suzie's wrecking yours. She's in the way. She's the problem. No one else, her.'

'Don't you think I know that?' he snapped back a little too loudly for her liking. 'Why the hell do you think I'm here?'

Amelia's expression hardened. 'Well then, do something about it. Are you playing games? Or are you willing to put everything on the line? Give that some thought and come to a decision. And do it soon. If our plan fails, which seems likely, just how far are you willing to go?'

## 25

Conflicted, yes, conflicted, that was the one word which best described his troubled state of mind, thought George, as he drove towards the church he'd once attended on a weekly basis, both as a child and an adult. He let out a loud, agitated yelp of deep frustration as he pressed his foot down hard on the accelerator pedal, increasing his speed well above the legal limit, desperate to get the morning's events over as quickly as possible.

George repeatedly blinked as his head began to ache, his mind still racing as he tried to make sense of his feelings, of why he was making the journey at all. He silently acknowledged that a part of him would have liked to be doing something else entirely. Work even, anything. Because the church, entering that building, and talking to a priest, would bring back memories that were best left in the past. But he felt he had no choice. Some things one had to do, however painful, however challenging. And this was one of those times. He had to man up, be strong.

George increased his white-knuckle grip on the steering wheel as he continued his rumination, gritting his teeth, screwing up his face, picturing a vision of hell, watching blue-yellow flames dance, dark smoke spiralling into the fetid air.

For all of his suffering at the hands of the priesthood and the hypocrisy he'd witnessed, he bemoaned that religion still had a hold on him, sinking in its fangs at the most inconvenient moments. Shit! Yes, fear and guilt were still so engrained in him. Always there, somewhere in the background despite his determined rejection, affecting his thinking, limiting his behaviour, eating away at him, beating him down.

However desirable a particular course of action, there was the fear of consequences, not just in this world, but the next. Was any of it real? Yes, no, yes, no? He didn't know the answer. But there was always that possibility. And some sins were more severe than others, weren't they? Surely, they were, yes? And now he was considering a big one. By far the most serious of his life.

George actively calmed himself as he approached the church, taking long, deep breaths, finding a free parking place in the street just a minute or two's walk from the dark Victorian stone building. This was it. The moment he'd been dreading. Come on, George, you can do it. In you go. Get it over with. It would be worth it in the end.

'Bless me, Father, for I have sinned. It has been over five years since my last confession.'

The plump, middle-aged priest moved to the edge of his seat, peering through the screen in the semi-darkness of the confessional, his brown plastic-framed glasses appearing too small for his chubby face.

'It's good to see you back at church, George,' he said with a North of England accent, utilizing harsher consonant sounds and shorter vowels than the Welsh. 'It's been far too long. Is there something specific you'd like to confess on this fine day?'

George pressed his face against the screen, looking the black-clad priest in the eye. His tight, white dog collar stood out even in the dim light, straining against his poorly shaven neck.

'I've been wondering...' George began, resisting the impulse to get out of there. To stand, open the door, run and never come back. 'Did you see the recent news reports about Father Hagan? The monster who ruined so many lives.'

George studied the priest closely, his eyes having adapted to the gloom. The priest had swallowed hard as he made the sign of the cross. He appeared uneasy, just as George had hoped he would. As if he couldn't get comfortable in his seat.

'Um, yes, yes I did,' the priest said. 'So very sad. I pray his suffering comes to a quick end. He's in the best place at the hospice. The nuns will ease his suffering as best they can until God takes him home.'

'Home?'

'Home to heaven.'

George gritted his teeth, snarled, clenched his fists. 'So, let me see if I've got this right? You believe even someone like Hagan, a man who preyed on the innocent, hiding in plain sight, indulging his perverted desires with no concern for his victims, can find redemption at the end of his miserable life?'

The priest nodded enthusiastically, his sagging jowls wobbling like a ghastly birthday jelly.

'No sin is absolutely unforgivable if the sinner repents and accepts the infinite mercy of God.'

George rhythmically tapped a foot against the worn floor-boards. 'Well, that's where me and God differ. I don't forgive Hagan. I hope the filthy, perverted bastard writhes in agony before burning forever in hell. You do believe in hell, don't you, priest? That's what you teach, isn't it?'

'Only God can judge.'

George let out a derisive laugh. 'So, if I do something considered terrible by the world, all will be okay if I say sorry, yes? Is that what you're saying? It seems so. As long as I'm not caught and prosecuted, of course. I don't think a criminal court would be quite as forgiving as you.'

The priest gave a slight cough, pulled at his collar, and cleared his throat. George could see the tension on his face.

'Where are you going with this?' the priest asked, his voice wavering. 'Is there something you need to tell me? You seem particularly troubled. I'd like to help if I can.'

George was slow to reply. Let the bastard stew, he thought, let him stew. 'Father O'Shaughnessy, that's your name, isn't it? Father Peter O'Shaughnessy?'

'You know it is, my child. But we're here to talk about you.'

George jerked his head back. 'Child?'

'A term of endearment, nothing more. I'm here to care for my flock.'

'Is that so?'

'It is.'

George spat his words. 'Didn't you used to run a youth club with Hagan? Didn't you take kids on camping holidays together? I'm sure I heard that somewhere along the line.'

'For a time, yes, yes, I did.'

'What, and you didn't once think any of those children were in need of protection? Did you turn a blind eye, Father? Or are you as evil as Hagan? Maybe you're a dirty nonce, too.'

The priest's voice rose in pitch and tone. 'I knew nothing of his crimes.'

'So you say.'

Another sign of the cross. 'I swear it in the name of the Holy Mother. Now, are you here for confession, or shall we bring this charade to a timely end?'

George pressed his hands together as if in prayer. It was now or never, he thought. Say his piece or get out of there. 'There is something else I wanted to talk about,' he said. 'About me, my life, my sins. Enough of you and whatever shit you've got up to. I came here looking for reassurance. And to some extent, you've done your job. I sin, confess, ask for redemption, and don't get caught. It's the Catholic way. A few Hail Marys and I'll be fine. As you said, I'll be forgiven.'

The priest's breathing became more laboured as he raised an open hand to his throat. 'What sin are you talking about, George?'

George lowered his eyes for a beat. 'You have an obligation of total confidentiality, yes?'

The priest nodded solemnly. 'I'm bound by the holy seal of the confessional. What you say here is between you, me and God Almighty. And that's how it will stay. Now, is there something you want to tell me? Because it seems to me there is. Best get it off your chest. I suspect that's why you're here, after all.'

'So if anyone asked, you couldn't tell them anything, right?'

The priest sighed, his frustration evident. 'The seal of the confessional is *inviolable*,' he said with conviction, emphasising the final word heavily. 'Now confess, tell me what you have done.'

'Do you know Suzie?' George asked. 'My wife.'

'Yes, yes, of course, she's a good woman. One of the most dedicated in my flock. I only wish all of the church's members shared her strength of faith. The world would be a better place if they did.'

George lowered his voice almost to a whisper. 'I've been having dark thoughts about her.'

Even in the dim light, the colour drained away from the priest's face, leaving him ashen. 'Sorry,' he said, 'what sort of dark thoughts?'

George let the silence hang there for a few seconds before responding. He briefly considered telling the priest he was considering murder but then thought better of it. How far could he genuinely trust the man to remain silent, despite his reassurances? And anyway, the priest had already been clear. If even an evil, perverted nonce was forgivable, then he was, too, whatever he did. If he was sorry afterwards.

George stood. 'Thanks, Father, I've said as much as I want to say. But rest assured, you've done your job. I sin, I repent, and then I'm forgiven. It's that simple, the Catholic way. I don't know why I was so worried in the first place... Oh, and one last thing, just to be crystal clear. If I ever find out you've told Suzie or anyone else what I said here, the police will know about your links with Hagan. And I'd be willing to say *anything* I need to say, sign any statement, to send you down for a very long time. So I'd keep your stupid mouth shut if I were you.'

## 26

George looked up from his surprisingly tasty microwaved ready meal as Suzie entered the kitchen, wearing a recently purchased red tracksuit with white trim, pristine sky-blue trainers, and a bright yellow, high-vis waistcoat-type jacket with silver stripes and no sleeves. She wasn't wearing the headband with a light given to her by Amelia, having previously told George she thought it looked silly, and a bit over the top given the rest of her outfit.

'Another walk?' asked George, showing only passing interest as he forked a mouthful of rice into his mouth.

Suzie smiled. 'My tenth evening in a row. And it's getting easier. I'm already getting stronger and fitter. I'm not panting nearly as hard when I'm going up the hill. And my legs aren't aching nearly as much afterwards. I never thought I'd say this, but I'm really starting to enjoy it. I might even start running in a few weeks' time. And maybe aim for a half-marathon in the spring if I think I'm up to it. Perhaps we could even do it together.'

George slurped down half a glass of tap water and then burped. He chose to ignore her suggestion. 'Same route as usual?' he asked.

'Past the White Lion, up the hill towards Kidwelly, turn right for

Broadlay, and then down the hill and back into Ferryside for home.'

George wondered why she felt the need to go into such detail, bigging herself up, making more of it than was justified. Just typical, he thought. Such an annoying woman. No wonder he was considering ending her life. She'd told him the exact same thing the day before, and the one before that.

'How's it going with the herbs?' he asked, making conversation. Asking another question he already knew the answer to. Anything to make the situation seem normal.

'Um, okay, I guess,' Suzie said with a pensive look. 'I think they might be making me feel a bit light-headed in the mornings, like I said before. So, I've decided to reduce the prescribed medication slightly slower than I originally planned. Maybe do it over a few months rather than weeks. It's the destination that matters more than the journey.'

'Really?'

'I think so,' she replied.

'Why don't you have a chat with your friend Amelia, ask her advice? She's the expert. It's not like you've done anything like this before.'

Suzie frowned. 'Why are you so interested all of a sudden?'

George shrugged. 'I am, that's all. You're my wife. Why wouldn't I be? I do care.'

Suzie approached the kitchen door, stopped and looked back before exiting. She kept hold of the handle. 'If you take a look at the graph I've stuck to the front of the fridge, you'll see it's my optimum time to conceive right now. When I get back, I'll have a quick shower, and we can go up to bed. I don't want to miss the opportunity. If we're going to have a baby, it's not going to happen by magic.'

George let out a sardonic laugh. 'Oh, very romantic, I'm sure.

Some women seduce with sexy lingerie, others with a beguiling dance, putting on a bit of a show. But with you, it's graphs. Well, I've never been a fan of maths.'

Suzie glared at him. 'You can drop the sarcasm. It's not appreciated.'

'All right, your majesty, I will perform like a trained monkey as soon as you're ready. Your wish is my command. But maybe you can actually move a bit this time. You know, rather than just lying there like a plank of wood with a hole in it for me to stick my cock in.'

Suzie walked slowly back towards him, then stood just a couple of feet from where he sat, her arms folded. 'You know what you did, George. At the party, to my sister, and with that woman at the restaurant you still haven't named. And I'm sure I don't need to remind you I feel betrayed. So, sex now is for procreation, not pleasure. And that's your doing – nothing to do with me. We'll take our clothes off as necessary and do what we have to do. But with no foreplay and no kissing. In fact, no affection at all. It's a necessary physical function to facilitate pregnancy, and that's it, no more than that. No doubt you remember our deal. You give me a baby, and I share my money. That way, we both get what we want. And maybe given enough time, I'll find it in my heart to forgive you. But nothing changes until the day I give birth.'

*That's what you think*, thought George, as she walked away towards the hall and the quiet road beyond. He so wanted her dead, so wanted her gone.

As Suzie closed the front door after her, George reminded himself that all he had to do was build up sufficient courage to act on his intentions. To do what he needed to do and get away with it. And then, once the dark deed was done, everything would change forever. He'd be an affluent man of leisure, living in luxury, indulging his wants to the nth degree with no interference from a nagging woman, who wouldn't know a good time if it slapped her on the arse. No more work and no more wife. Brilliant! It would be so good. And the sooner, the better.

George pictured Suzie dead and smiled. If only he could bring himself to end her life. It should be simple enough. He knew exactly what to do. He'd pictured the scene. Rehearsed it in his head time and again. But the doing wasn't nearly as easy as he'd hoped. The planning was one thing and murder quite another. There was always that fear of damnation, so deeply engrained, eating away at him, wagging an accusing finger despite the priest's reassuring words about God's forgiveness. And the police, there was always the police. He had to worry about them, too.

What would the consequences be if he killed her? George asked himself the question as he approached the dishwasher with dirty plate in hand. Getting away with it. That's what mattered most. In this world and the next. But was that even possible? Or would there be a terrible price to pay? Was it a risk worth taking? Yes or no? That was what he had to decide.

## 27

Suzie began striding up the long, steep hill towards Kidwelly in the light of a pale-yellow, three-quarter autumn moon partly shrouded in cloud, increasing her pace despite the effort of it all. Still a challenge, she urged herself on one determined step after another, her body warming despite a sudden downpour of stinging hail that quickly turned the hedgerows a sparkling white, the small pellets of frozen rain bouncing off the dark tarmac road before settling.

*Come on, Suzie, you can do it, girl, keep going; it's almost stopped,* she repeated to herself time and again as she walked on, head bowed, looking down to protect her face. *God, give me strength. Keep going, girl. Another half an hour and you'll be home in the warm. That's it, one step at a time.*

She began counting her steps now, one, two, three, etcetera, in her head, more as a distraction from the weather than anything else, as her internal dialogue came to an end.

Suzie paused very briefly by an old wooden five-bar farm gate set back a few feet from the road, just for a second or two, catching her breath before walking on again, not as quickly as before, but still making good progress as the hail lightened and then finally stopped almost as suddenly as it had started. She jumped, startled, and then laughed when a large red fox ran across the narrow country road in front of her. But it didn't impede her progress for very long as she hurried on, just 200 yards or so from the Broadlay turning she knew so well.

It all seemed so perfect; the rolling west Wales countryside strikingly beautiful despite the unseasonal chill. And Suzie felt tired but blessed. Fortunate to be there, to live in such a place. And to have a good friend like Amelia, too. A friend without whom she wouldn't be out walking at all.

Suzie heard the sound of a car engine starting just a fraction of a second before she saw the headlights switch on. She immediately stepped to the side of the road, over a small ditch, standing close to the high hedge, confident she'd be seen in her high-vis yellow jacket with its silver reflective stripes, sure she was safe, thinking the driver was likely local, someone she knew even. Danger was the last thing on her mind.

But as the car appeared around a bend in front of her, it didn't slow as she expected it would. It sped up, its powerful-sounding engine revving loudly in the cold evening air as it hurtled towards her, getting nearer and nearer, faster and faster. And the lights, those white lights were so very bright, on the main beam, never dipped. They dazzled her before she turned her head, urgently looking away with a sense of panic that quickly engulfed her, adrenalin surging through her system, increasing her heartbeat, sending blood to her muscles.

Suzie attempted to scramble up the steep hedge, the speeding vehicle now only feet away. But the icy foliage was too slippery, the hedge too vertical to find a foothold that held.

Suzie screamed as she slipped back to the road's edge just as the car reached her, hitting her full-on, bang, sending her tumbling high over its metal bonnet and bouncing off the windscreen with a loud thud that she heard just before the pain exploded in her head. She hit the road hard a moment later and rolled over and over as the car came to a gradual halt, then slowly reversed back towards her as she coughed up and spat out blood.

Suzie lay curled up in a ball, every part of her body aching, the pain almost too much to bear. She was barely conscious but still vaguely aware of her surroundings, of the liquid coming from her nose and mouth, pooling around her head on the hard ground, feeling warm to the touch of her skin.

As she lay there, it was almost as if it wasn't real. As if she was experiencing a nightmare construct of her subconscious mind. As if she would wake at any moment and all the pain would be gone. But even then, somewhere deep down inside, as she blinked her eyes, wondering why she couldn't see anything but blackness, she knew that wasn't true. She began to silently pray, begging God for help and mercy, to send an angel, as she heard what she thought might be footsteps walking towards her in the night. And then someone knelt at her side close to her head.

Suzie's initial semi-conscious dream-like reaction was one of relief that help had arrived, whether supernatural or of this world. But then she felt what she thought might be a hand touching her nose and mouth and then pressing down as she tried to struggle free. But Suzie had no strength left to fight or even to move her head as the light of life slowly left her body. She made one last gasping effort to suck in the cold evening air, but there was none to breathe. And in that instant, she knew she was about to die.

## 28

Detective Inspector Laura Kesey of the West Wales Police Force gave her life partner Janet a knowing look of apology when her official work phone rang a little before 9 p.m. in the comfortable lounge where they'd been watching episode three of an entertaining TV drama that had captured their attention.

Kesey paused the programme for the second time that evening, smiled at their young son Ed, who was playing age-appropriate computer games on his tablet, picked up the phone and headed to the kitchen, closing the door behind her.

Kesey reflected that life was almost always busy for a divisional DI, and it seemed tonight was no different. Rank came with responsibilities as well as privileges. And out-of-hours calls were common, particularly since the force stopped paying overtime to officers of her rank and above. It was something she had to put up with. It went with the job. And in all honesty, she wouldn't want it any other way.

Kesey held the mobile to her face, said hello, and recognised Detective Sergeant Raymond Lewis' gruff, Welsh, tobacco-ravaged voice as soon as he spoke.

'Hi Laura, sorry to bother you, love. We've got a fatal hit-and-run on the Ferryside to Kidwelly Road. It's bloody freezing out here. I'm there now, brass monkeys weather. I don't know what's wrong with me sometimes. I should have worn a coat.'

Kesey gripped the phone a little tighter. She trusted Lewis, and they were close friends as well as colleagues. But the call seemed unnecessary, an imposition even from him. And she knew Jan wouldn't appreciate yet another interrupted evening. She never did. And who could blame her for that?

Kesey spoke in a Birmingham accent, monotone, mainly hitting one note but tinged with just an occasional hint of musical Welsh. She made zero effort to hide her irritation. It wasn't in her nature. 'What the hell are you telling me about it for?' she demanded. 'How long have you been in the job? Thirty-plus years. Come on, Ray. Surely it's something you can handle yourself.'

She heard what sounded like a throaty groan before Lewis responded with predictable candour. He was never one to hold back. A 'say it as it is', man, a dinosaur still struggling to adapt to modern policing, but an officer who got results, if not always within the rules.

'All right, calm down,' he said. 'I wouldn't be ringing if it wasn't important. Amanda Donovan was first on the scene, traffic, after a call from a local woman walking her dog. Amanda didn't like the look of it. Thought it might be more than an accident and contacted me. She's sound, knows the job. So it had to be worth a look.'

Kesey sat herself down on a high stool next to a recently fitted breakfast bar. All of a sudden, she was interested. 'Okay, you've got my attention. Tell me more.'

She heard what sounded like a cough. 'Hang on,' Lewis said moments later, 'I'm just going to sit in the car. It's too damn cold to be standing out here freezing my balls off.'

Kesey waited for about thirty seconds or more without her sergeant speaking. And the seconds passed slowly. Every minute mattered when it came to her home life. Jan told her so often enough. It sometimes seemed she never stopped saying it. As if life wasn't hard enough.

'Are you still there, Ray?' Kesey asked.

'Yeah, give me a second,' he replied. 'I'll just get the heating on... There, that's better. There you go. I'm getting too old for this shit.'

Kesey repeatedly glanced at the wall clock, thinking Ed should already be in bed. The call was taking too long. 'Oh, come on, Ray,' she said. 'Say what you've got to say. I haven't got all night. You said it might be more than an accident. What are you thinking?'

'Calm down. What's the rush? I was just about to tell you. The dead girl's only in her twenties, terrible. I knew her, Suzie Reynolds. She worked at my bank. And her mum is friends with my ex-missus. They lived just a couple of streets away from us back when Suzie and her sister were kids. A very religious family – Catholic, I think, although I could be wrong. I've had a good look around and arranged for the body to be taken to the morgue. We're going to need a post-mortem on this one. I don't like the look of it at all.'

'What are you saying, exactly? The dead girl apart, you don't like the look of it, why?'

There was another brief silence, then another wet cough, before Lewis spoke again.

'I think she must have been out running. She was wearing sports clothes, a tracksuit, and trainers. But also a high-vis waist-coat jacket. There's no way she wouldn't have been seen. She'd been careful, taken the right precautions. And yet a vehicle still hit her on a straight section of a quiet road. Visibility was reasonably good; a bit of hail but no fog or heavy rain like you get up here sometimes. And there are no skid marks on the road, none at all. It doesn't look like the driver hit the brakes. And then the bastard drove off. Left her to die alone in the cold. No call for an ambulance, nothing. It reminds me of that case we had involving the domestic violence refuge a few years back. I think it's deliberate. She's got multiple injuries, bloodshot eyes. It looks like murder to me.'

'You think so, really? Murder?' Kesey asked, now on full alert.

'It's a definite possibility. That's all I'm saying. Something we've got to consider. Follow the evidence, as always. I made a few checks before ringing. One benefit of all this new technology we're stuck with. She was married to a bloke called George, who works at a local gym. You know, the big place about a mile from town. I had some dealings with him years ago, back when he was a student. Just a bit of pot, that's all, personal use, nothing serious. He was what? Eighteen or nineteen. I remember him being worried sick his mum would find out he'd been arrested. He kept banging on about it despite my reassurances.'

Kesey laughed. 'Takes all sorts. Not your typical criminal then?'

'He seemed like a decent enough lad, to be honest. I almost felt sorry for him. He accepted a caution without too much trouble. And that was the end of it. I sent him on his way. There's been no police interest since.'

'Does he know?' Kesey asked.

Another phlegmy cough. Then the sound of Lewis clearing his throat. 'Know?' he said.

She pictured Lewis lighting a cigar, sucking in the toxic fumes, the car full of grey smoke, and frowned. He'd have another heart attack if he didn't wise up.

'Does he know his wife's dead?' she asked.

'Not yet; I'm only ten minutes from the house. I was planning on paying him a visit after this call.'

Rather you than me, Kesey thought. Delivering bad news was never easy, however many times you'd done it. But all part of the job. No one ever said policing was easy.

'Give me another ring when you're done and tell me how it went,' she said, acutely aware Jan would disapprove. 'The husband might have something useful to say. And I'll contact Halliday, get his agreement for an early press release, ask for the public's help. You know what the chief super's like if he's not kept in the loop. I'd never hear the last of it.'

The sound of Lewis laughing. 'Still after that promotion, then?'

'Don't even joke about it.'

This time Lewis made what sounded like a groan. 'The man's a fucking idiot.'

Kesey grinned. It was a conversation they'd had many times before. She looked up at the clock again and sighed, thinking it was time to get on. Contact Halliday, have a quick cup of coffee, get Ed off to bed if Jan hadn't already done so, and then back to the telly. Lewis would ring again soon enough. There was always time for work.

## 29

Detective Sergeant Raymond Lewis sat outside Suzie and George's estuary village home in his unmarked police patrol car for almost five minutes before finally exiting the vehicle with a low groan as an arthritic ankle joint stiffened and ached. He'd been fit and uncommonly strong as a young man; a competent and enthusiastic rugby union forward who played for both the police and a local Carmarthen team. But so much had changed as time passed. Overeating, tobacco, stress and alcohol had taken their inevitable toll. And it now seemed the cold was more of a burden, as were the long working hours demanded by his job. But he reminded himself that retirement would come all too soon. And he still loved policing, however challenging, even after all the passing years. He made a difference, and that mattered. It made him relevant and worthwhile in a fast-changing world he sometimes feared might leave him behind. Work was about the only thing that gave his life purpose since his ex-missus had left. What would he be doing if not policing? Sitting in the rugby club or in front of the telly with a pint of best bitter in hand, that's what, drinking himself into a gradual stupor. Watching the seconds tick by for however long it took before the Grim Reaper finally called his name.

Lewis ground his glowing cigarette butt into the ground with the heel of a recently purchased black leather shoe, before slowly approaching the house one weary step at a time. He focussed back on work, pushing his melancholy thoughts from his mind as he took in the scene. There were two parked cars on the driveway, a high-end sporty saloon that, on brief inspection, looked in perfect condition, not a mark, let alone a bump, and a much older hatchback that looked well past its best, with several variously sized scuff marks and patches of red rust. But there were no dents at all, nothing that would suggest a collision.

Lewis made a quick note of both cars' numberplates in his police-issue pocketbook in case they were needed at a later date, returned the book to the inside pocket of his well-worn tweed jacket, and then quickly placed the palm of his right hand on the bonnet of each car in turn, while repeatedly glancing up at the house to confirm he wasn't seen. He knew he could come up with some excuse or distraction in the unlikely event George spotted him. But such things were best avoided if at all possible. The job was complicated enough without creating problems for himself.

Lewis had no reason to suspect that George Reynolds had played any part in his wife's death. In fact, he thought it an improbable hypothesis at best. But painful experience had taught him to cover all the bases. He relied heavily on a copper's instinct that rarely let him down. But there were procedures to follow, standing orders, a system that worked. And he never ruled anything in or out without very good reason. If you made assumptions, he reminded himself, a case could come back to bite you on the arse. True crime could be stranger than fiction. Always keep an open mind. That was best.

Both car bonnets were cold to the touch, so it seemed neither car had been recently driven. Although, having said that, Lewis thought his findings might be of no significance at all. The night was surprisingly chilly for the time of year. And well over an hour had passed since the traffic officer had contacted him. And there was no telling how long the victim had been lying dead on the road before then. So, there was more than enough time for a car bonnet to cool down.

If only he could be certain, but there were rarely any easy answers. All he could do was make his enquiries, ask his questions, and add one piece of the jigsaw after another until he finally knew the truth. Anything was possible where crime was concerned, anything at all.

Lewis knocked on George and Suzie's double-glazed front door, choosing to ignore the doorbell. He already had his warrant card in his hand when George opened the door a short time later. Hardly anyone ever looked at the card, and George was no different. So, Lewis returned it to his jacket pocket. 'Hello George, remember me?'

George looked back at the big detective with a puzzled expression as if he couldn't quite believe the evidence of his eyes. He had an almost empty glass of what looked like whisky in one hand. There was classical music playing somewhere in the house. Maybe, Beethoven, Lewis thought, but he was far from sure. Modern music was more his thing.

'Of course, I remember you,' George replied. 'But what, what the hell are you doing here? I thought that drug stuff was over with years ago. I didn't ever expect to see you again. At least, not on business.'

Lewis thought George looked nervy. The slight trembling seemed to be more than the cold. But the detective didn't read too much into it. People were often jumpy when talking to the police, even when innocent.

'It's got nothing to do with all that,' Lewis said. 'But we do need to talk.'

George lifted the glass to his mouth and drained it.

'About what?'

Lewis took a step towards him and touched his arm at the elbow.

'Let's not do this on the doorstep. Come on, in you go, lad; we can talk inside.'

George turned and walked back towards the lounge without comment, with Lewis following close behind. The detective noted there was nothing exceptional about the place. It was nice enough, well decorated and clean. Not like some of the shitholes he went into on the job. It seemed like an ordinary middle-class home. No red flags, nothing to ring any alarm bells. Much as he'd expected, there were no surprises there.

'Take a seat,' Lewis said. 'And I'll tell you why I'm here.'

A father had once collapsed, cracking his head when told of his son's death. The detective didn't want anything similar happening again.

But George remained slightly awkwardly standing as if uncomfortable in his own skin. 'I was just about to have another Scotch,' he said. 'Do you fancy one?'

Lewis liked a drink. He'd rarely wanted one more. But there was a time and place. 'Not for me, ta,' he replied reluctantly. 'You know, driving, on duty and all that. But you go ahead.'

Lewis waited for George to refill his glass and sit. It was time to tell what he was there to say. To give the information and watch George's reaction, weigh it up, and always look for clues. 'There's no easy way of saying this. Your wife, Suzie, was involved in a hit-and-run with an unidentified vehicle earlier this evening. She was found dead on Kidwelly Road close to the Broadlay turning about an hour and a half ago. Her body has been taken to West Wales General. I'm very sorry for your loss.'

Lewis had seen many different reactions in such circumstances over the years. Grief hit people in diverse ways. But at first, it was almost as if George didn't react at all. He sat in silence for about thirty seconds before finally raising his glass to his mouth and drinking. For the briefest of moments, Lewis thought George might look pleased. Was that the hint of a smile on his lips? But the detective quickly decided the answer was no.

'Hit-and-run?' George asked after draining his glass.

'The driver drove off after hitting her. Her body was found by a local person who dialled 999.'

'Who?'

'As of now, I can't give you that information. But I guarantee I'll do all I can to identify the person who killed your wife and bring them to justice. You have my word.'

'How do you know the person who rang didn't do it?' George asked.

'They were on foot, walking their dog.'

'Ah, okay, I see. But was it, was it definitely her? Suzie, are you sure it was Suzie? Could there be a mistake? She should have been home by now. But it could be a mistake, couldn't it?'

Lewis shook his head. It wasn't unusual for people to react with an element of denial. And it seemed George was no different. Although, he didn't appear as immediately upset as Lewis thought he might be. Perhaps it was the shock. Shock could do that. Sometimes, grief was delayed. He'd seen it all before.

'I'll need you to formally identify the body before a postmortem examination, but yes, I'm sure it was her. I don't know if you realise, but I've known your wife for several years, since she was a girl. Her mum is friends with my ex-missus. And Suzie also had a plastic bottle of tablets in a tracksuit trouser pocket with her name on it when she was found.'

This time Lewis was sure George had smiled. Just for a fraction of a second, as if he couldn't hide it. He hadn't parted his lips, and the expression left his face quickly, but it was definitely there before he spoke. Another grief reaction? Probably. People reacted in the strangest of ways.

'She took them for anxiety,' George said, looking past Lewis rather than meeting his eyes. 'The tablets. Sometimes too many, to be honest. I tried telling her to cut down. But I guess it doesn't matter now. It's all too late for that.'

Lewis made a scribbled note in his pocketbook with a plastic biro. 'Prescribed by her GP?'

George nodded twice, now looking the detective in the eye. 'Yeah, at Kidwelly Surgery.'

Another written note. 'Okay, thanks, that's helpful to know.'

'Why is there going to be a post-mortem?' George suddenly asked, now averting his eyes to the wall as if the thought of it might be upsetting to him.

'Unexpected death, procedure, it's not something that can be avoided in the circumstances.'

George made a face. 'When?'

'If we can get the identification done first thing in the morning, the post-mortem will take place later in the day. I've already had a word with the pathologist. Can you meet me at the hospital at nine? At the main entrance? Although, I can pick you up if it's easier. Whatever works best for you. Not everyone wants to drive in the circumstances.'

'I'll, er, I'll meet you there,' George replied. 'There's a couple of things I'll need to do in town afterwards.'

Lewis nodded once.

'Okay, not a problem. We're nearly done for now. But there are a couple of final things I need to ask you before I head off.'

George narrowed his eyes. He seemed more nervous now, agitated. As if the reality of the evening's events were slowly sinking in. 'What do you need to know?'

'What time did Suzie leave the house?'

'About, um, let me think, about a quarter to seven.'

'And that was the last time you saw her?'

'Well, yeah, obviously. I'd made her some food. We had a nice chat in the kitchen. And then she headed out.'

'She was out jogging?'

'She found the exercise helped with stress. I didn't really like her being out in the dark. I always worried it might not be safe. But she insisted. She was her own woman, never easily influenced. And now look what's happened.'

'Is jogging something she often did?' Lewis asked.

George nodded.

'Most evenings after work and sometimes at weekends. Although, it was more fast walking than running, from what she told me.'

'Did she usually take the same route?'

George was quick to reply. 'No, she liked to vary it, sometimes up towards Kidwelly and other times on the Carmarthen road past the garage. Even on the beach if it was light and the tide was right. I never knew which way she was going to go until she came back. She'd usually tell me then. But never before. I'm not sure she even knew herself until she got going. She said it kept it interesting.'

'You said Suzie suffered from anxiety. Has she ever deliberately harmed herself?'

George let out what seemed a scornful laugh. 'No, never; she wouldn't jump out in front of a car if that's what you're thinking.'

Lewis pressed his lips together. 'Sorry, just covering all the bases. I had to ask.'

'Suzie had a very strong faith. Suicide would be completely out of the question. Although, she was very sad after the last miscarriage.'

'Miscarriage?'

George nodded. 'Yeah, she had two.'

Lewis made another note in his pocketbook in blue ink, the page marked with a metal paper clip for convenience. 'Was she taking any other medication you're aware of?'

Another quick reply. As if there was an urgency to it. 'No, nothing, nothing at all. If she had been, I'd have known. We were close. We shared everything, no secrets. I can't, I can't begin to think what life's going to be like without her. Suzie was the love of my life.'

Lewis stretched out his aching right knee and gave it a rub. There was something about George's reply that Lewis doubted. He couldn't put his finger on what exactly. It was an instinct thing more than anything else. But there was definitely something.

'This might seem a strange question, but again, I have to ask. Can you think of anyone who might have wanted to deliberately harm Suzie? Anyone at all?'

George shook his head. 'No, that's ridiculous. It's crazy to even think it. Suzie was a lovely, popular person with lots of friends. I'm going to miss her terribly. She didn't have an enemy in the world. What you've told me has blown my world apart. The future seems very bleak without her. I don't know how I'm going to face it alone.'

'You don't have any children?' Lewis asked, already suspecting the answer was no.

'We were trying for a baby again but for some reason, it didn't happen for us. One of the greatest sadnesses of my life. Suzie would have been a wonderful mother. I was blessed to be married to her. I wish I'd died in her place.'

Lewis rose stiffly to his feet, thinking something wasn't right. George was saying all the right things, but they somehow didn't ring true. It was almost as if it were too much. As if George was putting on an act. Trying to create an impression to his advantage. Even when considering the effects of grief, his emotions seemed contrived.

'Is there anything I can get for you or anyone you'd like me to contact before I go?' Lewis asked, as he crossed the lounge towards the hall, ready to leave for home, a beer or two, a bit of telly and an early night.

'Do Suzie's parents know? Have they been told?'

Oh, shit, thought Lewis. Not another home visit to deliver bad news. Maybe get one of the uniform shift to do it. Yeah, what the hell? Why not? He'd done his bit. 'Not as yet.'

'I'll give them a ring,' said George, now on his feet. 'Or maybe I'll walk down there. Tell them in person. It's not far.'

'Do you want a lift?'

George shook his head. 'No, I'm good, thanks. I could do with the fresh air.'

'Sure?'

'Yeah, leave it with me. They love Suzie almost as much as I did. They've been good to me. It's the least I can do.'

Lewis reached into his jacket pocket and took out a small card with his name and contact details, black print on a white background. He handed it to George with an outstretched hand.

'I'll see you in the morning. And don't hesitate to give me a ring if you need anything, day or night. If I don't answer, leave a message, and I'll get back to you as soon as I can.'

'Okay, thanks, it's appreciated,' George replied. 'I'll be at the hospital at nine sharp. Is there anything I need to bring with me?'

'No, just yourself. You'll need to identify your wife but not touch her due to forensics. And some injuries to her head will be visible.

You'll need to prepare yourself for that. It's never easy. But it is important.'

'And you'll be with me, yeah?'

'Me and the pathologist.'

George slowly shook his head, but there were still no tears.

'I can't quite believe what's happening.'

A part of Lewis believed him, but only a part. There was still that nagging doubt that wouldn't let go. Something wasn't right.

'Oh, one last thing,' Lewis said, 'have you left the house at all since your wife went out?'

George sucked in his cheeks. 'Why do you ask?'

'You might have seen something without realising its significance, a car going a little too fast, that sort of thing.'

George shook his head vigorously. 'I've been in all evening. Didn't see a thing. Only wish I had. I do occasionally see someone speeding through the village. But not tonight. I'd have told you if I had.'

Lewis still didn't feel entirely persuaded. There was no obvious evidence to suggest George was telling him anything but the truth. But gut instinct could be a powerful thing. And that instinct was ringing alarm bells. George seemed more on edge than distressed. As if constantly on the defensive. Was that the sign of a guilty man?

'Okay, ta, at least I'm clear,' Lewis said, while feeling not very clear at all. 'I'll see you in the morning.'

As the big detective left the house, walking stiffly towards his parked car in the semi-darkness, he was telling himself he needed to know more about George, Suzie and their marital relationship. Was it as amicable as George had tried to make out? Or was there trouble in paradise? Maybe George killed his wife, but even if he didn't, there was undoubtedly something he was hiding. Lewis had never been surer of anything in a long police career. Something stank. He just had to find out what.

## 30

George watched from the lounge window at the front of the house, half-hidden behind the wall, peeping out through the blinds as Lewis ambled back towards his car. And at that moment, as the big detective climbed into the driver's seat, started the engine and drove off in the direction of Carmarthen, George decided he had good cause to celebrate. It seemed, he said to himself, that all his much-cherished dreams were coming true. The good times were about to begin. And hurrah to that.

George drank whisky from the bottle, did a little dance around the room, let out a loud cheer, and then approached the sideboard, where his mother's ashes were kept in a blue pottery urn next to the printer. He put down the bottle, picked up the urn, held it out in front of him with both hands and spoke to his mother as if she wasn't dead, as if the cancer hadn't taken hold, ravaging her body despite her many prayers. Where, he asked himself before speaking, was her God in all that?

'I've done it, Mother,' he said, looking directly at the urn with unblinking eyes that were welling with tears, not of sorrow but of delight. 'Did you hear what the fat detective said to me? Suzie's dead and gone. I'm finally free of the bitch. My patience has paid off. And I'm going to have all of it. The house, her flash car, the one she'd rarely let me drive, the investments, the life insurance, the lot. What do you think about that? Your screw-up son is going to be a rich man. Fuck the gym and my idiot clients. I won't ever need to work again.'

George imagined his mother smiling, nodding her acknowledgement and approval in his mind's eye, before he placed the urn back in its original position, a reminder of his grief for his mother, another reason for his loss of faith.

He picked up the whisky bottle and took another swig, savouring the malty spirit as it burned his throat. Amelia, he suddenly thought on spotting his phone charging on a shelf, lovely Amelia. He should tell her the news, share his good fortune. And then maybe meet up with her to celebrate together. Yeah, he could do with a shag. Something she was good at. One of the best.

George sat in Suzie's favourite armchair, the one she always chose, and then unfastened his trousers, pulling down the zip before ringing, thinking Amelia might have something sexy to say. Something to turn him on.

He grinned when he heard her familiar voice say 'Hello'.

'You're never going to believe what's happened—' George began, keenly anticipating the telling. 'I've had the police here. Here at the house. A detective called Ray Lewis, a sergeant. He's not long gone.'

There was an unexpected urgency to Amelia's reply. 'Oh my God, no, the police, why?'

George paused for a moment before responding, enjoying the tension, building up his part. He imagined a drum roll in his head, signalling his dramatic announcement.

'It's Suzie; she's dead.'

'What? Dead? When? How?'

'She went out for one of her walks, just like you told her to. And she was hit by a car earlier this evening. And she even had that high-vis jacket thing on. The yellow one. Talk about a lucky break. That's it; it's done. It's over. The bitch is never coming back. We've won.'

But Amelia didn't sound nearly as pleased as George thought she would. If anything, he thought she sounded more worried than excited.

'Did you do it, George?' she asked. 'Was it you? Were you the driver of that car?'

He shook his head despite her not being able to see.

'No, honestly, no,' he said with insistence. 'I actually thought about killing her. I even planned it. I pictured doing it in my head. I hated the woman with a burning intensity. But murder, I couldn't bring myself to do it. And now I don't have to. Isn't that great? Maybe there is a God, after all. It's one of the happiest days of my life. I thought you'd be as pleased as me.' There were a few seconds of silence that, to George, seemed to go on forever. He was beginning to wonder why he'd bothered unfastening his trousers. 'Amelia, are you still there?' he asked, emptying the bottle after another mouthful of strong spirit. 'Aren't you going to say something? I thought you'd be over the moon.'

'You can tell me the truth, George. It's me you're talking to, not Suzie. If you killed her, you can tell me. There's no need for lies. Not with me. Not between us. There'll be no judgement or blame. Not from me.'

George threw the empty whisky bottle to the carpet, where it bounced, hitting the sofa before coming to a halt. 'I've told you the truth,' he said. 'Nothing but the truth. And she's dead. Isn't that what matters? Who's done it isn't of any consequence. I don't know why we're even bothering talking about it.'

'Okay,' Amelia said, almost in a whisper. 'If that's how you want to play it.'

George resisted the impulse to yell or end the call. It now seemed Amelia was almost as annoying as Suzie. Sucking the joy from his life. Just like her! 'I'm not playing anything,' he said. 'I thought you'd be pleased. That's why I rang. I thought this was going to be fun.'

'I want you to get rid of the herbs. All of them, and the packaging, too. And don't just throw them in your bin. Dispose of them somewhere they can't be found. Or burn them, yeah, yeah, burn them. And do it as soon as we end the call. Don't put it off; no delays.'

'Why the hell would you want me to do that?' George asked, perplexed. It seemed the call was going from bad to worse. Not what he'd envisaged at all.

'If the police come back,' Amelia said, 'if they search your place, I don't want there being any links to me. And best get rid of your phone, this one you're calling me on. They might check that, too. You could throw it in the sea.'

George stood and began pacing the floor, one way and the other. His head was aching now, right at the base of his neck.

'Why would the police come back? What the hell are you talking about? You're not making any sense at all.'

'Oh, come on, think about it,' Amelia replied, speaking a little louder now as if to drive home her point. 'You're the obvious suspect. As far as the police are concerned, only one person will benefit from Suzie's death. And that's you. They will come knocking again. You can count on it. And you've got to be ready. So, do everything I've told you and be prepared. It's just a matter of time.'

## 31

It was almost eleven that night when Lewis finally picked up his phone. He'd watched the BBC Ten O'clock News while lying on the sofa, downed three cans of warm beer, and considered heading to bed after a quick bathroom visit, before thinking better of it. He could ring Kesey in the morning before heading to the hospital; of course, he could, but there were things he needed to get off his mind. Nagging thoughts that would keep him awake for hours if he didn't. And so, ringing the detective inspector, however late the hour, seemed to make sense.

Lewis sat up with a groan, held his mobile to his face and waited until he heard his boss's familiar Midlands drone at the other end of the line.

'What the hell do you want, Ray? I was already in bed. And you've woken Jan. This had better be good.'

Lewis opened a fourth can of beer with a metallic ping and took a slurp.

'You said to ring.'

After a few seconds of silence, he heard what sounded like a resigned sigh he'd heard before. 'Okay, fair point, get on with it. What have you got to tell me? And make it fast. I want to get back to sleep.'

'I saw George Reynolds at his home. Told him his wife was dead. Asked a few questions.'

'And?'

'He seemed very different to when I met him before. Almost like another man.'

Kesey was quick to reply, impatience betrayed by her tone. 'Well, that's hardly surprising, given you'd just told him his wife was dead. He's hardly going to be doing cartwheels. What did you expect?'

Lewis drained his can, crushed it in his hand, and then dropped it to the floor. 'No, you're not getting what I'm saying. I've given a lot of people bad news over the years. And this time was different. His reaction wasn't normal. He was on edge the whole time. Something's not right.'

'Oh, here we go again.'

Lewis screwed up his face. 'What the hell is that supposed to mean?'

He could hear the frustration in Kesey's voice when she replied. 'You'll be telling me about your gut instinct next. How it never lets you down. But it does, Ray, it does. Remember the Willis case? You didn't get that one right. It's evidence we need, not feelings and urges. I've told you all this before. When are you ever going to listen? You drive me nuts sometimes.'

Lewis massaged the back of his neck, taking very little notice of her argument. He chuckled quietly to himself. He was old school, and she was new, but they worked together well enough most of the time. 'I'll make a few background enquiries. That's all I'm saying. Check out the money situation, bank accounts, life insur-

ance, that sort of thing. See if he's got good reason to be in the
frame.'

Another sigh. 'Okay, yeah, fair enough, if you must. But don't go
spending too much time on it. And do it with subtlety. Don't go
blundering in and upsetting a grieving husband. I know what
you're like. You get fixated once you get an idea in your head.'

Lewis decided now was a good time to change the subject. 'How
did it go with the chief super?'

'Oh, shit, you had to go and mention Halliday. You'll be giving
me nightmares.'

Lewis smiled. 'What did he say?'

'It's all good,' Kesey replied. 'I'll do a press release about the hit-
and-run first thing tomorrow morning, and then we'll have a full-
blown press conference at HQ the following day if we need it. I
think that's a bit over the top, to be honest, getting everyone
together at this early stage. But you know what Halliday's like.
Anything to get on the telly. He loves the publicity. Thrives on it.'

'Tosser.'

'You've got that right.'

Lewis yawned. 'Okay, cheers, boss. I'll see you tomorrow.'

'I'll be in at nine. We can have another chat then. I'm stuck in
all day doing paperwork.'

'I'm meeting Reynolds at the hospital first thing for the identification, but I'll be in after that. With a bit of luck, he might let something slip.'

'Subtlety, remember that, subtlety. Don't go giving him a hard
time. You might just have it wrong.'

'How about we meet in the canteen for a catch-up at about
twelve?' Lewis asked, thinking the only person who had it wrong
was her. 'There's a big plate of egg, beans and chips with my name
on it. And it's your turn to pay.'

'I thought I paid last time.'

He laughed. She said the same thing every time. 'Night, Laura, give my love to Jan and Ed.'

'Will do; now get some sleep.'

## 32

Kesey was sitting at her office desk, working her way through the month's overtime sheets, a part of the job she hated, when her desk phone rang, offering a welcome distraction. She picked up the receiver on the second insistent ring.

'DI Kesey, CID.'

'Hello, ma'am, it's Ben; I've got a call for you.'

Kesey shook her head and blew out the air. 'How many times have I got to tell you? It's boss or guv. I'm a DI, not the Queen.'

'Sorry, ma'am. I'll try to remember.'

Kesey swore crudely under her breath. She'd been telling him the same thing for years. Maybe it was time to give up. It seemed he never got the message. 'Who wants me?' Kesey asked.

'It's a woman, anonymous call, wouldn't give her name. I did try.'

Kesey took a sip of strong coffee. It wasn't the best. But not bad for instant. A new brand she was trying for the first time.

'Did she say what it's about?'

'Something to do with the woman who was killed in the hit-

and-run. The caller saw the report on the Welsh evening news. She
asked for you by name. Said no one else would do.'

Kesey sat more upright, suddenly on full alert as adrenalin
surged through her bloodstream.

'Okay, put her through, and trace the call. We need to know
who she is. As quickly as you can.'

'Will do, ma'am.'

When the anonymous woman first spoke, Kesey noted an
instantly recognizable west Wales accent. It seemed she was local.
It was far from what Kesey needed. But it was better than nothing.

'DI Kesey? Laura Kesey?' the caller asked.

'Speaking, how can I help you?'

'The woman who was killed on the Kidwelly road, Suzie
Reynolds. I saw the report on the news. Your appeal for information. You're the officer in charge of the case, yes?'

'That's correct, yeah. Will you give me your name, please? It
would be entirely confidential. And it would be really helpful if you
would. I like to know who I'm talking to.'

'I can't do that.'

Kesey decided not to push it, fearing her caller might end the
conversation. It was a hard lesson learnt in a previous case, born of
experience. She picked up a pen and paper, ready to make notes.
'Okay, I'll respect your wishes,' Kesey said with reluctance. 'What
have you got to tell me?'

'I knew Suzie. I had done for years. And her husband, too.
George. I don't know if anyone has told you this, but they were
having problems. Serious problems. Suzie told me that herself.'

'Problems? What do you mean by problems, exactly? Please try
to be as detailed as possible.'

'He's a cheater, other women, lots of them, and he was always
trying to get his hands on her money. And I saw him out in his car that

evening, sometime between seven and eight, in his old Golf on the Port Way. On the night that poor Suzie died. The same road she was found. I think he did it. I think it was him. He ran her over. That's why I've rung.'

'You're certain you saw George Reynolds out in his car that night?'

'One hundred per cent, yes. It was him.'

'And it was definitely that same evening?' Kesey asked, thinking Ray might have got it right despite her doubts.

'It was. I've got no doubt.'

'Can you be more specific about the time?'

'I'm sorry, no. If I'd known the significance, I'd have looked at my watch. But I do know it was sometime within that hour.'

Kesey made a written note. 'I have to ask again if you're willing to give me your name? The information you've shared could be of crucial importance to the investigation. I'd like to take your written statement confirming all you've said—'

But that was it; the call ended, and Kesey heard no more. She tried to access the relevant information in the usual ways but wasn't surprised to find the supposed witness had withheld her contact details. There were still ways of getting her phone number, methods the police used. But even that didn't guarantee to identify the caller. Fingers crossed, Kesey said to herself. Sometimes you were lucky, and sometimes you weren't. It wasn't always just about good policing. Ray was right about that, too. He said it often enough. Sometimes you needed a break.

## 33

After first looking in his shared office, Kesey eventually found Lewis in the notoriously terrible police canteen at a little after eight the following morning. He was tucking into a predictably large and greasy full English breakfast, his plate piled high with bacon, eggs, mushrooms, beans and black pudding, all covered in copious amounts of brown sauce, a blob of which had found its way onto the table. Kesey looked at him with genuine concern as she sat herself down opposite, a cup of strong instant coffee in hand and a frown on her face.

'Morning, Ray; nice to see the diet's going well. Strange, that doesn't look like a healthy meal to me. What was it your doctor said? You need to lose about three stone?'

Lewis greedily forked some fatty bacon into his wide-open mouth, then wiped some sauce from his unshaven chin. 'Don't even start,' he said between chews. 'My wife used to nag me half to death, and now you've started. A man's got to eat.'

'Yeah, but he doesn't have to eat all that fatty stodge. It's not exactly heart-healthy. What's wrong with a bowl of muesli or a piece of brown toast?'

'I like my meat.'

Kesey let out a long breath, thinking it sometimes seemed the man she valued both as a detective and a friend was on a sure path to self-destruction. Another heart attack waiting to happen. 'I'm worried about you, that's all. You've been on a diet for months, and if anything, you've put on weight.'

Lewis took a slurp of milky tea, then wiped his mouth again with a hand. 'Any news on our anonymous witness?' he asked looking her in the eye.

Kesey knew he was changing the subject, a tactic he sometimes used when the topic of a conversation challenged him even slightly, but she decided to let it slide. It wasn't the first time she'd addressed his eating habits and no doubt it wouldn't be the last. She'd keep trying, although it never got her anywhere. 'Looks like our caller used a pay-as-you-go mobile, no contract, bought for cash. We've got the number, but that's it. It doesn't help us find out who she is.'

'Oh, shit.'

Kesey grinned. He always got straight to the point. 'Yeah, exactly,' she agreed.

'So, what happens now?' Lewis asked, swallowing another mouthful, rushing his meal.

'Our witness may have been full of crap, or there might be something to what she told me. Either way, it's not something we can ignore. I want you to bring Reynolds in, question him, put a bit of pressure on and see what he's got to say for himself. And get scenes of crime to have a really good look at his car, the Golf. If he did run Suzie over, there might be evidence to find. It may be our best bet.'

Lewis gave her a knowing look. 'I told you something wasn't right. I knew it. My instincts aren't so wrong now, are they?'

Kesey laughed. 'No, and you'll never let me forget it.'

'You've got that right.'

She rose to her feet. 'Just get it done, Ray. This morning, if you can. And let me know what comes of it. If George did kill his wife, I want us to nail the bastard. And if not, we need to find the person who did.'

## 34

DS Lewis left George alone in a cell at Carmarthen Police Station for almost two hours after his arrest before taking him to an interview room. The suspect had insisted on a duty solicitor who'd finally arrived. It was time to get on.

Lewis and DC Rhian Lee, a young detective under his supervision, sat across the interview room table from George and his lawyer, an efficient and experienced middle-aged woman with short greying hair whom Lewis had encountered many times before. Lewis noted George looked predictably nervous, seemingly close to panic, as he had on his arrest. And that, Lewis decided, suited him just fine. Here was hoping the lawyer wouldn't intervene a little too often. He knew from experience she sometimes did.

Lewis stared into George's face and kept staring as his suspect said nothing at all. 'Switch the tape on, Rhian. It's time we made a start.'

'Will do, Sarge.'

'Before we begin the interview, Mr Reynolds,' Lewis said, 'I need to remind you that you're still subject to caution. You do not have to say anything. But it may harm your defence if you do not mention something you later rely on in court. Anything you do say may be given in evidence. Is that clear to you?'

When George nodded once, Lewis thought his suspect looked close to tears. He was just about holding it together.

'For the tape, please, Mr Reynolds. I need to hear you say it.'

George glanced sideways at his lawyer and then said, 'Yes, I understand,' his voice filled with emotion.

It was clear to Lewis the pressure was already getting to his suspect. The big sergeant focussed on George, actively ignoring the lawyer, never looking away. 'You've been arrested on suspicion of murder. It doesn't get any more serious than that,' Lewis said. 'You could be looking at a life sentence. This is your opportunity to tell your side of the story.'

George gripped the table's edge with both hands, knuckles white, as if he feared falling. 'I haven't done anything wrong. I loved Suzie. I still love her. I would never have done anything to harm her. No one wants you to catch the person who killed my wife more than me.'

Lewis frowned hard. 'We have a witness who says your relationship with Suzie wasn't nearly as happy as you've claimed. Were there other women, Mr Reynolds? Did you have extramarital affairs? Because we're told you did.'

George's left eye began twitching at the corner. A vein on his neck was more pronounced. 'Whoever said that is lying.'

'Really? Why would someone do that?'

'Who was it?' George asked. A question Lewis ignored. 'I bet it was Suzie's sister. She's never liked me. It's the sort of crap she'd make up to get me in trouble.'

The lawyer whispered directly into George's ear. But George shook his head.

'No, no, I want to answer the questions,' George said, speaking more loudly now. 'I've got no reason to do a no-comment interview. I've done nothing wrong. Don't you get it? I'm an innocent man.'

It was clear to Lewis that George was becoming more irate and, the detective thought, increasingly likely to slip up. Time to up the pressure. Turn the screw. 'Did you leave the house on the evening of your wife's death?' Lewis asked next, leaning slightly forward, elbows on the table. 'When your wife was out walking. Were you in your car?'

'No, I've told you, no. I stayed in. The car was on the drive.'

'Are you sure about that? Because our witness says different.'

'If someone told you that, they're a lying bastard. Was it the priest, O'Shaughnessy? I wouldn't listen to a single word that nonce says. He's got it in for me. Always has had.'

Lewis hid his surprise, his face blank. Interviews sometimes took an unexpected turn. Something you couldn't prepare for. And he quickly decided to focus back on his questions, not to be distracted. If there were things to ask about O'Shaughnessy, now wasn't the time. This was all about George.

'Your Golf is being examined as we speak, Mr Reynolds. And if there's evidence to find, we'll find it. Now would be a good time to come clean.'

For the first time, Lewis thought George looked a little more confident as he answered. He rose up in his seat. He wasn't exactly cocky. But he was more full of himself. 'Examine the Golf all you want,' George said. 'And do a really good job of it. I'm glad you're looking at it. Because I know you won't find anything. I didn't run my wife over. So, there's nothing to find. I'm innocent. Why can't you get that into your head?'

Lewis began to doubt the anonymous witness' evidence for the first time. Although he then thought George might have washed the car, put it through a car wash. That might explain his newfound confidence. The slight rise in his spirits.

The lawyer tapped the table, disturbing the detective's train of thought. 'My client has made his position perfectly clear, Sergeant. He's told you he stayed in on the evening of his wife's death. And your evidence, if evidence it is, seems flimsy at best. Unless you have other questions to ask, questions unrelated to the Golf, I suggest we bring this interview to a timely end.'

Lewis remained entirely focussed on George, continuing the interview as if the lawyer had said nothing at all. It was a method he almost always adopted in such circumstances. Very little ever fazed him after all the years. Certainly not a solicitor doing their job.

'I've been looking into your financial situation, Mr Reynolds,' Lewis said, playing his next card. George visibly stiffened but remained silent as Lewis prepared to continue. 'You'll do rather well out of your wife's death, won't you?'

Another quiet word from the duty solicitor didn't stop George from answering, something for which Lewis was grateful. 'Money means nothing to me,' George said less than convincingly. 'If I could exchange everything I've got to have my Suzie back, I'd do it in a heartbeat. What does cash matter when I've lost my love? It doesn't bring her back.'

'Your personal finances are in a bit of a state from what I've seen. As of now, you've got debts coming out of your ears. And all the assets are in your wife's name. I've seen her will. Everything comes to you unless, of course, you're convicted. And then there's the life insurance. That was increased not long before her death. Any comment? That all seems like motive enough to me.'

George was quick to reply.

'Increasing the life insurance was Suzie's idea. She was conscientious about money. Always had been, even before working at the bank. The timing of the increase was a total coincidence. It had nothing to do with me. I never think about those things.'

'We've only got your word for that.'

George shifted in his seat. 'It's the truth. All I can do is tell you the truth. I saved Suzie's life on holiday. Has anyone told you that? She fell into a harbour in Tenerife, and I jumped in and saved her. She couldn't swim. I risked my life to save hers. Onlookers filmed it all. I can show you on social media. Why would I do that and then kill her only a short time later when back in Wales? That makes no sense at all.'

Lewis silently observed that obvious suspects weren't always the guilty ones. Sometimes it was somebody else. He decided the time was right to bring the interview to an end. He still thought it likely that George had killed Suzie, but now he was less sure. Doubts had surfaced, doubts the detective couldn't silence. And he knew there was far too little evidence to charge George with murder or anything else. It was time to release his suspect pending further investigation. The police needed more, a lot more. As things stood, the Crown Prosecution Service would drop the case like a stone.

## 35

On arriving home, George quickly downed a crystal glass of French brandy, having taken a train from Carmarthen to Ferryside Station and striding swiftly to the house from there. At least he hadn't been charged, he thought, as he threw down the strong spirit and then refilled his glass almost to the brim. Relaxation seemed beyond him. The day's events had shaken him. And as he sat there trembling, it proved impossible to think of anything else.

He'd been released and was home; that had to be a good thing. That was the end of it, wasn't it? Or would the police come calling again? Banging on his door. Dragging him off in cuffs. Locking him in a cell for God only knew how long.

George took a gulp of brandy, still in thought, searching for reassurance but finding none. DS Lewis seemed so sure of his guilt. Who the hell was the witness? Who'd say such things? A right bastard, whoever they were. Looking to destroy his life. Surely it couldn't be the priest, could it? Would any priest break the confessional seal? And particularly after the threats he'd made.

George sat back in Suzie's favourite armchair, still trying to make sense of the day's events as his racing mind beat him down.

He'd rung in sick from work from the police station, his one call feigning a migraine, and he fully intended to resign in style when Suzie's money was finally his. But now he asked himself if that day would ever come. Would all his cherished plans come to nothing? It had so recently seemed that fate had finally smiled on him. But now, so much had changed. Changed in the blink of an eye. Everything he'd hoped and planned for was potentially blown apart by some unidentified witness who claimed to have seen so much.

George grimaced, his gut twisting. He would get everything he was owed, wouldn't he? Unless he didn't. Like the pig detective threatened. What then? Surely that wouldn't happen, would it? Would it be riches or prison? It was one or the other. Life could become a living nightmare. Shit! What would be his fate?

George reached for his phone and searched for Amelia in his contacts, shaking from head to foot despite the mind-numbing effects of the alcohol, now thinking he needed a sympathetic ear. Come on, Amelia, answer, please answer.

He sighed with relief when he heard Amelia's sultry voice say 'Hello'.

'Oh, thank God,' he said. 'You won't believe the time I've had. I've been at the police station most of the day.'

There was an urgency to Amelia's quick response. 'The police station, why?'

George rushed his reply as if the telling would somehow relieve his angst. 'Some bastard told the police they'd seen me out in the car the night Suzie was killed and that me and her were having relationship problems. The police think I did it. I'm being investigated for murder.'

'Were you out in the car?' Amelia asked. 'Can the police prove it? You can tell me. Your secrets are safe. Nothing you tell me will ever be repeated.'

George wondered if he couldn't even convince Amelia, how the hell would he ever convince the pig detective? It was hard not to scream. 'No, for fuck's sake, no,' he said. 'I've told you no. I didn't kill her. It wasn't me.'

'I want to believe you, George.'

He dropped his head. 'I'm telling you the truth.'

There was a second or two's silence before Amelia spoke again. And when she did, it sounded as if she might be crying. There was a sniff, then what sounded like a muffled sob.

'So, what happens now?' she asked.

George noticed his hand was still trembling as he took another gulp of brandy, swilling it around his mouth before swallowing, keenly anticipating the alcohol entering his bloodstream, that chemical hit. 'I've been released under investigation, whatever the hell that means,' he said. 'They already know about the money, my debts, Suzie's will, the life insurance, the lot. The detective who interviewed me, a right awkward bastard, called it a motive. All I can do is keep denying I killed her if they arrest me again. I'm scared, absolutely shitting myself. I'm not afraid to admit it.'

Amelia sounded thoughtful. 'Hmm. I have to admit it doesn't sound good. You've got problems, real problems. Like I said before, you're the obvious suspect. And you haven't got an alibi. Nothing that would hold up in court. That's bad. You're right to be scared. Things really could go horribly wrong.'

Never a more accurate word, he thought. Shit! Amelia wasn't exactly offering reassurance. Maybe he shouldn't have rung at all.

'Worst-case scenario,' he said, 'I could be looking at a life sentence for something I haven't done. I could be banged up for years. The police will be back. I'm sure of it. They'll be back. And I'm innocent. I need you to believe that.'

Another silence. A little longer this time. 'Please try to calm down. I don't care what you have or haven't done,' Amelia finally said with a sigh. 'I don't want to lose you, and I don't want our plans to come to nothing. Those are the things that matter to me. That's it. And what I'm about to say might seem a little crazy. But hear me out. I really think it could work.'

'What are you talking about?' George asked, desperately hoping Amelia might say something that helped even slightly. He felt close to total panic.

'It was a film I watched a year or two back,' she said. 'A thriller. I can't remember the name. It came to mind while we were talking.'

'You're not making a lot of sense,' George replied.

'I can't give you an alibi without implicating myself, which would only cause other problems. But I could provide a useful distraction, make the police look in the wrong direction, smoke and mirrors, take the focus off you.'

George's spirits raised slightly. There seemed some logic to what she was saying. But he needed to know more.

'What? Nice idea, but how the hell would you do that?' he asked.

'I could ring the police station from a call box, there's still a few about, give a false name or no name at all, ask to speak to the officer in charge of Suzie's case, and say I had important information about her death.'

'What information?' George snapped back.

'I'd say I was having a drink in a busy local pub when I over-heard a man say it was him who ran Suzie over. I could say he was boasting about it. Laughing that the police didn't have a clue. I could even make up a detailed description and send the police off looking for a suspect who doesn't exist. At the very least, it would take the pressure off you. The police can only convict someone if there's no reasonable doubt they committed the crime. That's the way the system works. Innocent unless proven guilty. That was the pretext of the film. It's perfect. You'd be in the clear.'

George smiled as a light shone at the end of a dark tunnel in his

mind's eye, getting gradually brighter. 'You'd really do that for me?'
he said, now in tears himself. Tears of relief that there was at least
some hope.

'I would, and I will,' Amelia responded. 'But only on certain
conditions. I'd be taking on a big risk. And I'd need reassurance
that the risk was worthwhile. Actions as well as words. I don't think
that's too much to ask.'

George felt himself tense again, thinking another brandy might
help. What the hell was she going to say now?

'What conditions?' he asked.

And then it poured out of her, one point after another, almost
as if she'd prepared her requirements in advance.

'If I'm going to put my neck on the line, I must know you're fully
committed to me. And there's only one way I can think to do that. I
want us to get married. And quickly, I need that certainty if I'm
going to gamble with my freedom. I don't care about guests, and a
registry office would be fine. I don't need the whole church thing, a
white dress, and all that. And we could do it somewhere well away
from here, so no one needs to know. But I'd want you to start
making the arrangements today, no excuses, no delays. We'd have
the service in a few weeks when I've done my thing with the police,
and we're as confident as we can be that the deception has worked.
Is that something you're willing to agree to?'

George looked at his phone with an incredulous stare, a dazed
look on his face as he shook his head. *The devious bitch*, he thought.
So demanding, so conniving, but what other choice did he have?
Maybe agree now and then back out at a later date, once safe.

'If I say yes, you'll contact the police, yeah? Just like you said.'

'I will. And I'll do a convincing job of it. If anyone can get you
off the hook, I can.'

He felt his spirits rise. 'Then let's do it. Let's get hitched.'

'There's something else,' she said. 'Marriage is a part of it, but

not all. Perverting the course of justice is a serious crime. I'd be
taking a huge risk for you. So I'd need some financial reassurance.
want you to sell Suzie's house once the heat's off and it's yours, and
then we'll buy somewhere in our joint names. Somewhere big and
luxurious with a fantastic view of the sea. Maybe abroad or
perhaps the West Country. I used to go on holiday to Devon and
Cornwall as a child. There's no rush, we'd need to time it right so as
not to raise any suspicion, but I'd need to know it was happening.'

'Okay, if that's what you want,' he said, thinking it was only
words. That there was everything to gain and nothing to lose.

'And I'd want you to change your will leaving everything to me
as another sign of your commitment. So I'd know if the worst
happened, I'd be fine. And I'd do the same for you. We'd leave
everything to each other. You told me Suzie nearly died when she
fell in that harbour. And that got me thinking. We never know
what's around the corner. It could be you or me next, an accident or
illness. Life is so very unpredictable, and so this is important to me.
I need you to agree. I've got an excellent lawyer in Aber who'd sort
it out for us. Or there's plenty of information about how to do it
ourselves online if you'd prefer. As long as it's done, it makes no
odds to me. What do you think? Have we got a deal?'

George put down his empty glass and raised a hand to his face.
He felt backed into a corner. He was starting to resent Amelia
almost as much as he had Suzie.

'Wow, that's all a bit full-on, even for you,' he said. 'Not what I
was expecting to hear.'

'Just tell me your answer, George. Yes or no? Have we got a deal
or not? But remember, if the answer is no, I walk away now. That's
it. You never hear from me again. No call to the police, no distraction. You'd be on your own. We're either one hundred per cent
committed to each other, or we're not.'

The bitch, he thought, the cunning, manipulative bitch! But he quickly decided he had to play her game, at least for now. Nothing mattered more than that phone call.

'Um, yeah, I love you, so yes, you can have all you want. Just contact the police. Tell them what you said you're going to, and then we can sort everything out.'

'I'll give it a day or two, and then I'll ring if and only if you've started arranging the wedding. And don't even think about cheating on what we've agreed. I know exactly what you're like. But remember, I could always contact the police again if you let me down. I could tell them I lied. That you made me say what I said. That I didn't hear someone confess to the killing at all. That you were the guilty one all along.'

George's mouth dropped open as he reached for the brandy, discarding his empty glass and raising the bottle to his mouth.

George gritted his teeth in a snarl, then calmed himself. It seemed the bitch knew him almost better than he knew himself. He so wanted to say no, to scream no, to tell her exactly what he thought of her and her demands in crude expletives she couldn't fail to understand. But Amelia was holding all the cards. And prison was never a part of his plan. Like it or not, she was the best chance he had. Such a devious person, just like him. George swallowed his resentments, forcing them back down his throat in the interest of his freedom. 'Oh, come on, there's no need for all that,' he said. 'We're a team, you and me. I love you. Always have, since the first day we met. What are you wearing? I bet it's something really sexy. Are you naked?'

'Not now, George.'

He laughed sardonically, resigned to the inevitable, thinking her a necessary burden, another monkey on his back. 'I'll get online and start looking at options for that wedding,' he said, thinking he had no way out.

'You do that. And remember – you don't get a thing unless the police drop your case. I'm the difference between freedom, riches and incarceration. Me, nobody else, me. So, be very careful, and don't let me down. That really wouldn't be a good idea. We can both be happy together. We can live the dream. But only if you do what I say.'

# 36

## SIX MONTHS LATER

George lay on a soft white leather corner sofa close to a large picture window with an expansive sea view, looking up at Amelia in their luxury detached five-bedroom Cornish home. He held both hands on his aching stomach as he fought back the tears.

'I've been taking the herbs since we moved here,' he said, grimacing, 'and I'm still getting the pain. It's almost as if the move caused it. And it's worse today. Much worse, I'm in agony. And I'm feeling faint; my sight's getting hazy. I need an ambulance. Please call one. I'd do it myself if I could stand. I'm... I'm seeing stars. I'm close to passing out.'

Amelia held a glass tumbler containing a dark green plant concoction she'd prepared earlier to his lips.

'Please, try to relax. We've got everything we wanted. Suzie's gone, the police have long since lost interest, and the cash is in the bank. You needn't worry. Our dreams have all come true. And I'm here to look after you. Come on, take another sip. Drink. You need to trust me. The medicine will make you better. Open your mouth wide. All the pain will be over soon. And then we can get on with our lives.'

George turned his aching head and wondered why the effort was almost too much to bear. He had never felt weaker.

'I should have... I should have gone to the doctor long ago,' he said, his voice hesitant.

Amelia shook her head with what seemed a sympathetic smile.

'Come on now. Don't be so silly,' she said. 'I've repeatedly told you a doctor can't help you. The herbs are better for you than any tablets. Much more natural, treating the cause, not just the symptoms. Look at me. Open wide, another sip, drink it down.'

He opened his mouth just wide enough for her to pour in the sour-tasting liquid, then swallowed it down more in hope than expectation. The herbs never seemed to help. And even the effort of swallowing was exhausting. And that taste, awful.

He started to pant slightly, becoming more drowsy by the second. It sometimes seemed that health was even more important than money. And that came to mind now as he prayed for relief, saying the words in his head. Please, God, make it stop.

Amelia suddenly stood upright once the glass was almost empty, taking a backward step and looking down at him. And now George was certain something had changed. He thought he must have said or done something to anger her. But he wasn't sure what. There was something about her eyes that unnerved him. A reptile-like coldness he'd never noticed before. It was almost as if she was somebody else. Not the woman he thought he knew at all.

'That's it,' she said, 'we're done.'

'Done?' he asked, now even more confused by her demeanour.

'We've reached the end game. I think I've punished you for long enough.'

He screwed up his face, fighting the pain, trying to make sense of her statement.

'End game? Punished? What? Amelia! What are you saying?'

As she stared down at him, motionless, he noticed her eyes

lidn't blink at all. Her face seemed to lack emotion, blank, almost like a china doll.

'The worst of the pain will hit you soon,' she said ever so calmly. 'So, try not to worry. The anticipation can sometimes be worse than the pain itself. Think on that as you lie there weeping.'

His face was ashen when he responded, struggling to say the words, having to force them from his mouth. What the hell was she talking about? What did she mean? Was it a dream? A nightmare? She seemed so cold, so uncaring, and full of hate, not the Amelia he knew at all.

'P-punish me? But, but why?' he stammered, a stab of pain making him wince. 'What the hell are y-you talking about? What have you done? I d-didn't, I didn't kill Suzie, if that's what you're thinking. You're safe with me. I'm not a murderer. I've, I've told you the truth. If, if you've done something to me, it's, it's time to stop. Call, call for help.'

Amelia laughed, a cruel sound, head back, her chest rising and falling. Her voice had a hard edge, an unrecognisable bleakness that made him shake.

'Oh, I know you didn't kill Suzie,' she said with a manic grin, full lips drawn back, her overly white teeth in full view. 'Because I killed her. Not something I liked doing, but necessary. She brought it on herself. And who do you think rang the police to implicate you? That was me. Clever, eh? I was always going to cast you aside. It was just a matter of when.'

George raised his knees, clutching them with the little strength he had left, searching for even a crumb of physical relief as he groaned in woe.

'Yelp away all you like,' Amelia said with a sneer. 'Make as much noise as you want. It's almost half a mile to the nearest house. That's why I chose to live here. So, no one is going to hear you but me. Say your goodbyes. There's nothing to be gained by hanging on.'

Despite the room's ambient warmth, he felt so very cold. Icy cold as a shiver ran down his spine.

'Why? For God's s-sake, why?' he asked between sobs.

Amelia glared down at him as he slowly turned on his side. She was far more animated now, her face a picture of dark emotions.

'Men always let me down, every one of them, all bastards,' she began. 'My father was a vile pig of a man who made me and my mother's lives a misery. He was a misogynist, a narcissist. And so are you. When I first met you, I thought I liked you, that you might be different. You had the looks, the charm, the bullshit. But I saw through you soon enough, saw you for what you are. It was shocking how quickly you told me about Suzie and her money. But once you did, for me, it was all about that. I played you because I could. Because you deserved it. And now, everything is going to be mine. I'll never need a man in my life again.'

George's mind raced, searching for a means of escape, anything to change her mind. Was it worth trying to lie? One last attempt at deception? The final effort to con?

'But... but I love you,' he said, with all the faux feeling he could muster.

He flinched; far from helping, his words had enraged her. Her face took on an animalistic snarl that he silently acknowledged was terrifying... totally terrifying. He closed his eyes, not wanting to look.

'Love?' she said, her voice venomous, the pitch raised almost to shouting. 'You're a dirty cheater. You cheated on Suzie, and you cheated on me. But I'm not nearly as forgiving as Suzie was. I knew another man like you. An ex who died, too, screaming in distress, full of manipulative pleadings that didn't get him anywhere at all.

And now it's your turn. With me, cheaters pay the price. Love? You don't know the meaning of the word.'

George made one final effort to speak, blubbering as his world became an even darker place. 'An ambulance. My chest, my chest is h-hurting. It's, it's hard to breathe. Please, for God's sake, call for an ambulance.'

Amelia sat at the furthest point of the sofa away from his head, still looking at him, one long leg resting over the other. She began to laugh. Then a girlish giggle.

'An ambulance? Oh, I don't think so,' she said, 'not after all my efforts. It's amazing what one can forage in the hedgerows and woodlands in the British countryside. There are any number of poisonous plants in the area, some of which are almost impossible to detect even with specialist tests. And I chose you some of the best, a combination to make you suffer over the months and now, finally, something special to bring your worthless life to an end. It's highly doubtful the authorities would ever discover how or why you died. But just to be sure, I've typed out a suicide note on your laptop naming that one final fatal poison and saying the guilt of Suzie's murder became too much. And all typed with thin latex gloves on, of course. You chose such an obvious password. So easy to guess. And the police will only find your fingerprints if they ever look. I'll print the note off and press it against your cold, dead fingers once you're stiff. I'm the clever one, you cheating bastard. I win, you lose. Do you think I liked having your filthy cheating hands all over me? No! Not for a minute. Sex with you was a means to an end. Something I tolerated. What do you think of that?'

But George didn't think about it at all. He began to pray quietly, under his breath, and then he screamed out as the pain again became unbearable, coming in waves, peaking as if a raging fire was burning in his gut and a demonic hand tearing out his heart.

He thought he saw Amelia stand to walk away in a blur when

the hurt finally subsided, an eight compared to a ten. And then suddenly, he could see nothing at all as the remaining light faded the bright sunshine filling the room seemingly turning to black as a stabbing pain exploded in his chest and fired down one arm.

One last searing scream and it was almost over. 'Please, God,' he whispered, 'forgive me my sins. I'm sorry, I confess.'

And then, as all went momentarily silent, George was greeted by an all-engulfing fear of hell in his final moments. George Reynolds pictured scorching flames and devilish figures in his mind's eye, strange creatures grasping him with bloody clawed fingers, pulling him towards them with gnashing teeth flashing screeching like demented banshees before he drew his last breath.

# ACKNOWLEDGEMENTS

With thanks to my editor, Isobel Akenhead, and to the rest of the brilliant Boldwood Books team.

# ABOUT THE AUTHOR

**John Nicholl** is an award-winning, bestselling author of numerous darkly psychological suspense thrillers. These books have a gritty realism born of his real-life experience as an ex-police officer and child protection social worker.

Sign up to John Nicholl's mailing list for news, competitions and updates on future books.

Visit John's website: https://www.johnnicholl.com

Follow John on social media:

 x.com/nicholl06

 facebook.com/JohnNichollAuthor

 bookbub.com/authors/john-nicholl

instagram.com/johnnichollauthor

# ALSO BY JOHN NICHOLL

The Sisters

Mr Nice

The Cellar

The Student

The Cop

The Victim

The Bride

The Holiday

**The Carmarthen Murders Series**

The Carmarthen Murders

The Tywi Estuary Killings

The Castle Beach Murders

The Dryslwyn Castle Killings

**The Galbraith Series**

The Doctor

The Wife

The Father

# THE
## *Murder*
## LIST

**THE MURDER LIST IS A NEWSLETTER DEDICATED TO SPINE-CHILLING FICTION AND GRIPPING PAGE-TURNERS!**

**SIGN UP TO MAKE SURE YOU'RE ON OUR HIT LIST FOR EXCLUSIVE DEALS, AUTHOR CONTENT, AND COMPETITIONS.**

SIGN UP TO OUR
NEWSLETTER

BIT.LY/THEMURDERLISTNEWS